THE INDOMITABLE LADIES
OF AMIENS . . .

Amiens, not Paris, was the true capital of the Great
War, and it had been the heart of the Western Front
all through 1914.

At the peak of a desperate advance the Germans
were able to bring their guns to within eight miles
of the city; in fact close enough to fire and scatter
high-velocity shells and shrapnel through the homes,
stores, shops, and warehouses. The determination
and impact of the British counterattack saved
Amiens, and the few people who refused to be evacuated came up from the cellars chanting the defiance
born at Verdun: *"Ils ne passeront pas!"* But it usually was the women and girls who displayed this
indomitable spirit, and when they crept cautiously
to the edge of the city and stared toward the east,
they looked over the broad graveyards of British
youth.

SQUADRON FORTY-FOUR

BY ARCH WHITEHOUSE

MODERN LITERARY EDITIONS PUBLISHING COMPANY
NEW YORK, N.Y.

To JAMES WARNER BELLAH
With many thanks for his suggestion
and permission to use his short story,
FEAR, as the basis of this novel.

BOOK ONE

ANTICIPATION

January 1918

☐ The five Sopwith Camels, outlined against the gray sky in a loose V formation, were led by one that flaunted two light-green streamers on its tail. The aircraft and their gay insignia provided the only color of the day as they zig-zagged, back and forth, over the ravaged villages that might have been part of some battered Lilliput. Péronne was a thumb-smear below. Cambrai lay off to the north-east, a shapeless smudge of brick-red devastation. Just ahead, Arras, a gaunt pile, was castellated with groups of monolithic shafts that thrust up defiantly from its pattern of destruction. The dull, early afternoon was as still as clotted cream, blotched here and there with patches the color of moldy bread.

Condensation appeared at intervals on the corners of the Triplex windscreens, or gathered along the trailing edges of the lower wings before flicking off like discarded pearls to disappear beyond the tail planes. There was no sunshine; only the inky blobs of antiaircraft fire furnished any contrast to the composition. Through gossamer streaks of mist, the Arras-Bapaume road appeared and disappeared into the dun browns and grays of the battle-ground. This melancholy world was what the men below had been fighting for since the summer of 1914.

This was the modern Inferno.

There was one particularly loud cough that seemed to arouse the flight leader to action. He waggled his wings and started to circle, spreading his little formation wider. The circling continued for more than a minute, just as buzzards contemplate their prey, then the leader nosed down suddenly aiming his blunt nose at some indistinct pattern of earthworks. Once his intent was established, the rest of the flight ruddered into a tighter design until the five machines appeared to be wired to an invisible arrowhead.

The winged bolt was cruel and lethal, for it was armed with twenty Cooper bombs carried in racks below the wings, and ten Vickers .303 guns that spurted six hundred rounds per minute. The explosives were designed for enemy strong points, artillery batteries, or heavy road transport; the machine-gun ammunition for the frail bodies of men.

Captain Hoyt, the leader, was a gaunt, dark-visaged man, the product of three years of uncompromising discipline. He had been assigned a low-level, ground-attack mission, and he had found his target. It was his duty to destroy it; life was as simple as that for Captain Hoyt.

Phelps-Barrington, who held forth at the outer tip of the V as deputy leader, was a compact, aristocratic man. He wished they could go down, get rid of their bombs on something large and rewarding, and clear off. Phelps-Barrington would rather risk his neck at higher altitudes.

A man, named Trent, flew at the opposite corner, and had already pushed up his goggles, the better to inspect the ground below. Trent was a specialist in railroad operations, and the enemy could not disturb, repair, or add to any section of track in this area without his knowledge.

Hoyt slammed through a three-belch burst of antiaircraft and nosed down more sharply. The other pilots saw him raise his right hand just above the line of his windscreen and wave it back and forth as a command for a general attack. A hundred men were to die on that signal.

"What the hell has he spotted now?" muttered Mac-Clintock who sat off the left wingtip of Hoyt's Camel. He turned an inquiring glance across at the pilot who held down the other wing position, but there was no answer there. Mallory, a big, burly man who fitted a Camel cockpit neatly and snugly, grinned and shook his head. The leader was on another of his determined missions, and if the rest of the flight got through the next ten minutes they would be lucky. MacClintock shoved his goggles up and scrutinized the sky above. That was his job. He was expected to keep a close watch for any enemy aircraft that might pile in from above while the Camel pilots were concentrating on working over the landscape below.

"Damn it all!" MacClintock gasped, once they were low enough to draw enemy ground fire. "How the hell does he do it? A minute ago I would have sworn that that road was completely deserted, but by God, there're half a dozen motor lorries huddling under their camouflaged tarpaulins. They're not even moving!"

Trent had turned away and was streaking along a few dozen feet above a narrow-gauge railroad line, daring the wild fusillade of tracer bullets streaking up from the ground gun positions. "They keep adding to this system, but what for?" he asked himself, and pulled his bomb toggle, releasing two Coopers and hoping they would explode amid a grouping of trucks and construction equipment. Trent never could quite bring himself to blow up lengths of completed track. He had supervised the laying of too many systems on the London, Midland & Scottish Railway, and fully appreciated what it took to put them in.

He curled away from the narrow-gauge line and passed directly under Phelps-Barrington who was following Mallory in his attack on the transport lorries. Two were already burning, and, in an attempt to get under way, a third had plunged across the road, gone out of control, and now lay on its side in a ditch.

"Come on! Come on!" MacClintock was screaming. "We can't stay down here all day. Get on with it, Hoyt. There's a formation of Jerry Hannoveraners moving in from above, and they're two-seaters, remember."

Lacking interplane communication, Mac watched Hoyt who was again circling, obviously picking out a prime target. "Come on, Hoyt! What the hell are you looking for now?" He saw his skipper nose down sharply, and then hoick into a violent climb that should have ripped off the wings. There was a terrific explosion below, followed by a gigantic flower pattern of green and scarlet flame.

"Jesus Christ!" MacClintock gasped. "He's found an ammo dump. How does he do it?"

Swinging in to follow Hoyt, Mac saw Mallory doing crazy split-ass turns through a maze of tracer bullets as he tried to tack onto Hoyt's tail. Phelps-Barrington was roaring along what had once been a hedge, his guns raking the remaining stubble to fork out any enemy troops huddled there for sanctuary. Hoyt came back toward the circling pack and fired a white Very light, ordering them to re-form. Daring the opposition, he turned and coursed deeper into German territory to avoid the enemy balloon defense, and the damnable cables looping down from the kites, until he had gained enough height to clear the treacherous curtain on their return to their own lines.

"Well, thank God!" MacClintock breathed, once they were back in some formation. He grinned across at Mallory, and went back to his sky watching. "Those bloody Hannoveraners are still moving into position." He shoved a red signal cartridge into his Very pistol and fired the spluttering ball ahead so that it would catch Hoyt's eye. When the leader turned his head, Mac pointed up to where six German two-seaters were flying a parallel course some three thousand feet above.

Hoyt nodded and looked up, studying the enemy formation. He pondered on the situation for a minute, and after rocking his wingtips twice, made a sharp turn and headed back toward the enemy reserve area again.

"Good!" Phelps-Barrington mused. "He's going back to get some more sky, or just enough to make a proper attack on those swine. You take two-seaters from behind and below, and in that way put the stopper on the rear gunners. Good old Skipper."

But when the Camel flight had turned once more and headed back where Hoyt hoped the two-seaters would be, there was no sign of them. Evidently sensing what he had planned, they had curled away in a wide arc and returned to safer territory. With that, Hoyt decided to fill out his patrol time providing protection for any British aircraft engaged in other duties. He found a lone R.E.8 doing an artillery shoot over the enemy back area and sat over him until the observer fired a green signal and headed back toward Albert. Following that, the Camel leader took over a three-ship formation of Armstrong-Whitworths that were obviously carrying out a photography show and when they were through and had paid their respects for the support, Hoyt made one more covering patrol of his area and decided to head for home.

2

The road was the military link between Amiens and Albert, a dreary, sodden streak in another exhausting day, but except for the acrid whiff of cordite there was little evidence that the world was engaged in combat; and there was no indication that the weather would clear. Through the windscreen of the Crossley tender the scene was being washed through with a cold needling rain that chilled men to the marrow.

The R.F.C. vehicle had been picking its way along the pot-holed highway for more than an hour. Its leaf springs, long since lacking lubrication, squeaked, and the engine complained and groaned in its effort to make headway. An early thaw, backed by the intermittent rains, had all but eliminated the boundaries of this once superb thoroughfare. The foliage and the marginal poplars had been leveled by shellfire, and in their place a single file of khaki-clad figures slouched along, heading for some mysterious base of operations. At intervals these desolate tribesmen made vain efforts to uphold a half-remembered dignity.

"Why the 'ell don't cher look where yer splashin' yer blinkin' muck?"

The driver of the equipage, 2nd Class Air Mechanic Magthorpe, replied in the spirit of the times. "Sorry, matey, yer don't want to look too posh when yer get up the line, do you now? They might recognize yer."

"Well, keep yer bloody tup'ny bus on the blasted road!"

"If you knows where the road is, put a bit of stick in it so I can find it, will yer, chum?"

The remonstrative voice followed in the wake of the tender: "You just slapped most of it in my mate's face."

An MP sergeant flat-handed the tender to a halt, and with a professional air shoved his head and arm into the front seat. "When you get to the bend up ahead, driver, you'll have to pull off and take the left-hand road. There's an ambulance train halted just beyond, and a battery of Long Toms behind that. Better make that bend fast!"

"Right you are, Sergeant. Fast it is."

Lieutenant Paterson, who shared the front seat with Magthorpe, looked very young, very clean, and very remote. For the first few miles he had held himself aloof from the activity and intercourse of the groundlings, and as the mist beyond the segments wiped by the rubber blades evaporated, he studied the murk above with an affected professional eye.

Magthorpe said from the corner of his mouth, "You won't see much activity this far back. Them 'uns don't come over 'ere."

"So I understand, but you'd know better than I."

Encouraged by this unexpected appraisal, Magthorpe became philosophical. "Still, I do like to see a man take 'eart in 'is work. But you take me, sir. My 'eart's not in this bloomin' tender. My 'eart's in them turnips over there. These French don't know 'ow to grow turnips. They let's 'em grow by themselves. That's no way to bring out the best in turnips."

Young Paterson reflected and finally agreed. He turned to get a more complete view of the driver. "How did you become a chauffeur?"

Magthorpe sniffed and assumed a beatific expression. "Fortunes of war, sir. *Mis*-fortunes, rather. My lady, 'er at Apthorpe 'All, she went and bought one of them 'lectric motors. One wiv batteries. She'd become quite old an' didn't like to drive be'ind 'orses. I rather think she thought it was warmer, being all glassed in like that, but whatever it was, she made me learn to drive the blasted thing—and what's more, sittin' in there wiv 'er, I 'ad to take a bat nearly every day. Then like an ijit, when I 'listed, damned if I didn't go and put it all down on me papers. You know what 'appened then!"

Lieutenant Paterson had switched his interest to the popping of a motorcycle splashing up from behind, as a dispatch rider tried to force a passage between the tender and the infantry replacements trudging along the right-hand side of the road. When the bike had gone through, he resurrected Magthorpe's monologue. "What happened?"

"Well, sir. I was on cookhouse duty up at the squadron until old Barnwell goes sick. 'E got the measles, an' they made me take over as driver—temp'ry in 'is place, an' damned if I ain't bin confirmed in me rank, an' 'ere I am, just about as far away as I can get from the only thing I really know. If that ain't the Army!"

The young pilot agreed. "Yes, that sounds like the Army all right. They seem to have a special genius for that sort of thing."

"They do that, sir."

An MP stood teetering on a flat stone in the middle of the road. He bellowed at the dispatch rider, "Where you going?"

"Headquarters, 14th Brigade, Sergeant."

"Righto. Come on through."

A muffler-wrapped infantryman inquired, "Who's invitin' who to tea?"

"Not you, my lucky lad."

The MP wallah glanced under the tilt of his tin hat and addressed the infantry mob: "What lot are you?"

"Steelbacks, Sergeant . . . the Northamptons."

"All right then. Close up now. You look more like a lot of bleedin' Belgian refugees. Move up to the next bend and take the road to the left into Albert."

"Whot about the spring offensive?"

"That's your department, chum."

"Good old Steelbacks!"

Once the tender had churned into a fairly clear piece of road, Paterson reopened the intercourse. "What kind of a squadron is this I'm going to?"

"Number 44, sir? Why, just like any other Camel squadron."

"I suppose I shall seem awfully green, shan't I?"

"Green? I'm afraid you 'ave me there, sir. What do you mean, green?"

"Oh," smiled Paterson, "that's an Americanism. It means . . . not experienced . . . er . . . a newcomer."

"Oh," nodded Magthorpe and then turned and looked the youngster over once more. "Are you an American, sir?"

"Yes. From a section we call *New* England. But our family is *Old* England away back."

"But America's in the war now, isn't she? Why didn't you join up with your own lot?"

"For several reasons. First, as I said, we have family ties with Old England. Next, I wanted to join the Royal Flying Corps, so it was simple for me to go from New England into Canada. The R.F.C. had a recruiting office in Toronto. And here I am."

"Well, I'll be blowed! Fancy you going all the way up to Canada to join the Royal Flying Corps. It takes a bit of understanding, really."

"Oh, it's not unusual, you know. Lots of Americans joined the British cause long before their own country declared war," explained young Paterson. "I'm glad I did, but naturally I wonder how I shall do, now that I'm out here."

"If you arsk me, sir," the driver responded thoughtfully, "you'll do all right. You're the sort we want. They all feel a bit uncertain . . . green is it? . . . when they first come out, but it soon wears orf. The boys'll be patchin' up Archie 'oles in your plane a'fore the week's out, an' you'll be tellin' 'em 'ow to do it."

"All that within a week?"

"Roight! An' by the time spring's well along, you may be a flight commander. You know, things 'appen fast in

Camel squadrons," the driver added with a knowing air, and blew to aerate his mustache.

Paterson said thoughtfully, "Yes, so I've heard. What about Major Tremaine? How many Huns has he?"

" 'Uns? 'Uns, sir? My word, I don't know. Never 'eard any of them say. They don't go in for much of that talk up 'ere you know. That's the French idea—aces wiv medals all the way down to their bellies. They even wear them when they fly, or so they tell me."

Young Paterson exploded, "You mean to say they don't go after them—the Huns, I mean?"

"I should think they do! Give 'em billy-ho, too! But wot they worry about from wot I can make out, is time. The blighters are watchin' the clock like 'awks, sir. You try to take five minutes from them, an' you'll get yore bloomin' 'ead chopped orf."

"Oh, I see," Paterson said with a deflated air. "You mean they think more of the time in their logbooks than they do of the Huns they bring down?"

"Of course, sir. That's bloomin' important when you're out for another pip on your sleeve. Oh, they've got medals, too. Lots of 'em, but mostly they get 'em for bringin' the bombers back and doing trench strafing."

Paterson stared dead ahead. "It's quite different from what I expected. Many casualties lately?"

Magthorpe managed a wry smile. "Not too bad. Wot wiv Christmas just over and what you might call the 'oliday spirit, we 'aven't had many casualties lately. In fact, the only one we've 'ad is Mr. Slyne whose place you're takin'."

"Oh? What happened to Mr. Slyne?"

"Well, we don't quite know, sir. 'E went orf yesterday arfternoon, regular patrol, an' 'e didn't come back. We should 'ear of 'im eventually."

"Of course."

As they bumped along, Paterson caught a particularly offensive smell, and he glanced at Magthorpe for some explanation.

"It's 'orses, sir. To my mind, it's dead 'orses wot smells the worst. There don't seem to be anything you can do about dead 'orses. Dead 'orses seem to 'ave so much insides, and they bloat something awful. You might think you could burn 'em, sir, but some'ow when you gets through the outer layer, it only 'elps to make the insides smell worse. As the French say, 'piquancy,' sir. Some'ow burnin' adds piquancy. 'Orses is a problem, I must say."

Paterson stared off to the left. "Those aren't horses over there."

"No, sir. You're right. They must 'ave bin wiv the 'orses. Them's Canadians."

The young pilot reflected on that and flicked cigarette ash from his trench coat. "By George, I must look very clean and new . . . and very much out of place."

"Well, yes, sir, in a manner of speakin' but then most flyin' gentlemen does, compared to the PBI, but I allus say, let 'em. I says, let flying gentlemen do what they want to do, even when they *ain't* flying. I still says they deserve it. Let 'em 'ave 'ot shaving water. Let 'em 'ave baths. Let 'em 'ave sheets on their beds. Let 'em all 'ave whatever they want."

"You seem quite sympathetic toward flying officers. Isn't that a bit unusual?"

Magthorpe continued as though no comment of any sort had been made.

"Sittin' up there all alone at fifteen thousand feet, cold, and wiv nobody to talk to, an' wiv only a few wires and bits of wood between them and the 'ereafter, ain't no fun. The worst thing must be not 'avin' anybody to talk to."

Paterson smiled. "It would be to you. You're a devoted conversationalist, aren't you, driver?"

"You take the PBI—the poor bloody infantry. They're wet and lousy, but they're allus close together, an' they can talk. No, sir! I says let flyin' gentlemen 'ave their baths *and* their clean clothes, an' good luck to 'em."

"You put it very clearly," Paterson agreed, and wondered what Magthorpe would do when the war was over. Would life ever be the same? Would he find what he had been fighting for? And what would his lady at Apthorpe Hall think of this widely traveled gentleman?

" 'Course, we ain't got much of what you might call real comfort up at Number 44, but we're snug. 'A' and 'B' Flights *and* the major are down at the old barn, 'way on the other side where the village once was, an' they got their 'angars set up down there too. There wasn't room for 'C' Flight, so 'C' took over some old sheds at the far end of the cornfield." And with that explanation Magthorpe broke into a guffaw. " 'Course, it don't look much like a cornfield now, but it *was* a cornfield. You'll see when spring comes along."

"You mean when I'm a flight commander?" Paterson asked with a smile.

"Corn in Egypt, as the sayin' goes," Mr. Magthorpe added.

The wind was veering to the northwest and had diminished to a light breeze that slowly drove ragged flocks of murky clouds across the sky. The whiff of smoke and cordite had again replaced the odor of burned horseflesh, and Paterson sensed that the standard features of the war were being moved into the scene.

"You know, driver, I've enjoyed this run, but if I had anything to do with this war, I'd have you sent back to England," the young pilot said with studied determination.

"Oh? Just what do you mean, sir?"

"I'll bet you're a first-class gardener and ought to be

back in England growing food, instead of being out here tender driving."

Magthorpe's face took on the expression of a puzzled beagle. "I couldn't go back, sir. I tried to stay in England, workin' on the land, like they told me, but I'm a Kentish man, sir, an' you can 'ear the guns in Kent."

"Can you really? I never realized . . ."

Magthorpe assumed a more relaxed position behind the wheel. "All night long and all day long—when the wind's right—you can 'ear them very plain. It got so I couldn't keep me mind on me work 'arf the time. In fact, it got so I could 'ear 'em when the wind *wasn't* right." He looked uncomfortable again, but went on. "I think they was sort of inside me, them guns. An' guns some'ow bring out all the things they tried to teach me in school—what schoolin' I 'ad. I was allus rememberin' old Admiral Drake playin' 'is game of bowls when them Spanish ships was comin' up the Channel. Alfred burnin' the cakes. Things like Waterloo, sir . . . An' they tell me Agincourt ain't so far up there."

Young Paterson found himself sitting tense with sweat forming in the hollows of his knees. "By golly, that's right! Agincourt! And you were always thinking of those historic occasions?"

"I can't say I rightly *thought* of 'em," Magthorpe explained with ancient caution. "It was the guns that brought 'em out, an' made 'em real. An' as soon as I 'eard 'em like that, I didn't care who laughed at me for takin' the king's shillin'—I dropped me spade an' I went into Dover an' took it, an' 'ere I am."

"I know exactly what you mean," young Paterson pealed, anxious to renew his association with his schoolboy heroes. "And just as you say, Agincourt can't be far away from here. Have you a map? I believe it is only fourteen miles from Saint-Pol where good old Henry V said:

> *'If we are marked to die, we are not enough
> To do our country loss; and if to live,
> The fewer men, the greater share of honor.' "*

" 'Enry the Fifth said that?" Magthorpe inquired. "What was 'e talkin' about?"

"Actually, Shakespeare put those words in his mouth, and what he was saying was that the English were trying to break through to Calais, but they had only ten thousand men against sixty thousand under Charles d'Albret, constable of France."

"Ar, but didn't we have some brave archers?"

Paterson went on: "Their position was flanked on either side by woods, but with a front so narrow the masses had to be drawn up thirty men deep."

"My word!" gasped Magthorpe wondering what this was all about.

"That was excellent for purposes of defense, but ill suited for attack. Thus, the French leaders warned by the experience at Crécy and Poitiers, resolved to await the English advance."

"You must 'ave done a powerful lot of readin', sir," Magthorpe said, "but that's your schoolin', I suppose."

"But England's archers first drove pointed stakes into the ground before them to stop the French cavalry charges. And as the rainy night passed—it was raining in this area, just as it is today—they bared their arms and chests to give fair play 'to the crooked stick and the grey goose wing.' That's Shakespeare again."

"Crooked sticks . . . grey goose wing?" inquired Magthorpe.

"He meant bows and arrows. How I loved that phase of English history when I was in prep school."

"Oh, I see. 'Bows an' arrers.' Fancy that, now."

"Our history prof said the victory at Agincourt ranks as

the most heroic of all land battles England has ever fought. I've read every word of it, over and over, and who knows, maybe that's why I went up to Canada and joined the R.F.C.," Paterson went on. "Let's see—the archers were disposed in six wedge-shaped formations . . ."

"Why, that's 'ow our Sop Camels fly today, sir. In a wedge, just like that."

"Exactly! Each was supported by a body of men-at-arms. They kissed the soil in reconciliation to God, and, crying loudly, 'Hurrah! Saint George and Merrie England!' planted their stakes and loosed their arrows."

"An' is that 'ow we won, sir?" Magthorpe said, his beady eyes begging for more.

"The French were crowded upon the field, standing in three dense lines, and neither their crossbowmen nor their battery of cannon could fire effectively. Under the storm of arrows they had to charge down the slope, and plodding heavy in their armor were soon floundering in a quagmire."

"Just like this bloomin' old road."

"The long bow destroyed them all. Horse and foot alike went down; a long heap of armored dead and wounded lay on the ground over which reinforcements struggled bravely, but in vain," recited Paterson breathlessly. "Oh, Agincourt was always my favorite history topic."

"Come to think of all that," Magthorpe said, "there's somethin' funny about this road. There are times, going back and forth in this old Crossley, when it don't seem to be me at all. I sometimes feel it's somebody else."

Paterson frowned. "Who does it seem to be?"

"I can't exactly say, sir, 'cause I can't quite see who it is."

"Think! Think hard," young Paterson said, his soul full of hope.

"Well, sir. I seem to 'ear things. Very often I can 'ear

'orses 'oofs cloppin', cloppin', cloppin', an' I can 'ear a light jinglin'—but not a very 'eavy jinglin' . . . not like heavy steel."

"Equipment . . . chain mail?" Paterson suggested, almost whispering.

"It only 'appens about twilight . . . and sometimes early in the mornin'," Magthorpe smiled, and blue patches appeared in the sky like quarters of heraldry. "At any rate, sir, not real armor, like in the pictures of them knights in our old schoolbooks. I think it's just a long sword an' a sort of tight-fittin' 'elmet an' a leather jerkin." He turned and matched Paterson's stare. "You can think a powerful lot of things out 'ere when it gets sundown, sir. It's old, France. Old in history an' fightin.' "

They reflected on that observation in companionable silence until Magthorpe came back a few centuries and pointed up through the windscreen. "There they are, sir. They be comin' back from Agincourt . . . 'ark at me . . . I means the afternoon patrol. Just beyond that hayrick, sir. 'Ere they come. One—two—three—four . . . and five."

Paterson nodded as the indistinct frontal outline of five Sopwith Camels came into view. "How many went out?" he asked.

"Well, that's 'ard to say. I left before they took orf."

"What flight is it?"

"That's 'C' Flight, sir."

"How may pilots in 'C' Flight?"

"There was five, sir—when I left to pick you up."

"I see. I wonder if they downed any Huns."

"I wouldn't know, but it's a ragged formation, seems to me. Almost anything could 'ave 'appened."

"Thanks."

"You're quite welcome, sir."

3

Three infantry officers sat at a galvanized-iron table huddled in the corner of a shattered wall of an *estaminet* in Albert. If they leaned over toward the right and peered through the ravaged window frame they could see the hapless Virgin of Albert Cathedral hanging from the battered tower, a position she had endured since the early days of the Somme. Local tradition had it that when the Virgin came down, the war would end.

The three men in khaki were stamped out of the same mold. They wore G.S. tunics with leather buttons, and all were spattered with dried mud. All three had the weariness of war etched under their eyes with the same tool. In every *estaminet* in the British sector small groups such as this spoke on the same subject.

"A spring offensive? God help us! I tell you, the new draft hasn't even had box-respirator drill. They thought the zone tapes were something they had to stand on. We had three casualties from bayonet wounds in the crawl-through rehearsal, getting to the sunken road. God only knows what they'll do when they're sent over with a bag of bombs."

"If there's anything I hate, it's an attack rehearsal. They frighten me to death."

"Right! They map the whole thing from Flying Corps photos. Then you go over every inch of the ground with the dry method, and after it's all finished, everything clicks nicely into place and the attack is a howling success—except for the minor item that the damned pilot who took the pictures was photographing something twenty-five miles away from where he should have been."

"Comes under the head of diversionary action."

"We're going to be early this year, aren't we?"

"Before the frost is out. No more Cambrai mud bath."

"They're evacuating beds at Etaples already—they tell me."

"Oh, that's just routine."

"No, that's not routine. That's panic."

"What do you mean, panic?"

"Staff panic. You mark my word. GHQ is starting early this year because they're afraid Jerry is going to start earlier. May I ask when a staff officer was ever worried about mud?"

"Did you make that one up, or did you hear it?"

"I can't tell any more."

"Well, there's confirmation. There goes another new R.F.C. pilot."

"Saved! Another round of drinks, eh?"

"That's my idea of a war. Riding around in your own private taxi, and saying, 'Sorry' when you muff it."

"My God! Things must be bad at home when they're sending out middle-aged pilots of nineteen. What's the war coming to?"

"I wish something mild would fall on me so that I wouldn't see you chaps again until some time around June."

"How about that wall? Looks a bit bulgy to me, and it's sagged about three inches since we've been sitting here."

"It must be marvelous to have a technical education."

"Oh, it is. *Garcon encore trois!*"

"Carthage must be destroyed."

"Gentlemen, I give you a toast. The eternal triangle—the spring offensive, the wall, or Number 9 clap hospital at Rouen."

4

It was strange, this talk about a spring offensive, because no one in a responsible, but safe, position believed that the enemy was capable of staging another push. Since long before the Battle of the Somme, the Royal Flying Corps had met the challenge of the Boelcke Circus squadrons, and had almost driven the Imperial German Air Force from the skies. The new Sop Camels, the S.E.5s, and the indomitable Bristol Fighter had chased the knights of the Black Cross as far back as operational range would allow. Cambrai had proven the new tanks, and it was only a matter of time—and weather—before the final surge to victory could be started. So sure of this was everyone in command that the creak of saddlery, the panting of officers' chargers, and the dust of cavalry was abroad in the land.

The war correspondents knew, but were not permitted to speak—until there was no space to display their forebodings. By then, they were telling the dreadful tale of breakthroughs, the loss of the Somme crossings, the threat to Paris, and the fight to hold the Channel ports. The war correspondents had remembered what had happened at Caporetto the autumn before when Sir Herbert C. O. Plumer and his Chief of Staff, Sir John Harington, had been sent to Italy with many of Great Britain's best divisions, leaving a dangerous gap in Sir Douglas Haig's western front command.

No sooner had this thin khaki line been filled in, than General Foch, weeping over the fact that some of the older classes of the French Army had been under arms since 1914, next begged Haig to extend the British lines north and south of Saint-Quentin, and the Fifth Army, under General Hubert de la Poer Gough, was saddled with this additional responsibility.

Once the new ground had been taken over, there were a few short weeks of respite and the appreciation of an almost pastoral countryside. What a change from the mud of Flanders! Down here were living trees, acres of green fields, and vistas of lush meadows, regardless of the fact that the battle-scarred Saint-Quentin cathedral could be seen with the naked eye. For days, the troops searched for the reason of the solemn quiet, for beyond the odd burst of harrowing fire, and the inky boom of antiaircraft guns, the somnolence was seldom disturbed.

But the war correspondents knew there was a great movement of enemy troops westward from Russia where surrender and revolt had put an end to the war in the east. They also looked about for evidence of up-to-date trench systems and support lines, but General Foch's men had used all their power in upholding the Great Tradition at Verdun, and the veterans of the Class of 1914 had been content to dig standard trench and traverse systems, and lightly man them against the none-too-belligerent Saxon divisions.

This was the general situation prior to the March Push. If you had an afternoon off, you could arrange a picnic lunch with a friend or relative who had been transferred to the new battle front before Saint-Quentin. The British divisional recreation men held various sports events, boxing bouts, and soccer matches. Here and there, troops of cavalry enjoyed practice gallops or brushed up their mounted sword drill in the warm hope of reviving the glory of the Boer War.

Only the war correspondents predicted a spring offensive. General Sir George F. Gorringe of the 47th London Division thought that most concern was due to the fact that GHQ "had the wind up." "It's all bluff, you know," he assured everyone. Another general, temporarily in command of the Irish Division, held much the same view, and was most explicit that such an enemy effort would be utter folly. Mr. Bonar Law, Chancellor of the Exchequer, looked down his thin nose and sneered: "I am skeptical of any German offensive."

Finally, enough intelligence officers pooled their opinions and facts, and the war correspondents argued that at least England should be told; the people ought to be prepared. GHQ was convinced eventually, and by February 23, the evidence pointing out the gravity of the situation was passed by the censors. But England was enjoying a warm and early spring; no one on that side of the Channel was frightened. By now the horrors of the Second Battle of Ypres and the Cambrai show had been forgotten. The theatres were crowded, dances were in full swing, and London was alive with clean-uninformed Americans whose pockets were bulging, and whose interest in the war was novel and naïve. Unfortunately, the war correspondents were not permitted to present all the facts of war, its naked realism, horror, and loss, nor did they risk delving into the deeper psychology of the conflict; their simple warnings carried no weight.

5

The adjutant's office, a dusty compartment huddled in one corner of 'C' Flight's hangar, bore a high effluvium of stale tobacco, wet leather, engine oil, and decaying canvas. To prove it was an administrative working area, a battered desk that had been resurrected from some forgotten business, was jammed against a side wall. On it, at opposite ends, were two-cut-down ammunition boxes, and the nose section of a twenty-five-pound Cooper bomb filled in as an ash receptacle. A narrow strip of discarded Army blankets was tacked across the flat working space. Two of its upper drawers were missing, while the third was usefully employed as a footstool. A prehistoric instrument, acting the role of a telephone, teetered at one end of the desk, an the whole melancholy tableau was boxed in with drab walls and two doors that creaked no matter how often their hinges were lubricated.

The squadron clerk peered out over the uneven ridge of a broken nose, his abstract haircut giving him the appearance of a third-rate prizefighter. He wore the shapeless bag, popularly known as an R.F.C. maternity jacket, a pair of dirty breeches, unevenly wound puttees, and highly polished military bluchers more suitable for an investiture at Buckingham Palace than an active service squadron. Like most members of the "other-ranks" fraternity, he subscribed to the theory that if his boots were clean, the rest of him was equally acceptable.

Polished Boots was manning the telephone and conferring with the adjutant, Lieutenant Chamberlain, who sat with his slim buttocks on the raw edge of what had once been a French Provincial chair. Captain Hoyt, the flight commander, stood peering through the half-open door which led into the hangar, trying to see beyond the fretwork of wings, struts, and wires of three Sopwith Camels sheltered there for servicing. Hoyt was tired, ratty-minded, and in need of a shave. Although of medium height and fairly compact, direct from his bath he would have looked relaxed and at least three inches taller. In his present state of mind he seemed hunched up and shrunken.

"Where the hell is that MO swab merchant?" he growled for the third time. "Mallory has been in agony out there for half an hour."

"Was Mr. Slyne wearing a general service tunic, sir?" Polished Boots interrupted, holding the transmitter end of the instrument under his armpit. "An open tunic?"

"I'm damned if I know," Lieutenant Chamberlain snapped. "What do you think, Hoyt?"

The skipper turned to the clerk. "Who have you got there?"

"It's the 15th Metra-Loors . . . between Toul and Nancy, I think, sir."

Chamberlain looked up from several patrol reports scattered across his desk. "Have they got an engine number?"

The clerk gave his attention to the telephone once more, blinking through his attempt to transpose military French into the mother tongue.

"I can't remember what kind of tunic he had on," Hoyt fumed, and went back to the half-open door. "Poor bloody Mallory. Must feel like a winged grouse."

"Oh, I see," the man at the telephone responded, and peered at Chamberlain with the expression of a bemused carp. "It wasn't the tunic, sir. It was the engine that was open—full open. He's burned, sir." He gave his attention to the instrument again. *"Avez-vous le nombre de l'engine?"*

Hoyt and Chamberlain consulted an equipment list. "Ask them if 15464 is right?" Chamberlain nodded . . . "15464 . . . right."

Polished Boots jerked the instrument from his ear. "Oops! They've buzzed orf again."

The crunch and wheeze of a Crossley tender outside stirred up the roar of a Clerget engine being tested out on the hangar apron. Hoyt listened, straightened up, and began to pace the floor. "There's that Japanese cigarette case of his. That'd go through fire. Good metal of some sort. The gold and the decoration would melt and leave little channels. He could have had that with him. They might look for it. If it *isn't* Slyne, we can't go all that way to Toul. Must be a hundred miles away. This is a bloody big war, as I remember."

This reflection was interrupted by a knock on the outside door. "Come in . . . Come in," Hoyt growled and turned to stare at the closure. "What's all the blasted noise out there?"

The slim, well-tailored figure carrying a neatly folded Burberry over his arm entered and snapped a posh parade-ground salute. Hoyt gulped, stared, and acted like a schoolboy who has suddenly found himself in a milliner's shop.

"Paterson sir. G. K., Second Lieutenant. Reporting from Pilots' Pool for duty with Forty-four."

Hoyt cringed, hooked a forefinger over his chin and seemed to hold his breath. He took time to light a cigarette, and then tossed his bewilderment to Chamberlain.

"I've only just arrived, sir," Paterson added.

The adjutant raised a careless finger in acknowledgment of the youth's correct military approach. "Oh yes. How do? Bring your logbook and all the necessary?"

"Yes, sir. Everything, sir."

"Good! Chuck 'em on the desk here. Do you mind?"

The young American carefully placed his wad of credentials down as ordered and snapped back to attention. Hoyt winced at the display and turned his annoyance on the squadron clerk who was still trying to restore contact with the French machine-gun detachment.

Chamberlain smiled up at Paterson and said pleasantly, "Please break off. This isn't Cadet School. We're rather careless here."

Paterson relaxed and said: "Very good, sir," and backed toward the dusty side wall and glanced at a set of aircraft-recognition prints. He spotted the new Pfalz and tried to remember whether it was French or German. Seen free of the discomfort of the tender's seat and out of his trench coat, Paterson was a slim, wiry youth of better than average height. He was blessed with the lean face of the budding athlete, a young animal who has not as yet realized his full potential.

Hoyt took him in out of the corner of his eye and

reached several knowledgeable conclusions. He decided that Paterson usually stood wide-legged when puzzled or uncertain, holding his hands free, and when ready to take a stand or speak his mind would turn slightly sideways to face his opposite number over his left shoulder. His smile was a winner, once it had blossomed to its full, but this warmth came on a slowly rising wick. The newcomer, whatever his background, was naïve, and unfamiliar with this world of war, tension, strange sounds, vile smells, and the uncertainties of existence. But there was a mark of breeding in him that thrived on adversity, and he probably was at his best in a losing game, relishing the conflict, rather than its outcome.

Polished Boots muffled the instrument and addressed Hoyt. "It *is* Mr. Slyne, sir. It's a Clerget engine, 15464, and Fort Garry Horse collar insignia." He clapped the phone to his ear, and offered further evidence. "Oh, and the metal parts of a Sam Browne belt, *and* the cigarette case, sir."

The skipper sighed, and then bowed politely to Paterson who was trying to interpret the exchange of words. Hoyt explained. "We've lost one of our men—yesterday's patrol," and with that spoke quietly to the clerk. "Tell them to hold everything as it stands. I'll go over tomorrow and make identification for burial. Oh, and thank them for all their trouble, will you please?"

Polished Boots belabored the line with, *"Merci beaucoup, M'seer. Laissez rester toutchose. M'seer l'Capitain Hoyt arriver domain matin a bon houre pour identifier. C'est notre pilots, je pense gu' gu'—oui—oui—Merci—Merci."*

Captain Hoyt endured the closing remarks, and added, "Intercourse at the international level is a wonderful thing," and with that point established returned to the door leading into the hangar. "Well, thank God! The poultice wallah has finally turned up. A retarded case of senility would work him into a real sweat."

"Oh, Paterson," Chamberlain began again, "just give me a note or two on yourself, d'yer mind?" He reached for a slip of buff paper and began mumbling and scribbling. "Let's see . . . Paterson, G. K., Second-Loot. Next of kin?"

"Dr. Paterson, sir. Joshua Paterson."

"That's the name of your father?"

"Yes, sir."

"Address?"

"Mine Hill Road, Salisbury, Connecticut . . ."

"In America?" Chamberlain gasped. "Christ, Hoyt, we've found an American, at last!"

"Connecticut, U.S.A.," young Paterson added.

Hoyt turned back from the hangar door and took another look. A fine-looking boy, he decided. Old Joshua is probably a good general practitioner out there; his mother a lovable and gangling busybody whipping up all the local charities. The kid looks and talks like he's been to a good school and is probably the idol of a damned good family.

"So you're one of the American volunteers, eh?" the adjutant inquired, sucking the end of his pencil. "Funny thing, you're the first that's come our way. The R.F.C. used to get a lot of your chaps, but since America came into the mess, I suppose they join up in their own service."

"That might explain it, sir," Paterson smiled back. "In my case, I always wanted to join the R.F.C. and as soon as they'd take me, I went in. After all, you had something to join up for."

"I know what you mean. We're still looking for those fleets of twenty thousand warplanes your newspaper boys have been promising. Ah well . . . let's get on with it. Your age, Paterson?"

"Nineteen and one-twelfth, sir."

Plaisted, the bright-booted clerk, reached over to pick up some squadron records and personnel sheets. "Are these Mr. Slyne's, sir?"

"Right! Now clear out!" Chamberlain roared and returned to Paterson. "You'll find an empty cubicle in the 'B' block. That's the middle row of huts. You're lucky. The roof leaks in only three places."

Hoyt flicked his gasper into the Cooper-bomb tray and broke in. "Correction. Four places," and smiled at the young American.

"I'll have your duffel trekked over shortly," the adjutant explained. "I suppose the driver stacked it up outside the door."

"Is that all, sir?" Paterson inquired. He looked disconsolate and neglected until the captain turned and shoved out his hand.

"I'm Hoyt, skipper of 'C' Flight. I'm going to snatch you now, before 'A' gets you." He checked with Chamberlain. "That's all right, isn't it, Charlie? Tell 'em I intimidated you."

The adjutant shrugged. "Righto!"

Hoyt took that to mean agreement, and he clamped Paterson's elbow, steering him toward the door that led into the hangar. "Let's have a look round."

6

They threaded their way through the knock-kneed Sop Camels, blunt-looking creations that seemed to resent the intrusion. There was whiff of war about them, a combination of stale blood, burned oil, the stench of cordite, and the acrid fume of machined metal.

"You, of course, have had some time on these?" Hoyt

inquired as he caught Paterson's eager glance toward the battle-scarred planes.

"Oh yes, sir. School types, of course, but I did the gunnery course at Frieston. I have fifteen or twenty hours on Camels."

"Lucky man. I was taken off Pups one morning and sent out to strafe roads leading into Cambrai an hour later. That was my first glimpse of a Camel."

"Holy smoke! How did you manage?"

"I'm still here."

"Yes, of course."

"Funny thing. We were messing about this side of Cambrai this afternoon, just taking a look-see. You must come over and find out what happened. Mallory was Number 4 . . . Never saw a thing. It just happened. You'll see what I mean."

They sauntered over to where a small group had gathered near the open hangar doorway. Mallory, a square-faced man with a shock of sweaty black hair, sat tense on a straight-backed chair. His jaw was locked, his eyes closed, and he was bare to the waist. He still wore his Bedford cord breeches and hip-length flying boots. The wounded airman's helmet was perched loosely on his head with the ear flaps turned up. It was uncomfortably cold but Phelps-Barrington, a tall gangling pilot with tight curly hair, was holding Mallory's tunic up over his right shoulder and across most of his bare back. The medical officer was experimentally probing several puncutres in the wounded man's shoulder.

Hoyt said quietly, "Now you can see why I was keen to get you. Can't tell how long it will be before Mallory gets around again, and I've got one vacancy in this flight already."

"You mean, this . . . and the man who was burned . . . all happened this afternoon?"

"The man who was burned—that was yesterday."

"I see. Not two in one day."

"Not this time."

Mallory's putty-colored face was streaked with Castrol and cordite smoke. His lower lip trembled and his neck glistened with sweat as the blue-jawed medical officer swabbed his left arm and shoulder with iodine.

"Christ, that stings!"

The MO agreed. "I know it hurts, but you've got to put up with it. Four lovely holes there, just like the mark of some animal's claw. Fascinating. I'll get you an anti-tetanus shot and we'll slap on an emergency dressing."

Mallory winced, and watched the injection being prepared. He shook his head slowly. "Never saw a damn thing, Doc. There we were, coming home, and the next thing I knew there was this business through my arm."

Phelps-Barrington drew the loose tunic up more snugly. "And those slugs came right down on through my lower right-hand wing," he contributed.

Mallory gasped as the hypodermic point went in. "What is that, a knitting needle?"

"It is a bit dull, what?"

"Yes, what?"

Hoyt said, "You'll see a lot of this sort of thing, you know, but you get used to it. The important thing is that he got back."

"Yes, he got back, didn't he?" Paterson felt that there was a decided lack of human sympathy in the whole proceeding until Phelps-Barrington tenderly drew up Mallory's tunic to cover the wounded shoulder and arm, then leaned over and grinned at the exhausted pilot. "You going to be able to teeter-totter now?"

"Why not?"

"Well, let's be off then."

In a gesture aimed to relieve the tension,

Phelps-Barrington turned to the medical officer and said, "And now, my good man, if you will let us know your fee, we'll send in his panel card. In the meantime workmen must have their beer," and he waved a gracious hand toward the doorway for Mallory to precede him.

Hoyt turned Paterson away, and called to a flight sergeant who had been standing in the shadows while Mallory was being attended to. "Sergeant!"

"Sir?"

"This is Mr. Paterson, Sergeant."

"Yes, sir. Mr. Paterson, sir."

"Sergeant Opperdyke's our flight sergeant, Paterson."

Paterson nodded and wondered why all NCOs looked like characters out of Bruce Bairnsfather's cartoons.

Hoyt went on, "We're having a new Camel sent up from Depot tomorrow. That means D-6812 goes to Mr. Trent with that engine from . . . er, '74 . . . D-6418 is Mr. Paterson's plane with Mr. Trent's engine. Oh . . . er . . . Mr. Slyne is down at Toul."

Sergeant Opperdyke brightened and said, "Is he, sir?"

"A complete washout."

"Oh. I'm sorry, but I understand, sir." Opperdyke attempted to relieve the situation by turning to Paterson and explaining, "There's your D-6418 over there, sir. She's a very good Camel. A *very* nice bus, sir. In fact I rigged her myself."

Paterson glanced at a very battered war bird, one with many fabric patches, a torn wheel fairing, and minus an inspection panel, but she looked very clean and efficient around the engine and machine-gun mountings.

"Well, I'd say she's been broken in," Paterson observed.

"She'll be put in first-class shape, sir, and we'll start on the engine change right away, sir."

"Quicker than that," Hoyt said, "and tomorrow Mr. Paterson and I will go joyriding and see what we can teach each other."

"Very good, sir." Opperdyke saluted and stepped back, allowing Hoyt and Paterson to pass on toward the hangar door. As he broke off, he turned and bellowed: "Izzard! Bream!"

A toolbox clattered and a voice responded, "Coming!" Deeper in the cavern of the shed someone began a tuneless ditty:

> *"Around the corner*
> *And under a tree*
> *The sergeant major*
> *He says to me . . ."*

7

The 'C' Flight skipper and his new pilot stood in the vague oblong of the hangar door and stared up into the fading light. There had been a light snow flurry earlier, but with the veering wind it suddenly broke into a blizzardly squall that faded the afternoon light to the color of casket satin. Hoyt passed his cigarette case, and they both lit up. As he heeled out the match, Hoyt heard himself saying, "It's a queer war, Paterson, full of queer things, and the queerest of these is charity; in case you were wondering why I didn't see Mallory back to his cubicle." He took a long drag on his cigarette. "What was your school, Paterson?"

"Back home . . . in New England? I prepped at Hotchkiss which is nearby, and from there went on to Yale. I was only a freshman at Yale, of course."

"Hotchkiss . . . anything to do with the machine-gun chap?"

"Everyone asks that. As a matter of fact, sir, Hotchkiss School was established with funds provided by Mrs. Maria H. Hotchkiss, widow of Benjamin B. Hotchkiss, inventor of the Hotchkiss machine gun."

Hoyt smiled. "You certainly started out with a martial background."

"Well, no. They don't make much of the association at the school," explained the youngster.

"You're a long way from Hotchkiss now," Hoyt went on, "and if you don't mind, we'll dispense with the sirs. That all right with you?"

"Sorry. I'll try to remember . . . sir."

"You'll get used to it. Remember your first day at school?" Hoyt began again. He tilted his head back, and Paterson saw him for the first time in profile. The skipper was a man of medium build, and with more than his share of chest expansion. His nose was thin and sharp, the type sometimes called aristocratic. His eyes were slate-blue. "This is that first day, all over again."

"It's not exactly what I expected," Paterson said.

"War never is. I came out to France early in 1915 with a cavalry regiment, and pictured myself galloping all over Artois with about six Uhlans stuck on a lance. I soon had all that knocked out of me, and wound up swinging an entrenching tool."

Paterson smiled. "Artois! I like the sound of that word. Reminds me of *The Three Musketeers*. I read it over and over."

"There's none of that sort of thing today," Hoyt said sadly, "but never mind. You'll have a good time if you play the game according to the rules. Forget the war as it is fought in the weekly pictorials. There are all the medals in the world, and you'll get plenty of opportunity to earn them—if that's what you are after. But don't forget, when the column is all figured up, the numbers you put on the Time Board are the most important."

"That's the part that has me puzzled, sir. This time business. I've devoted all my efforts to becoming a good pilot and a marksman. I arrive out here and discover it means nothing."

"That's where you're wrong. We want good pilots *and* good marksmen, God knows we do, but every time you go into the air out here you have a definite job to do. Do the job first. If the Huns get in your way, and if there's time, you can enjoy yourself. But the job comes first. The rest is all poohbah!"

"I understand, sir, but it kind of knocks some of the props from under me."

"Well, don't let it dry up your enthusiasm. As I say, they fill you up with poohbah at the training 'dromes and again down at Pilots' Pool. They always do. It's part of the system. I advise you to take what you want of it for what it is worth, and forget the rest. If you want to know anything, come to me, and I'll give it to you as straight as I can. I've been here for four months. When I came I was pukka dud and afraid of uncertainties. You get over that very fast. Oh, by the way, first chance you get, report to Gavin McRae, the squadron gunnery officer. You'll find him across the field at the armorer's shed around three o'clock every afternoon."

"Gunnery, sir? But I had all that at Grantham."

"That's what you think. We know better. Most of you haven't the slightest idea how to clear a bulged cartridge. Old McRae will take care of you."

"Yes, sir."

Hoyt slitted his eyes and vetted the youngster once more. "Don't be too disillusioned. We're not out here for ourselves and we're not out here to be heroes and get our names and photos in the newspapers. The V.C.s are few and far between. I don't know anything about causes, or who started the war, and I don't care. I'm preaching 'C' Flight and the lives of five men. You saw Mallory back there in that chair. It was teamwork that put him there, as rough as it was." He flipped his second cigarette through a high arc into the snow. "Just a slight closing of formation, a wave of someone's hand, somebody else dropping back and climbing above to protect his tail from any stray Hun that might waylay him on the way home. That's what I mean. *Esprit de corps* is a cold, hard phrase, but call it what you like, it's the greatest lesson you have to learn. Never give up a man. They call me an old woman for all my concern and fretting. Take it or leave it." Hoyt dusted his hands together and abruptly changed the subject. "I'm as filthy as a pig. Come on, let's get curry-combed."

As they hurried away another voice, filtered by the sandpaper hiss of the slanting snow, screamed, "Where the hell is that bloody man, Bream?"

8

The cubicle assigned to young Lieutenant Paterson was typical. Its walls were drab and dun, against which stood two folding military cots, bare and comfortless. Two orange boxes, retrieved from the book house refuse heap, were set up to form something resembling a bookcase. Before one of the cots lay a rug that had been devised by splitting the legs of two flying boots lengthwise and binding them together, fleece side up. A small window looked out on the darkness, and bunched at one side of it was a canvas curtain that could be pulled across to observe blackout precautions. And to give a touch of the times, a printed sign nailed to the right of the window read:

Customers Are Reminded That
Each Gentleman Must Pay for
His Own Drinks

Magthorpe's voice outside announced the arrival of Paterson's gear. "Kit bag for Mr. Paterson—and his trench coat. Mind that trench coat, I've got the belt buckle through the 'andles."

"Right you are," another voice grated, and Air Mechanic Portwine staggered in, carrying a regulation kit bag, and the trench coat. He dropped the heavy bundle on the floor near the cot on the left-hand side. He took his time unbuckling the kit bag, taking out the kapok bedroll, issue blankets, and all the folding equipment a British officer is usually burdened with: a folding cot, folding chair, folding wash basin, those complex metal and wood frameworks covered over with a bilious-green canvas. To do all this, he had first to dismantle the equipment already set up, and which had been left behind by a previous tenant. When all the blacking, wrenching, and folding had been completed, the batman moved toward the door with one final glance around the cubicle.

At this point Hoyt's voice was heard in the hallway. "Here we are, Paterson. This way." Portwine recoiled as the door was unceremoniously kicked open.

"Everything's ready, sir," the batman announced and stood aside as Hoyt and Paterson walked in. The newcomer glanced at Portwine and then looked around the inhospitable cell.

"It isn't much, but it's home to most of us," Hoyt said.

"It's quite all right. I shall be quite comfortable."

"Well, slick up a bit. In the meantime I'll scrape off the outer layer of silt. Dinner will be in half a tick. Better make sure you have all your things here."

Paterson turned toward the door, and looked back at Hoyt. "That batman. Wasn't he an observer?"

"Aerial gunner. He's here on light duty with us."

"Oh, I see. I thought he was wearing an observer's wing."

Hoyt moved to the doorway and said, "You'll be cozy enough here," and smiled pleasantly. "Ever have the wind up?"

Paterson stiffened perceptibly. "No!" he said with some hesitancy.

"Lucky man." Hoyt closed the door.

As he moved about the cubicle, checking his kit and the general layout, Paterson pondered on the personality of Captain Hoyt. He realized that his skipper could be a good companion, but in sharp flashes he reflected the determination of the relentless taskmaster. He had never met anyone quite comparable to this sage-eyed man, and decided that he had better devise plans to cope with Hoyt's varying moods. While he contemplated this situation, he hung his haversack on a rusty nail, opened its flap and took out a roll of toilet articles. These he laid out on a narrow shelf nailed to the underside of the window sill. A small shaving mirror was hung on another nail protruding from a bare beam.

The batman returned with a large white enamel pitcher of hot water. He nodded to Paterson and set the jug near the wash-up conveniences. Looked at from the rear he was a slim-hipped youth with sloping shoulders. His tunic was neat, clean, and had evidently been retailored to fit far better than the run-of-the-mill bags issued to the mechanics. His puttees were neatly wrapped with the tape above the ankle, instead of above the calf as cavalrymen affected. Paterson sensed that here was a man who with better luck could have been a commissioned airman. He wondered what had interfered.

"Hello." Paterson smiled. "What's your name?"

"Portwine, sir," the batman answered in a hoarse whisper.

"You're an aerial gunner?"

"Yes, sir," Portwine replied with the same speech difficulty.

"Not flying any more?"

"No, sir. Not at present."

"I see . . . but not so many sirs. All right?"

"Just as you say, sir."

"How old are you?"

"Just turned twenty. Do you want me to pour your water in the basin?"

Paterson began to unbuckle his Sam Browne belt. "That'll be fine. I want to brush up a bit before dinner."

Portwine arranged the wash basin and continued in his husky voice. "I could set up your cot, but it would be wiser to use the other frame over there. That would save yours. These new patent cots give along the seams in a week or so, and they're no good at all. It's important . . . in case you want to sell your gear, for any reason. You can get much more for it if it hasn't been used."

Paterson considered the other cot. "Nobody sleeps there?"

"Not at present."

"I think I'd rather use my own, thanks."

"I take it you'll be filling in for 'C' Flight, eh?" the batman inquired while Paterson unbuttoned his tunic and unknotted his tie.

"Of course. This is 'C' Flight's quarters, isn't it?"

Portwine pondered on that and said, "That's right, and besides 'C's got the present vacancies, so I'd better put your name on the call board, eh?"

Paterson nodded and felt a warm concern for this man

who had once been on active flying, and he wondered what had brought him to this menial station.

"Now let's see. That's the M.M. ribbon, isn't it?"

"Military Medal, sir."

"You got it . . . in the air?"

Portwine glanced down at the ribbon as though it was something he had not noticed before, then looked up, smiled, nodded, and placed his left-hand fingers against the side of his nose, thus hiding his observer's wing and the decoration with his coat sleeve.

"Wouldn't you like to go back to flying?"

"I would if I could, but it's my neck . . . here." Portwine turned his head sideways, pulling the high-fold collar away to show a decided welt that ran from below his right ear and up into the scalp at the rear of his head.

"Oh, I see. That one came damned close, eh?"

Portwine straightened out his collar, and stared down at the toes of his polished boots. "It was rather funny, in a way. I was flying aboard a Fee . . . You know Fees?"

Paterson nodded. "Pusher types . . . Nacelle . . . Observer sits in front of the pilot. But they don't use them out here any more, do they?"

The batman shrugged and went on, "I was transferred from a line regiment. I was hot stuff with a Lewis gun, but I'd never been in the air before. It seems they needed machine gunners."

"That was last year during the Bloody April business, I presume."

"It was a bit bloody, as you say, sir. First they showed me how the air gun sights worked . . . They are different, you know. I remember I arrived there about lunchtime, and I was a bit peckish, but our flight was taking off right away, so I had to go. They showed me how to climb up on the edge of the nacelle and fire the rear gun over the top plane. That was all the training we got in those days."

"Good God!"

"Well, then we went up . . . in the air, I mean," Portwine continued in his pained, hoarse voice. "I remember how pretty it all was down below. There was sunshine all across the fields, just like you can see from Knob's Hill. Everything clean and even, like the fields in England." The batman stood fumbling for words. "That was south of here, of course."

Paterson felt like a tourist stalking through a historic cathedral while a worshiper fingered through the Book of Common Prayer. As he waited for Portwine to resume, the walls were outraged by a voice that rose from the next cubicle. Someone was singing and glubbering through a good sloshing wash-up,

> *"At seventeen he falls in love quite madly*
> *with eyes of tender blue.*
> *At twenty-four he gets it rather badly*
> *with eyes of a different hue.*
>
> *At thirty-five we find him flirting gladly*
> *with two, or three or more.*
> *When he fancies he is past love,*
> *it is then he meets his last love . . ."*

then suddenly broke off into a bearish growl: "Will you, for God's sake, stop taking my towels? I don't know what you need towels for; you never wash anyway."

A strident falsetto in the same cubicle completed the popular ditty from "Bachelor Gay": *"And he loves her as he never before."*

Both Paterson and Portwine awaited the climax to the chorus, then the young pilot said, "Go on."

"Well, you know how things happen in the air, sir."

Paterson looked sheepish and admitted that he was a bit new to the game.

"Well, they happen fast. There's always a lot of colors and wings—sometimes some smoke. Now, I *do* remember smoke and black crosses, and I remember what they said." Portwine wiped his lower lip with his tongue. "Or was that later on another show? No . . . no, I think it was that one."

"What did *who* say?"

"I climbed up . . . I think, and I brought the sights on him just a they had told me. I let him cut into the outer ring, and then I fired! I meant to give him ten . . . like they said, but I froze on, and I gave him twenty . . . maybe thirty . . . maybe thirty . . . perhaps forty. Then for a minute everything was all yellow flame. I closed my eyes and when I looked again, I couldn't tell whose it was. Sometimes I think it might have been one of our Fees."

"What do you mean—a Fee?"

"One of ours. I didn't see any crosses afterward."

"But you must have known who came back."

"Quite right, sir, but we also know who didn't. Mr. Winslow didn't." Portwine stood with his fingers interlocked, as if straining against some inner conflict. "You . . . you . . . you don't think I shot Mr. Winslow down, do you, sir?"

"What are you trying to say, Portwine?" Paterson stood with his hands in the warm water pondering whether to continue his wash-up, or to dry off and start again. "I don't understand."

The batman began to fold Paterson's tunic, seeking a new focal point, but turned once more with his wistful appeal. "You don't think I did, do you, sir?"

"Of course you didn't. How could you? Even a beginner would know the difference between a Fee with cocardes and some Hun bus bearing black crosses."

"I think it had black crosses."

"Of course it did. You wouldn't be here if you had shot one of your own machines down . . . would you?" A jolt of anguish burned across Paterson's chest as he tried to assuage the other man's wound.

"Wouldn't I?"

"Well, naturally you wouldn't."

"No. I suppose they would have done *something* to me," Portwine muttered and busied himself with setting up Paterson's new cot. "No, that's right," he agreed. "I certainly wouldn't be here, would I?"

"You've got to keep thinking that way, Portwine," the young pilot said as he watched the batman putter about with the bedding. "You should try to concentrate on getting back to flying, you know."

"Hello, I've taken the wrong cot. This is Mr. Slyne's." Portwine husked and almost managed a smile. He folded the unwanted gear and carried it across the room. At the door he turned and muttered, "You don't think I did, do you, sir?"

Before Paterson could offer further assurance, a loud voice from the next cubicle announced, "I like 'em with short hair and long legs. With large breasts and small hips. With their clothes off and their stockings on . . . and in bed!"

Paterson digested the proclamation with cherubic concentration, then swilled his face with soapy water, and toweled vigorously. As he reknotted his tie, a rotary engine cylinder, employed as a gong, began to clank at the other end of the corridor, and a disinterested voice announced: "Dinner!" followed by a rushing of feet, the slamming of doors. The hutment shook with the prospects of another mealtime.

9

As Magthorpe had explained earlier, 'C' Flight's hangar, messing, and personal accommodations had been incorporated into a series of sheds, barns, and unclassified military shelters that were grouped at the far end of Number 44 Squadron's flying field. From the air, the complex took on the shades, pattern, and disorder of some disturbed insect settlement, through which at intervals crawled a limited number of winged termites, mechanical beetles, and antlike figures, all bent on some mysterious exploration. Only the dreary smoke garlands twining up from the cookhouse, the officers' mess fireplace, and the dilapidated metal chimneys of the living quarters gave indication of human existence.

Amid this shaggy collection of huts were quartered Captain Hoyt and his Sop Camel pilots. There, too, Captain Frost, a general practitioner of no particular skill or intellect, was usually huddled in a shelter that had once held some outmoded dairy equipment. Here he treated odd cases of ringworm, diarrhea, lice, second-degree burns, suspicions of syphilis, and malingering at all levels.

Another kiwi was Lieutenant Harboard, an ancient warrior who rightly deserved the distinctive title of veteran, having decades before commanded a regiment in some long-forgotten campaign in India. True to his heritage, Harboard had crept out of his hoary chrysalis of retirement and answered Kitchener's call. Here in France, he was the junior subaltern, taking responsibility for transport and squadron stores, and was known as the Equipment Officer.

In addition, there was to be found, if one searched diligently, an adjutant who also served as the squadron's Recording Officer, but Lieutenant Chamberlain was generally devoting his time to the demands of Major Ivor Tremaine at the squadron headquarters at the opposite end of the field. A few NCO mechanics, cookhouse toilers, mess stewards, and batmen completed the establishment.

To some extent, 'C' Flight was a small, compact organization, jealous of its limited sovereignty, quietly satisfied to fight the war on its own terms whenever possible. Stepchildren they were, but they reveled in their isolation and independence, the greatest of all human benefits without which no other advantage can be enjoyed. At the same time, contrary as it may seem, this independence relied greatly on depedence and trust. Their armor was honest thought, and simple truths supported their utmost skill.

Here was an exemplary jewel of the Royal Flying Corps, a nucleus of a new military arm that was being forged into an efficient weapon of what was to become known as tactical aviation. 'C' Flight had little concept of this budding history, for when the airplane had sprouted guns at its ports and emerged as a winged weapon, progress in the art of war-in-the-air had flashed across the front with the speed of a fletched bolt and there was no time to digest what was actually taking place.

Number 44 Squadron's mess was established in an ancient Adrian hutment, a forerunner of the prefabricated hovels that were to mark military habitations following the First Battle of the Marne. At best, it was a ramshackle example of such improvisation, shapeless, drafty, damp, comfortless, and unfit to offer shelter to a flock of pipstricken Buff Orpingtons.

An old refectory table stood along one side, spread with a grease-spotted, red-plaid tablecloth on which was set a biscuit tin of weary evergreen foliage, the ruins of a Stilton cheese, a mixed display of cutlery, and places for eight diners. Toward one end of the room a Dutch-type stove, lacking most of its decorative tiles, glowed moodily, providing limited heat, a few wisps of smoke, and pungency usually associated with urine-sodden horse blankets. Six assorted lounge chairs, salvaged from God knows where, stood around this pillar of comfort in studied disorder. Protruding from an unfinished plank near the door, a number of tenpenny nails, hooks, and pegs provided accommodation for an untidy display of Sidcot suits, hip-length boots, trench coats, leather flying jackets, scarves, caps—and a woman's poke bonnet.

The walls, composed mainly of whitewashed boards, were decorated with a variegated display of prints torn from *La Vie Parisienne, Tatler, The London Illustrated News,* and the *Christian Advocate.* At some earlier period, a patron with an eye for the ludicrous had created a frieze, running the four sides of the cavern, in which he had used cutouts of famous statesmen, clerics, actresses, noted military figures, leggy Kirchner girls, and musical-comedy stars whose costumes left little to the imagination. By judicious clipping, and an eye for juxtaposition, this wag had created the impression of Gertie Millar booting Papa Joffre high in the crotch. Daphne Pollard was wrestling with the Archbishop of Canterbury, Admiral Beatty waddled through the bunny hug with a *La Vie Parisienne* charmer, and over the buffet Mary Pickford was unashamedly changing clothes with General "Boom" Trenchard.

In contrast to this lighthearted frippery, Number 44 Squadron was burdened with two standard characters, a breed sired especially for R.F.C. messes. Both were ancient bonifaces drawn from some late eighteenth-century whelk stall, or perhaps they had matriculated at the fish-and-chips school of cookery. They seemed to use a mysterious method of locomotion that enabled them to pass from one point to another without moving their feet, and were known as Shuffling Wally and Shuffling Joe. They seldom spoke in the mess; they obviously were fed up and far from home. They had never been able to understand this modern madhouse, and had given up trying.

The officer personnel were already gathering for the evening's fare. The flying men were Captain Hoyt, Lieutenants Trent, Phelps-Barrington, MacClintock, and Mallory who was still awaiting transport to a base hospital. Shuffling Joe and Shuffling Wally were doling out plates of something that looked like stew and smelled like the byproduct of a tannery. The walrus-whiskered Lieutenant Harboard, was, as usual, reliving his earlier days. Captain Frost, the medical officer, sat stirring something in a cloudy glass. The others were either dawdling with the meal or wolfing it like jackals.

"Of course," Lieutenant Harboard expounded, gesticulating with a forkful of potato, "in those days things were quite orderly in lower Burma. As a matter of fact you couldn't be sure of a decent show until you got fairly well up into the north country."

"Steady, the Buffs!" MacClintock broke in.

Harboard ignored the interruption and continued. "Even the Civil Administration was orderly. South of Delhi we didn't have to make people talk because it never mattered down there whether they had anything to say or not. That part of the country was fairly well consolidated after Sir Frederick Roberts' time, and that isn't so far back you know. When I speak of making people talk, I speak of an art. The art of bringing that meticulous amount of physical discomfort to a man's body that will cause him in return to give you the exact information you require . . . and which his mind holds. I remember in North Peshawar in the eighties when we were brigaded with the 17th Shikaris, we drew fourteen feet of intestine out of a local Indian gentleman, and thereby saved fifteen hundred British soldiers."

Ignoring this nugget of military history, Captain Frost turned to MacClintock, "So the first Tommy says to the old sweat, 'How do you know? You meet the tart, she takes you 'ome, biles a kettle of 'ot water and takes you upstairs. She's blinkin' sure you are all right, but 'ow the 'ell do you know that *she's* all right?' Of course, the old sweats have one way of finding out—something involving an old copper penny . . ."

"I've heard that one, but I've never given much testimony to it," MacClintock said offhandedly in his rich Scottish burr. He was a broad, squat man with unruly sandy hair. For some personal reason he wore a black tie and had retained the cutaway tunic of his old regiment, the Argyle and Sutherland Highlanders. Beneath his greasy wings could be discerned the ribbons of the Military Cross, and the Distinguished Conduct Medal, an NCO award he won at Neuve-Chapelle in 1915. He half-closed his eyes and pondered on an incident of the afternoon. "I'd gie a lot to know how they qualify two-seater pilots nowadays. Take yon laddies at 119. They select the rendezvous, but they don't get there. They go out to take pictures of Hun battery positions, and all they come back with is an out-of-focus view o' their own lower wing and an autographed cabinet photograph of Gladys Cooper. They go out to bomb a dump, and then call us up to find out whether they hit it or not." He roused from his critical reverie, and bellowed, "I'll bet I know what happened to Foxhall. He's down in Germany and is tryin' tae get through to us on the telephone, asking us to send a lorry over to pick up his crash. He's that daft. I'd rather be a staff officer than a two-seater pilot."

Ignoring the wide spread of conversational topics, Phelps-Barrington said to Mallory, "I hope you'll leave those phonograph records. I have been trying to pick out the new tunes on the piano. Funny, I thought I knew them by heart from my last leave."

"I'll get some new ones in Blighty."

"Did I tell you about Frobisher who fell so hard for the girl who played 'Madelon' that he woke me up at three in the morning to go back to London with him and be his best man?" P-B chanted on. "We got there, cleaned up, bought a ring with a diamond the size of a Vickers muzzle-cup, and had breakfast with her at Gatti's where she and Frobisher got into such a hell of a row over the kippers—and how many saccharine tablets he ought to put in his tea—that the whole thing broke up in a riot, and I had to pay the check while he chased her across the street. She made the Charing Cross gates in the best time for the course, and hopped the first train out to get away from the bloody fool, and the show didn't open that night because the train took her to Folkestone. She didn't have any money to come back with."

Trent sat with his face mounted on one cupped palm. "Look here, Harboard," he demanded. "How long are a man's intestines?"

"I'm sure I don't know," the old gaffer said, fumbling for his pipe.

"But you ought to know, if you're going to pull 'em out. That's the fallacy of the whole British colonial policy. They send too many regular soldiers out to India to pull out men's intestines. They ought to send a railroad man. I can tell you how long a man's intestines are. Twenty-five feet, Mr. Harboard, with a possible variation of a foot or two either way, depending on the man, and I don't have to shave every morning as soon as I get up, to know that. And I don't have to have my buttons polished, and my belt polished, and my boots polished, and I don't have to stand up on Guest Nights and raise a glass of port for which I am paid sixpence a week to buy, and drink to the King's health. And it wouldn't make any difference, as long as I *did* know it, whether I had ever been to the Gaiety Theatre in all my life, or had Upper Tooting Cycling Club engraved on my calling cards. Regular Army officers, Mr. Harboard, would be all right if so many of them weren't gentlemen."

Lieutenant Mallory who had been sitting in numbed silence fondling his wounded arm, contributed to the program with, "Look here, Frost, if you'll promise me one thing, I'll do something very nice for you. In you won't say to me when the ambulance comes to take me down, 'Mallory, old cock, old cock, it isn't when you're sober that I worry about you, it's when you're drunk. When you're sober, you're all right, but when you're drunk, you'll put your maggot where you wouldn't put your walking stick when you're sober.' If you won't say that to me when they come to take me down, I'll take up a subscription among the nurses to send you through medical school."

"My friends," Phelps-Barrington intervened, standing like a long-beaked heron amid a pattern of weeds, "they say that the air at St. Moritz is like wine this winter. Mind you, it's always like wine, but this year they say it is like fine, very old wine, and running Cresta is much less dangerous than photo patrols or doing artillery observation aboard an Ack-W. Would you consider it bad breeding for me to insinuate that Captain Foxhall is *not* trying to telephone for a lorry? After all, we don't know what Lazaret-6 in Cologne is like, but we certainly know what this particular bit of France is like at this time of year; and whereas we don't know what German prison fare is like at the present moment, we *do* know"—he rose to his feet— "that if Corporal Fairbrother, who at present is doing duty as chef of this exclusive dining club, doesn't stop trying to disguise that last batch of 1894 steak-and-kidney pie with

onions and Worcestershire sauce, I'll have him lashed to
the undercarriage of my tricycle and flown through an Archie burst!"

And with that, Shuffling Wally moved into position as
Phelps-Barrington, with a courtly bow, handed over the
offending offal.

It was at this point that young Paterson made his way
through the curtained doorway and stood uncertain and
alone until Captain Hoyt took over and made the introduc-
tions.

"Come in. Come in, Paterson. You're just in time."

The flight commander moved around the table and took
Paterson's elbow. "Captain Frost, this is Mr. Paterson, a
replacement."

"How do you do, sir," Paterson responded.

"I'm fine. How are you?"

"That's enough," Hoyt broke in. "This is Mr. Mallory,
you saw him out at the hangar. Trent you met in the corridor when I took you to your cubicle. Here we have Mr.
Phelps-Barrington *and* Mr. MacClintock."

Phelps-Barrington, with the gleam of a lewd cockatoo,
bowed solemnly, and Hoyt led the newcomer up to Harboard. "This is Mr. Paterson, sir. Mr. Harboard is our
equipment officer, Paterson. He commanded the East
Suffolk regiment until he was retired in 1900."

Old Harboard bowed to the youngster, and muttered,
"Other times, other manners, Mr. Paterson. I was junior
subaltern here until you arrived. Many thanks for my
promotion."

"Happy to oblige. My cousin is in the East Suffolks—
2nd Battalion. He's just been given command."

"I presume he's an elder cousin, Mr. Paterson. It's a
bit startling to an old peacetime soldier to find battalions
commanded by thoroughly experienced old veterans just
turned twenty."

"My cousin is twenty-four, sir. He's my English cousin. Our part of the family is in America . . . Connecticut. So I'm his American cousin."

"I hope his father is not worried about his career."

There was no time to compile an answer, as Phelps Barrington broke in with, "As long as I don't like the food, I hope none of you mind if I draw this conversation into somewhat serious channels which may serve to pass the time pleasantly until the tender leaves for Amiens, and I can get on with my delightful career of debauchery. By the way, Captain, what are we going to do with the Legion of Honor?"

"Major Tremaine hasn't decided yet," Hoyt said.

"When Napoleon was at Elba," Frost offered, "they put the Legion of Honor on their horses' tails and rode through Paris."

"That's out. I can't ride a horse," grumbled MacClintock.

"And what happened to the six Croix de Guerres?" Trent broke in.

"Oh, Wing was very polite about them," Harboard explained. "Wing said that Number 44 had just been going along on its regular duty, and that it felt that any official recognition of that fact would be superfluous."

"Well, it was something along that line," Hoyt admitted.

Captain Frost muddled his drink. "Very intricate, diplomacy. Wing bowed when they said it. The French bowed and were so overcome with the extreme modesty of Wing that they raised the six Croix de Guerres to one Chevalier Order of the Legion—and because the luncheon had been so pleasant. Now Wing has initialed the whole matter and referred it to us, because you damn well can't refuse the Legion."

"Precisely!" snapped Phelps-Barrington. "Now I may have seen 'A' and 'B' Flights in the air the other day, but I was probably mistaken. Still, I insist that they have more time to walk around wearing medals than we have." He rapped decisively on the table and stood up again, "But to-night, gentlemen, the whole situation has altered. We have in our midst a man who can use that medal. We have a man who leaves shortly for light and gaiety and the smiles of women, God bless them! We have a man who deserves every possible aid in the business of legitimate seduction, an art in which he has heretofore been most unsuccessful."

He bowed solemnly to Hoyt. "I move, Mr. President, that the Legion of Honor be conferred on Mr. Mallory, and that it be pinned directly above the bandage which stanches the flow of his heart's blood from the grievous wound he received this afternoon in the service of King and Country."

"Thanks, I've got a medal," Mallory said.

Phelps-Barrington recoiled, gulped, and yelled: "Steward! Take every gentleman's order, and give the chit to Mr. Mallory—he's *got* a medal!"

"They're all wrong on that business anyway," Trent stated. "Those brackets they want to cover are from December 15 to December 29. Between those dates Number 44 Squadron escorted that French artillery-observation squadron only three times. I was on every patrol myself. There wasn't a casualty in either squadron, and there wasn't a satisfactory photograph taken because 119 Squadron was put to work on the whole thing, starting the afternoon of January 2, and working right through to the eighth when we did those three flights that Sunday afternoon and had to have the flares out to get down from the last one."

The wounded Mallory twitched in his chair and proclaimed: "The Brighton Special leaves Charing Cross at seven forty-five A.M., stopping at Sevenoaks, Batten Ball, and Lower Slapton. Half prices for children and household pets—including chambermaids. Bicycles without lamps, ninepence. There will be two flags displayed on the last coach until darkness falls, upon which they will be replaced by red and green lanterns. The guard will take orders for tea and we warn once more that gentlemen over nine-stone-four may not sleep in the luggage racks. At suitable intervals the engine's whistle will go, Toot! Toot!"

Needled by this labored satire, Trent replied, "Let me tell you one thing. When this bloody war is over, I'll have a job to go back to. I'm the only man in this mess who had a real profession before the war. That's why I'll get through. When you've worked on a railway, you do things right and you do them on time. You do them the way they ought to be done. You pay attention to detail."

Phelps-Barrington countered with, "I was in a very nice wreck on your railroad once. There were fifteen people killed outright and about eighty seriously injured. The acetylene tanks on the three forward coaches exploded and the engine driver was properly grilled." He turned and pointed a severe finger at Mallory. "And let me tell you there is nothing quite like a well-grilled engine driver . . . with a cooked tomato and a sprig of parsley."

"Oh I say," Harboard cried. "Were you really, P-B? How'd you come through it?"

"Pelmanism. The new art of memory control. After six lessons I could even remember the date of my own birthday."

Hoyt tried to orient Paterson with, "Trent isn't quite right on those dates. There's some mistake somewhere. We escorted this French squadron more than three times."

"I take it they want to give out a decoration, and there's some question as to who ought to have it."

"Right! Nobody wants to take the ragging."

Mallory turned on the medical officer, "By God! You

told me I could have four whiskies without my nose bleeding, but I've had only two, and it's started already!"

"It's probably the stew," the MO explained. "I didn't count on that."

Phelps-Barrington walked over to Paterson, and said, "When are they going to start the spring show this year? Did you pick anything up on your way through? Is it going to be early?"

"I didn't hear anything," Paterson answered turning to him.

"It's going to be early. You mark my word," Harboard contributed.

"His great toe aches," MacClintock explained, "just as it did in 1884 when the East Suffolks had their square broken at Khyber Pass."

Phelps-Barrington took up the cue, "Steady the Suffolks! And there where Britons fought and spilled their blood until the plain ran red; there, mark you, stands the little white schoolhouse where all the little black children from Kabul to Kandahar—and some of them not so black —come pattering on bare feet to learn that in Yorkshire it's Yorkshire pudding, but in Birmingham and points south, it's *baked* pudding!"

"Oh, come, Mr. Phelps-Barrington," Harboard chided.

"Your servant, sir." The tall pilot bowed.

"Mr. Phelps-Barrington, we who have watched our years run all too swiftly down the River of Time, realize, if we are wise, that younger men must take our places. There should be no sadness in our hearts. There should be only a desire to guide those youngsters in the paths of righteousness. Also, Mr. Phelps-Barrington, may I point out that in Leighton Buzzard and Woburn Sands it is also *baked* pudding!"

MacClintock threw his arms around Phelps-Barrington

and sobbed, "And the men of the First Shikaris picked up their subaltern—dead."

Amid all this banter, Captain Frost, who was obviously tight sought out Paterson. "Young sir, this medical officer had to take about four snifters this afternoon in order to get his hands steady enough to probe Mallory. If you think I'm drunk, you're very right. Spring offensive *is* going to be early this year. They're moving in ammunition already, and they started parts of Corps rehearsals before Christmas. Everybody knows that. But that doesn't really prove anything. What proves anything is tags."

"Tags? What do you mean tags?"

"Bundles . . . bales of 'em. Everywhere you look, if you look in the right places, you see tags."

"What kind of tags?"

"Royal Army Medical Corps tags. Tags with lots of little words down the left-hand side. Take off a man's leg, check one little word. Take off a man's arm, check off another little word. If he gets hit in the belly, check off another little word. If you gotter get hit, Mr. Paterson, take my advice. Get hit in the buttocks."

"Oh, you mean wound tags—tags for the wounded."

" 'Course I do. My own idea, wasn't it? Recommended the whole thing. Put it down in writing months ago and sent the whole matter through. We use only three tags now. Before, with so many people thinking out so many systems, the more you cut off a man, the more tags you had to hang on him. Anybody can see where that leads to. You reach a point in any surgical tour of duty where the number of tags has gotten so great, you haven't enough man left to hang 'em on. Result, the whole system collapses. I'm the man who foresaw the whole expediency. I'm the man who reduced it all to three tags. One there. One there. One there. Understand?"

Paterson smiled at him. "Well, I'm trying to."

"Not only that, but I foresaw something else. I foresaw that if I didn't get attached to the Flying Corps, I'd be working so hard taking care of infantry casualties, that I wouldn't have a chance to develop any more ideas like that, so I got myself transferred to the R.F.C. where nobody gets wounded—except, of course, people like Mallory here, and they don't count. He'll be back flying again, shortly."

"What do you mean, nobody gets wounded?"

"My goodness! What do *you* mean?"

"I mean, of course people get wounded."

"I mean, of course they don't. It's the exception."

"Oh, come," Paterson argued.

"You just try it."

"What do you mean, try it?"

"Well, in the infantry there's always a chance of being somewhere, sometime, where you know something's coming through—if you stay there long enough—and you can put a hand there and get pinked. If you don't care about dancing, you can put a knee there. But you try anything like that in the air." Captain Frost pounded the table. "It just can't be done. In the air you've got to be killed, or be bloody lucky."

Paterson pondered on that until he heard Trent say, "Heard anything about Slyne, Skipper?"

"Yes."

"How near Toul was he?"

"Right there."

"What'd I tell you?"

"I forget. What did you tell me?"

"I told you he was hit. And the wind was southeast and he thought the Meuse was the Somme. The bend at La Fère is exactly the same as at Damvillers. He was hit, wasn't he?"

"Not in the tank."

Trent looked puzzled. "Not in the . . . Oh, I see. I'm very sorry. Slyne was on his way to being a very good man, Skipper. He was in his second year in the engineering school at that place in Canada."

"McGill."

"I believe that was it, and his father was a division superintendent on the C.P.R."

"Do you want to go over there tomorrow?" Hoyt asked him. "We're washed out so far."

"Yes, yes. I'll do that. Let me see, his engine number was 15464, wasn't it?"

MacClintock said, "If this keeps up Number 119 will have more British planes to its credit than the whole German Air Service. What the hell were we doing down there at Damvillers? Looking for 119? We're always looking for 119."

The telephone rang at this point, and MacClintock anticipating the message, cried, "I'll bet it's Foxhall."

Shuffling Joe went to the instrument, and after some vague mumbling turned and nodded to Hoyt. "It's for you, sir. It's Squadron."

"Oh, it must be Foxhall," MacClintock persisted. "He wants a lorry to come and pick up his crash."

Hoyt spoke but a few words, then hung up.

"Wash-out, Skipper?" Phelps-Barrington said with anticipation.

"Wash-out."

"Who is Foxhall?" Paterson asked.

"Our albatross."

Paterson smiled. *"Rime of the Ancient Mariner?"*

"Good boy!" Hoyt said admiringly. "Actually, he's a 119 Squadron flight commander. He's down somewhere on the other side of the line."

"You mean in the Jerry lines?"

"Somewhere between Jemappes and Boussu, a place called Hornu," Phelps-Barrington added.

"Why don't you offer to work out the map squares for him?" Trent said with some contempt.

"Well, I'm not going to try to cover him up."

"But if you don't know a thing for certain, you hadn't ought to say it," the railwayman reproved mildly.

"I know he's down at Hornu, and I know his wheels rolled after he landed. And I know he didn't fire a white light, which he could have done, and I know he took a new observer, too. But if you don't agree with me, you can go over to 119 and ask Bobby Storrs. You can ask Richardson—and it will cost you six whiskies—but ask Urquhart himself. Maybe they won't tell you, and if it was my squadron, I wouldn't either."

"Oh I hate two-seater pilots," MacClintock grumbled.

Young Paterson attempted to unravel this tangle of inferences. "What's this all about? Do you mean that this man Foxhall went down and had himself captured?"

Phelps-Barrington raised his eyes piously. "Out of the mouths of babes and sucklings."

MacClintock switched the subject by asking, "Where did you do your gunnery, laddie?"

"Ground course, at Grantham. In-air gunnery at Frieston."

"Anything new on the No. 2 stoppage? Are they teaching anything more practical than hitting the crank handle wi' a great braw club?"

"That's usually a bulged cartridge, isn't it?" Paterson probed cautiously.

"I believe it is."

"Well, for one thing they feel the auxiliary loading handle can be improved, but they also advised us to test our own cartridges. I think that is one of Billy Bishop's suggestions."

MacClintock smiled at Phelps-Barrington, and remarked, "I think we're going to like Mr. Paterson. Have the goodness not to take him to Amiens until I have completed his preliminary education."

"And while we're on bulged cartridges, Mr. Paterson, did you see Marguerite on your way through?"

"On his way through what?" the MO intruded, but before that query could be answered Shuffling Wally intercepted Hoyt with, "Driver's here with a tender, sir."

"Amiens!" Phelps-Barrington pealed.

Shuffling Wally touched Mallory on the shoulder. "Ambulance, sir. At the hut block door."

As Harboard watched the group flutter toward the clothes rack, he muttered, "The Spanish took Amiens in fifteen-something. Caesar probably took it at least once. It was taken again in 1870 by the Prussians. I suppose if you are drunk enough, you're liable to run into almost any war in Amiens."

MacClintock was arguing at the coat rack. "That's not your trench coat. That's my trench coat. I suppose this is your red tippet, also."

"I can't stand the bloody place since they cut up the main line," Trent expounded. "If it is necessary to cut a railroad, it ought to be cut cleanly by some special arrangement, so you can use what's left after the war. This way, it means too much patching up."

"I'm sitting with the driver," sang Phelps-Barrington.

"I'm sitting on his lap," MacClintock added in the same key.

Continuing the horseplay, they grabbed the swaying medical officer, and arm-in-arm barged toward the door, but were brought up sharp when the frame proved to be too narrow for completing the three-man egress. In the momentary delay, Phelps-Barrington held Captain Frost off and demanded, "And what, may I ask, do you do in Amiens?"

"You may not!"

Hoyt wrapped a scarf about his neck, and then went back to Mallory. "Would you like me to go down with you, old man?"

"You might, yes."

"Come on, Paterson. We'll take Mallory down to Number 4 Base, and watch him go bye-bye."

"That's the hospital?"

"Righto." Mallory beamed. "I'll stand you both a nurse."

"What about you, Trent?" Hoyt inquired.

"Thanks, no. I'm staying with the Old Army. We're going on to the King's Levee—full-sized decorations, breeches, and silk stockings. And with silver buckles on our shoes."

"Do you know," Harboard beamed. "The first time I went to a King's Levee, I was presented by Major General Sir Laurie Murchison Hart-Urquhart-Hart-Hart, and on the stairway something happened, and the next thing we knew we had the Sirdar Hardoo Soong who happened to be the vice-president of the Punjab Association, and he had another fellow with him who was lost and he turned out to be the police surgeon of the Warwickshire Constabulary."

Mallory wagged his head, and said, "North of the border a sheer is a shire, and south of the border a shire is a sheer." Harboard continued his reminiscences, "And there were two Seventeenth Lancers blokes, the member from Little Ealing and a Dominion secretary."

MacClintock returned to the open doorway, took a stance and pointed his finger at Harboard. "What did Solon say to Croesus?"

The old soldier smiled, closed his eyes, and responded with, "Solon was the wisest man in the world, and Croesus was the richest. When Croesus asked Solon what he could do to be happy, Solon stood back from him a moment, and said, 'That man is happy who has sons and whose sons have sons and who himself is allowed to die on the field of battle.'" He turned to Hoyt, "May I ask you, Captain, if the Flying Corps may be presumed to be upon the field of battle?"

MacClintock thumped away from the light in the doorway as the telephone rang once more. Hoyt scowled, but went to the instrument.

"Yes sir . . . Very good, sir. Right you are. Right . . . Right, yes, sir. I suppose you have been told that Mr. Slyne is down at Toul, sir. Yes, sir—burned. Then you'll arrange for one of the 119 Squadron pilots to take Captain Frost over to identify him for burial . . . Right, sir."

Hoyt hung up with deliberation, and then turned to the door and called out suddenly, "MacClintock! Phelps-Barrington! Where the hell are they? I say, driver! . . . Oh, never mind."

Trent stood up and asked, "What have you got, Skipper?"

"We're washed in again. It doesn't matter, much. They'll be back." He turned to Shuffling Joe. "Send in the caller."

While matters settled down again, and trench coats were buckled for the run to the Base hospital, Portwine responded to Shuffling Joe's cries. Hoyt produced a smile. "Hello, Portwine. How are we feeling today? You're keeping up that neck exercise Captain Frost suggested, aren't you?"

"I'm quite all right, sir."

"Good! Four-thirty A.M. call—in the morning."

"I'm to call everybody, sir?"

Hoyt turned and glanced at Paterson. "Like to go out with us tomorrow?"

Paterson was adjusting the belt on his trench coat. "Well, I don't quite understand what you mean by *like*. What am I here for, anyway?"

"You're here to be broken in gently—as a pilot—and to be taught how to stay alive as long as possible, but I'm damned if I know how to teach it to you, so it just occurred to me to ask you that question. The only other thing I can think of is to say to wait until the next day, and then take a joyride."

"I'll go with you tomorrow, thanks."

"Good man!" Hoyt then tapped Trent on the shoulder. "You're watch officer, Trent, vice me. Be back in two hours." He flicked a finger toward Harboard. "Good night, sir." He turned to Mallory. "How are the pins, old man?"

"Do you ever think about yourself?" Mallory asked. "You've got a concept in your mind about Captain Hoyt. You see Hoyt standing apart from Hoyt—approving and disapproving Hoyt's actions, but you're a great skipper, and for your information, the pins are all right, old man."

Harboard watched Hoyt, Mallory, and Paterson ease out of the doorway, and then resumed his memories. "I remember once when we were over the border. As a matter of fact we were operating without specific orders and weren't so damned sure whether the native troops were loyal or not, but as a matter of fact, you could almost always count on the loyalty of any native Indian regiment . . ."

10

At four-thirty the next morning preparations were under way for 'C' Flight's scheduled intrusion of the enemy skies. A coil of oily smoke rose from the cookhouse chimney, and a vagrant breeze brought a tang of chloride of lime from the latrines. An armament man decided that the coming dawn was an ideal time for testing recalcitrant machine guns at the butt, and the high screech of cordite and reamed bullets tore across the intervening space like a tool-steel blade through harsh metal. The rope and pulley gear that opened the hangar door sounded like the *plap-plap-plap* of ghostly galleons, and the creak of aircraft dollies was reminiscent of coster barrows on their way to Covent Garden market. In a minute a Klaxon horn, a new weapon in the war of nerves, would be aroused, if only to test its availability for the rest of the day. No hoped-for rain pattered down, but through the leafless trees a small rosy cloud began to take form in the east. It was the sort of dawn that threatened an unusually fair day.

Minus his tunic, but comfortable in a heavy blue soccer sweater, Portwine had hauled out Shuffling Wally to help in the morning patrol calls. His whispery voice was never forceful enough to arouse the sleeping pilots, so one of the Shuffling types usually accompanied him to help complete the onerous duty.

In the cubicle they first came upon Captain Hoyt's door, and Wally put his knuckles to the panel. "Captain Hoyt, sir . . . *Captain Hoyt*. It's four-thirty o'clock, sir. It's the caller, sir."

"Right you are, Portwine," the skipper responded although he had been roused by Shuffling Wally's voice.

"Mr. MacClintock, sir," Wally muttered when they had reached the next door.

"Oh, hell," the Scot replied. His bed creaked, and he added, "I don't know what this is all about, but tell Cookie I want three rashers of bacon this morning."

The two callers continued to bang on the door. "Mr. Phelps-Barrington, sir."

"He's getting up," MacClintock grumbled.

"We're washed out!" Phelps-Barrington yelled.

"No, sir. You're flying, sir. It's on the board."

"Flying hell. I'm in bed!"

"I know, sir. Get up, sir."

MacClintock's voice added to the harangue. "What the hell do they want?"

"They want you, I think," Phelps-Barrington mumbled.

"I wants you both, sir," Shuffling Wally implored.

"You wants us both, gentlemen. Sir is singular."

Hoyt broke into the early morning discussion. "The caller is right, P-B. We're flying. Come on, Mac."

"What the hell for?"

"There's a war on!"

"Mr. Trent, sir. Mr. Trent, sir," the caller continued.

"Number Four's leaving for Brighton," Phelps-Barrington taunted.

"Coming. Where's the hot water?"

"Mr. Paterson. Mr. Paterson. You're on call, sir."

"Coming."

Twenty minutes later Hoyt's flight was wolfing fried eggs, wads of toast, tea, jam preserve, and spoonfuls of condensed milk. Trent was grumbling about a rigging problem that had come up: "The bloody mechanic said he had taken up on the wash-in about one degree, and says she ought to fly level now. He said it was very hard for him to tell how much to take up, from just my say-so. Then he said that if I could take him up in the air—knowing that I can't—he could tell better."

"I'd love to take one of those blighters up some time, but they slack it, knowing that there's no room in a single-seater."

"They had two-seater Camels at Cranwell, for training purposes," explained Paterson. "As a matter of fact, I had about half an hour of dual time on the two-seater before I was turned loose. It helped, but it's not really the same."

"How could it be?"

"They have no right to botch-up a Camel like that," Trent argued. "As she is, she's the best bus anyone will ever put into the air in this war. Christ, has anyone here tried to fly one of those French Spads? They maneuver like a Leyland lorry. They're bloody rugged, mind you, but they handle like an asthmatic billboard. But that's the French for you. They either design the Nieuport which comes apart in a good wind, or they make Spads."

"The Americans seem to like them," Paterson interjected.

"Americans? What do they know? They were all brought up on something called a Curtiss Jenny. Now I ask you, has anyone here seen a Jenny?"

"I was trained on one," Paterson said ruefully. "I agree, she's a real clunker."

"Our old D.H.6 looks like an S.E.5 alongside a Jenny," continued Trent. "But it's the American production-line system. They make the wings by the mile and saw them off by the yard."

"Hear! Hear!" remonstrated Hoyt. "I don't think you ought to apply that old chestnut to any American product. We used to say that about the old 'Clutching Hand.' Can't you think up a new one?"

"You wait until you see a photograph of a Jenny," Trent continued and looked around for his flying gear. "Like the cove who when he first looked at a giraffe, said 'I don't believe it!'"

"I'll never forget the first time I saw a Sop Camel," mooned MacClintock.

"Will you ever forget the first time you *flew* one?" Phelps-Barrington broke in, as he scraped a blood speck from his egg.

Young Paterson leaned forward. "We had an elderly Canadian at Cranwell . . ."

"A redundancy," interrupted Phelps-Barrington. "All Canadians are elderly. They are not whelped until they have passed their twenty-ninth birthday. It's a bit tough on the mothers, but there you are . . . the indomitable patience of the great open spaces."

"This Canadian," Paterson continued, "landed after his first solo in a single-seater Camel. He climbed down in something of a daze, and when we asked him how he liked it, he suddenly grinned, and said, 'She's wonderful! I love her. There's one bus I shall never get killed in. Do you know, I was five miles behind her from the minute I took off until I landed. It's the safest war plane I've ever flown.'"

"How's he making out?"

"Well, as a matter of fact," explained the youthful pilot, "shortly after that, he was sent home on compassionate leave. I never did find out the reason."

"You know, Paterson," Trent said over the edge of his cup, "you come to us as a real breath of fresh air."

11

The six Sopwiths were lined up outside 'C' Flight's hangar, a morbid exhibition of vultures of the new age, brooding and threatening in the slowly rising dawn. One or two were silent except for the drip of condensation from their upper trailing edges. A brace stood shimmering under the light vibration of their idling propellers, with a spark-flecked fiery breath coughing through the maw of the engine cowlings. Two more were undergoing starting ministrations with shadowy mechanics twirling the sword-blade propellers as they chanted their litany: "Switch off, petrol on . . . Switch on, contact!"

These 1918 model Camels were powered with a 130-horsepower Clerget rotary engine that produced a top speed of 113-miles-per-hour at 6500 feet. Above 14,000 feet the rotary power began to fall off because of the primary carburetor system, and up there the Camel was somewhat handicapped at altitudes where enemy power plants were more efficient. Because of this she had been assigned to these new low-level missions and the S.E.5 was expected to take over the action at the higher levels.

Paterson went back to his cubicle, riffled through his flying gear, and sorted out his gloves, overshoes, goggles, and scarves. As he came across a small silver picture frame carelessly wrapped in cheap tissue paper, he hesitated, studied the photograph for several seconds, wiped his elbow over the glass, and with some hesitant resolve set it up on the orange-box cabinet. The faint gleam from a naked, overhead bulb fell on the face of a young girl; a sturdy-chinned brunette, with wide-set eyes, a saucy mouth, and nose to match. Her hair was cut short—Irene Castle style, and she wore a neat, tailored blouse that was smock-stitched to bring out the detail of the yoke. The subject had written in a neat, but bold hand in the lower right-hand corner, *"To Gerry—With affection, Daisy."*

Young Paterson studied the pixie face for an instant and then snickered into a pleasant expression. "You little devil," he muttered, "I'll bet you'd love to go on this expedition. It would just suit you. I wonder what we're ever going to do with you." He considered the possibilities while buckling the calf strap of a pair of short flying boots. A khaki sweater had replaced his tunic, over which was drawn his Sidcot suit, a one-piece utility garment that could be hooked into an electrical heating circuit. The power for it was supplied by a propeller-driven generator mounted on a forward center-section strut. He hefted an automatic pistol that had been wrapped in an oily, flannel rag, but after figuring it might be useful if he had to force-land in Germany, he decided that a full clip of ammunition would be insufficient to shoot his way back to the Allied line, so he dropped it in his haversack.

He picked up his helmet, rolled his goggles inside, and wadded the lot with his gloves under his arm and went out. He came upon MacClintock in the corridor who stood sleepily hooking his hip-length flying boots into his breeches belt. His short flying jacket was folded in the loop of his arm, and his helmet teetered precariously on the back of his head.

"They're blooding you early, eh lad?" Mac said trying to maneuver a cigarette to the other side of his mouth.

"There's never much doing on early patrols, is there?" Paterson said while buttoning the upper portion of his flying suit.

"That's one theory. Still, you can get bad weather, a switch in the wind, a storm that should have turned up an hour before, or engine trouble. Bloody fitters can't be trusted until well after their lunchtime."

"Well, I've got to do my first job eventually. I've been practicing long enough."

"That's the spirit, laddie. We'll look out for ye. That's one thing ye can be sure of when Hoyt has the streamers. He'll never give a man up."

"So I understand. It's quite reassuring."

MacClintock linked arms with the young pilot as they headed for the line. "What's it feel like? You're going on patrol on your first full day in France. Ye've never fired a shot at Jerry or heard a shot fired, have ye now? Ye've never even seen a Jerry in uniform. Prisoners of war, maybe, somewhere in Blighty, but never a real fully armed German; yet they're askin' ye to fly a Sopwith Camel over the line, and could be ye'll have to shoot two Vickers machine guns at a Jerry who'll be aiming two Spandau guns at you. Just what does it feel like?"

Paterson was trying to pat his helmet into place with his free hand. "Funny, you should ask that. When I woke up this morning, I felt as I used to on Christmas when I couldn't wait to go downstairs to see if the tree had been put up . . . Now I feel just as I did the first time I explored a cave in the rocks down at Ogunquit, Maine. I was scared to death, dreading that I wouldn't have the sense to get out before the tide came in and drowned me."

"You're a good boy," MacClintock said affectionately. "You've got yours screwed on right. That's worth more than all the heroics and bravery."

"From you with the M.C. and the D.C.M. that's a compliment. What does it feel like, being awarded a decoration for courage . . . devotion to duty . . . whatever it is called?"

MacClintock flipped his cigarette ahead of him, took three more strides, and then rammed his heel at the soggy ember. "Don't let medals fool you, lad. You know the Victoria Cross is cast from bronze cannon captured in the Crimean War. With its bit o' ribbon and bar pin it's actually worth nine-pence-ha'penny—an' laddie, that's all it is worth. Every man who comes out here and stands his ground is entitled to one, but they are given only to heroes —usually dead heroes."

"But the ribbon must indicate something."

"To whom? The chaps who are fighting with you have their own ideas whether you are brave, or a coward. The civilians back home have no idea what goes for heroism or courage. They see your bit of ribbon, and the first thing they ask is, 'What did you do to get that one?' but there isn't any answer."

"But," Paterson persisted, "a decoration at least indicates that a man has proved his courage."

"Courage? What is courage? You can't turn it on or off like whisky out of a vat. Young Albert Ball was awarded the V.C. for destroying forty-three Jerry aircraft. Major Hawker was also given the same decoration, but he probably didn't do in more than ten or a dozen before he himself went down. Where are the standards? The fact of the matter is that it didn't take half as much courage for young Ball to score his forty-three as it did for Hawker, who was much older, to get his ten or a dozen. What is courage in one man, is simply animal instinct in another."

"But what about your particular case?"

"Me? I'm no hero. I got my D.C.M. back in 1915 . . . Neuve-Chapelle. I was a member of a machine-gun team. We were holding a position, and when it was all over I was the only one of the seven men left alive, so some bewildered ass at Regimental HQ decided something should be done to commemorate the action, and I was given the Distinguished Conduct Medal. Distinguished conduct, my ass! I was too scared to get out and crawl away. In fact, I was left alive, because I was sheltered by three or four poor devils who had sprawled over me when they were cut down. You call that heroism, courage—or distinguished conduct?"

"No, that is commendable honesty," Paterson replied, "but what about your Military Cross?"

"Since I am burdened with honesty, I shall have to say that my M.C. came through when I had been here but a couple of weeks. I have no idea what excuse was written into the *Gazette* report. I haven't downed coveys of Fokkers or Albatri. I can't recall being unduly offensive on any particular occasion. I just take my quota of bombs and drop them where I think they'll do the most good, or where Hoyt orders, and trust that I am earning my rations. In the hallowed halls of Whitehall, such activity is considered devotion to duty. Whether I live or die isn't particularly important. I believe most V.C.s are given posthumously." MacClintock suddenly halted and raised his arm across Paterson's chest. "You want to see an example of true courage? Take a look at Phelps-Barrington over there near the corner of the hangar."

"Whatever is he doing?"

"What he does every morning before he goes on patrol; sticking his finger down his throat to make himself vomit. He does that just as regularly as he tests his engine. Purest evidence of human funk, but he'll go, just the same."

"The poor devil," Paterson whispered. "Can't we do something?"

"Christ, no! You show any compassion, and he'll kick your brains out."

"Wouldn't a spot of brandy . . . ?"

"No. Nothing!"

When Paterson reached the line he found Captain Hoyt in consultation with Sergeant Opperdyke. "Now you're sure Mr. Paterson's bus is quite ready?"

"Everything just as you ordered, sir. I've got that old engine from '74 put into 6812, sir, and Mr. Trent's engine is in 6418, but it's going to need a top overhaul in about twenty hours, and so is your engine, sir."

"Don't worry about mine. I can nurse it along," Hoyt said petulantly.

"We just got a message from Squadron that Captain Archibald of 'A' Flight is going to fly up that new Camel. Will you sign the receipts and blank now, sir? We've got to indent for four new tires on account of those two that were on Mr. Slyne's, the one on your . . . er . . . mishap, sir, and the one our gentlemen damaged the night they had the fight with the Very pistols, sir. Would you care to sign for Mr. Slyne's plane now? Captain Archibald says he'll drop by Toul and identify Mr. Slyne on his way through to the Aircraft Acceptance Park. Then we have two men on the carpet at eleven. Washing their shirts in issue petrol, sir."

"Oh, my God! I'll take that up afterward."

"When you get back, sir," Sergeant Opperdyke said, as he always did on such occasions.

"Thank you, Sergeant. You're very kind." Hoyt noticed Paterson. "Ah, there you are, Paterson. You quite ready? Your bus is marked 'R' . . . mine, you will notice is 'M' but I also carry two streamers. Phelps-Barrington, flying 'N' will be carrying one."

"As subleader, sir?"

"Right. Now there's nothing to this, you understand. You must have done some formation flying, and you'll be flying Number 3 behind my left shoulder. Keep in close, watch the man behind, and I'll make the first few turns easy till you begin to feel at home. We won't go looking for trouble. We're on a routine show. No bombs—nothing."

"But suppose some Huns do turn up, sir. Don't we have a crack at them?"

"That will be for me to decide."

"But if it is a routine show . . . no particular job to do, aren't we expected to act offensively?"

"All will depend on the conditions, the situation, how much fuel we have, and how far over the line we are. I want you to forget the pot-hunting and the victory scores. I want you to forget that you came up yesterday, and I want you to forget all you were taught back home. Anyway, it's all poohbah! Don't worry about antiaircraft fire. It'll buffet you about perhaps, but it won't hurt you. If anything does happen, follow me. Don't pay any attention to anyone but me."

"I take it then, I am to do no shooting."

"No shooting. If you come back here claiming a Hun, I'll . . . I'll disown you."

"I'll do just as you say, sir."

"Good! Hold out your hand . . . full arm's length."

Young Paterson held out his arm, and Hoyt raised his own palm until it lightly touched the tyro pilot's hand. "Good! Steady as a rock. That's fine. Now let's get going. We pick up formation at three thousand feet over the field. Don't be late."

"Just a routine patrol, eh?" Paterson muttered and shuffled away resenting the implication that Hoyt would not accept combat because he was burdened with a replacement pilot. It was one thing to be a newcomer, a junior subaltern, as old Harboard put it, but it was something else entirely to be wet-nursed through a routine patrol. If only there was some remote hope of pooping off a short burst at some faint-hearted Jerry, there would be something to look forward to, but as MacClintock had pointed out, he had never heard a shot fired at a German. It was all very discouraging.

He found his Camel which was marked with a large white letter 'R,' and the instant he put his foot in the stirrup, a strange dread assailed him. He flicked his belt over, and tightened it for security rather than comfort. An impersonal fitter yelled, "Switch off . . . petrol on, sir!" Paterson replied mechanically with the same words, pumped up his fuel pressure, waggled his joystick, treadled the rudder bar, and pulled up the C.C. gear piston handle while the mechanic turned the trop to suck gas into the cylinders.

"Contact!"

Paterson flicked the switch and responded, "Contact!" and was relieved to hear the engine start with the first swing. He eased the throttle back, adjusted the fuel flow until the Clerget hummed into a smooth rhythm. He polished his new goggles with an old silk handkerchief he kept in his breast pocket, but the lenses were still absorbing the early morning mist.

By then Hoyt was taxiing out for the take-off, MacClintock was following him, and Trent's engine was going through a final test run-up. Paterson turned to make sure a mechanic was holding his tail down, and then gradually eased the throttle bar up the quadrant. The rotary responded beautifully, and its high scream was recorded by the rev-counter needle, and finally flickered well up near the 1400 segment. He nodded professionally to the fitter, and waited until the chocks were pulled away, then worked his way clear from the line and moved out to the middle of the field. The wind sock was as limp as any discarded prophylactic sheath for which it was often named.

On early morning shows, Number 44 Squadron did not take off in formation; those displays were reserved for full daylight. Thus, with a final wave to Trent who had preceded him, Paterson hurried to get into the air. He eased the throttle up, held the joystick forward to keep the Camel's nose down, and to gain speed as she bounced over the uneven turf. Gradually, the undercarriage thunder eased, and he drew back the stick, and, once satisfied that he had the power, zoomed and tried a steep left-hand climbing turn. With a gasp, he saw his wingtip just clear something that looked like a hedge, but the Camel held her course, and with a glorious sense of accomplishment Paterson kept her in the climbing turn until he saw the flickering lights of the mess and cookhouse below him.

Enjoying a new sense of command, Paterson leveled off, and waited for the compass disc to settle down. He went full out toward the east, then turned and began climbing, all the while watching for the exhaust splashes of the other

machines. The early light, faint and creamy, was seeping
through the fields, flowing through the gashes in the hedges, and putting new tints on the walls of the villages.
When he had picked out the airdrome again, he turned
wide and was amazed to find himself less than sixty yards
from the other four Camels. He spotted Phelps-
Barrington's 'N' bus moving wide to let him through to tag
on to Hoyt's left-hand elevator. He tried to increase his
power, but in fiddling with the fine adjustment lever, he
had set up an uneven series of poppings, and he began to
fall back. He experimented, keeping wide of the formation, and finally the Clerget behaved, and by nosing down
to pick up speed he moved gradually into his assigned
position. By this time MacClintock was on the opposite
side while Trent and Phelps-Barrington took up the two
rear corners.

"Well, this is more like it." Paterson beamed. "Just like
the old days at Cranwell when we used to make up
Sop-Pup formations and show off over Sleaford, or swank
about over the seaside at Skegness. That was fun."

Hoyt was a stolid, methodical leader. He made certain
his flock was huddled behind him, then set his nose on
some battered scar ahead, and climbed at a modest rate,
continually turning his head left and right to watch both
Paterson and MacClintock. The two light-green streamers,
his bars of command, were tied to the king posts of the
elevators, and they stretched flat out in the slipstream,
flickering lightly at their extreme, fringy ends.

In a few minutes the flight was over a gloomy mass,
faintly recognizable as a town, but it was badly battered,
the streets having no pattern or design. Ahead, the sun
raised a gilded shoulder to warm the earthy murk, but the
ground below was still under the filter of an uncertain
dawn. It was difficult for Paterson to distinguish any

standard features of a battleground. No front-line dumps, no M.G. pits, no zigzag of communications trenches. The roads linking the shapeless village masses had little definition, and quickly melded into the universal daub of the morn. A few shapeless clouds seemed to be floating up from the southwest, probably on a freshening wind, but it was hard for a newcomer to analyze any of the topographical or meteorological evidence. There was too much to do keeping a position in the formation.

When a few features of the front line emerged through the vague draperies of the dawn, Hoyt began to zigzag gently from side to side. Paterson caught himself sideslipping into his leader's tail assembly, and realized that this front-line Camel was much faster and trickier than anything he had flown in England. He had a minute or two of quaking panic, but when MacClintock gave him a friendly salute, he thought that he probably wasn't performing too badly, and he snuggled his rump deeper into the bucket seat and took a lighter grip of the joystick.

Hoyt made a left-hand turn, a wide safe change of direction, and seemed to be heading north. This drew a sudden blast of explosive above and ahead that made Paterson cringe. He had been watching faint, indistinct splotches of yellow flame and wondered what had caused them, pondering the possibility of an unexpected thunderstorm. Then there was another, closer and louder, and it was evident that the yellow flame clusters were part of the phenomenon.

"This must be Archie, and if it is antiaircraft, we must be over Jerry areas. Well, this is what I came out for."

Hoyt began to dart about more actively, and Paterson responded remarkably well. He was sitting relaxed, holding his gloved hand lightly on the top of the joystick; his toes, not his insteps, were moving the rudder bar, and everything was working smoothly. The light was improving, except for the murk the antiaircraft bursts had dotted about the sky.

At the high point of this content, Paterson was jolted against his belt as machine-gun tracers passed a short distance over his head and went cartwheeling all over the sky. He turned sharply, caught the sound of gunfire, but was deeply relieved when he realized that the interruption was only Trent testing his guns. Then Phelps-Barrington warmed his and rammed a sparkling lance ahead into the murk.

"Wonderful thing, when you think of it," Paterson mused, "how they can synchronize a gun, firing six hundred rounds a minute with the position of a two-bladed propeller which, in this particular instance, is twirling at some twelve hundred rpms. That chap Constantinesco must be a bit of genius. I could never figure out a problem like that."

Paterson checked his C.C. gear handle, making sure the hydraulic pressure line that controlled the speed of the guns was at its correct position. He pressed the twin triggers on the joystick, fired two short bursts from both Vickers, and felt alert and aggressive. MacClintock's guns answered the hunting cry and pumped a sparkling burst into a bolster of Archie smoke.

The planes closed up into a tighter formation, and Paterson was pleased to note that he was riding in as close to Hoyt's tail as was MacClintock. So this was war flying. Snuggling in close, keeping the guns warm, daring the antiaircraft opposition, and sharing the game with fine companions.

"Hello! What's wrong now?"

Paterson sensed some telltale odor, an acrid heat, and his eyes immediately went to the rev counter. A threatening whiff with an oily tang worried him when it was followed by a distinct smell of scorched metal. His mind assumed he had an overheating engine, some lubrication breakdown, but as he watched the rev needle the Clerget still held her power. That damned hot breath was coming from somewhere, and the metallic tang revived a previous nightmarish flight in which he had snapped a tappet rod on an old Avro trainer—the same outraged metal whiff and the odor of scorched oil that had ended in a forced landing—one he would long remember.

He peered over the coaming of his cockpit, trying to interpret the blue-yellow glow from the trunked exhaust. The flame was clean and true, but the stench was still there, though the rev counter showed no hint of trouble. The annoying recurring waves of heat frightened him. "I wonder how far over we are," he said to himself, setting up inner panic. "Hoyt should have taken time to give me some idea of the area we were to work over, so I would know how to get back to our line in case something like this happened. Damn it, I don't even have a map!"

A new contribution of Archie bursts broke up his plaintive reverie, and Hoyt zigzagged through the black pillows of smoke. Paterson held his position, but was sweating profusely; the back of his helmet was sopped with perspiration. He wondered how the time was going, and stared at the watch, set in a metallic fixture, trying to figure how long they had been in the air, but the hands were indistinct. They seemed to be indicating 3:30, and he remembered that he had forgotten to wind and set it.

Making a 180-degree turn, Hoyt led them southward, and the gleam from the rising sun flashed golden shafts from their engine cowlings and the main-spar bulges of their lower wings. More antiaircraft bursts seemed to concentrate on piling up a pyramid of smoke clouds behind them. The formation had spread wider now and Paterson relaxed and glanced about studying the activities of the other pilots. After concentrating on something indistinct below, he kept looking back toward Phelps-Barrington, as if seeking some confirmation. MacClintock was in no way interested in anything on the ground; his head was swiveling back and forth, watching the sky above in all directions. Trent appeared to keep his head sheltered close behind the tiny Triplex windscreen. He probably was concentrating on something mechanical or jotting down figures or notes on a pad fastened to a small shelf he had screwed to a fuselage member.

Paterson saw Hoyt glare back at Phelps-Barrington, and the subleader raise his shoulders in an exaggerated gesture of mild perplexity, upon which Hoyt suddenly nosed down and went screaming through several thousand feet of altitude. The newcomer was taken by surprise and for a few seconds found himself abandoned by the formation, and flying on a level course with a tight bracket of Archie bursts all around him. When he finally realized that Phelps-Barrington's tail with its single streamer was well below and apparently heading for the battered ground, the youngster let out a low cry, rammed his stick forward and went full tilt after the pack.

He managed to move between Trent and Phelps-Barrington by the time Hoyt had eased up, and when Trent peered across and held up a flat hand, Paterson was content to remain in the turbulence of Hoyt's slipstream. It was bumpy and uncomfortable, but there was some satisfaction in being back in the safety of the pack.

Hoyt leveled off and began a wide circuit well below fifteen hundred feet. Phelps-Barrington sat looking intently over the left-hand side of his cockpit while Hoyt peered in the same direction over the right-hand side of his. While sensing the chatter of machine guns and the harsh scream of heavy metal, Paterson wondered what in heaven's name they were looking for. Whatever it was, it apparently held no interest for MacClintock: the Scot was still concentrating on the sky above, and Paterson finally realized that this was how 'C' Flight operated. While the leader and subleader sought out important information below, MacClintock assumed the responsibility of watching for Huns attacking from above. What Trent was supposed to be doing had not as yet evolved in this battle program.

Now the opposition below burst into a belated frenzy, and along with the machine-gun hate they were blasting off strange yellow-green objects that seemed to crawl up from mysterious bunkers below. They came on with slow and maddening deliberation, a tangled skein of blazing balls linked together with white-hot chains. No matter how slowly they moved, each twirling garland seemed destined to loop itself about someone's propeller. They never did, but months of active-service flying seldom, if ever, relegated these "flaming onions" to the discard of unimportance.

"What the devil are we doing down here?" Paterson quaked, and snapped his head from side to side until he felt his helmet fold chafing his neck. He searched for some explanation from Trent who now was engrossed with a narrow-gauge railroad line below. He turned and looked over at Phelps-Barrington and then his eye caught the bulbous outline of a kite balloon. It hung above them, a short distance ahead to their right, and the new pilot wondered whose it was, for his anxious eyes could spot no identifying mark. He continued to wriggle up to his proper position off Hoyt's shoulder, hoping the skipper would turn and attack the kite, when his eye caught the glint of a length of steel cable drooping down in a slack loop from the balloon rigging. The coppery sun, peeping out over

Saint-Quentin, had wrapped the tether with a plating of green-gold, and left it as distinct as a yellow crayon streak across a dun canvas.

"That blasted cable could be dangerous," Paterson complained as he ruddered to get clear of Trent and Phelps-Barrington. "Anyone could run into that thing." He was still sliding into his assigned position when he suddenly realized that MacClintock who was still keeping watch on the sky, could be heading straight into the balloon tether. Aghast, he watched Mac turn and wave a friendly welcome as he eased into his Number 3 position. Paterson screeched dry-throated as he saw the Scot's Camel stumble, falter, and snap savagely into a sharp, flat turn.

"My God, Mac!" Paterson cried. "Didn't you see it . . . ?"

As the formation swept on, Paterson turned and looked back, and to his horror saw that Mac's scout seemed to be snaffled by some invisible chain. It bucked, floundered, and rolled against this mysterious force, helpless to rid itself of the inexorable entanglement. Added to the nightmarish tableau were two blossoms of saffron silk, below which dangled two black-booted figures.

Staring back over his tail assembly, Paterson tried to watch Mac's tragic departure, counting every twirl of the trapped Camel and cringing against a terror that tightened something harsh and gritty inside him. He noticed that Trent had taken over MacClintock's wing position, and Phelps-Barrington had ruddered over, transforming their original V into a tight diamond formation.

To the newcomer's dismay, and outraged sense of decency, no one made a move to go back to see if anything could be done for their comrade. "We should have gone back," he argued. "We should have gone back," but Hoyt continued to fly straight on, still looking down as if searching for some telltale movement of troops. Only Trent seemed to show any interest in the smoky blossom where Mac's Camel must have piled up on a winch. Phelps-Barrington had taken over the duty of searching the sky above.

Hoyt led them back to five thousand feet, and flew on as far south as Bapaume. After the grim incident of the balloon cable, everything seemed unhurried and peaceful. The antiaircraft barked intermittently to keep itself in voice, but it was careless and inaccurate, probably because of an area of low-hanging mist. The patrol was becoming something of a joy ride. High above, a slack formation of Dolphins was grinding away for greater height, and a tight and well-disciplined V of Bristol Fighters came into view from a distant Archie barrage. From all indications, Jerry was lingering long over his morning *ersatz* coffee and sawdust sausage.

The diamond formation tightened up as though a drawstring had been pulled to reduce a pattern of pegs. Hoyt spotted a couple of R.E.8s doing an artillery shoot, and patiently circled them for some minutes; his idea of spreading a thin layer of assurance. An ancient Ack-W, as Armstong-Whitworths were called, seemed to want to join the party but when a bracket of antiaircraft blossomed, it turned away. It probably was hauling some old-maidish general on an early morning tour of his front, a daring escapade for which he unquestionably would be awarded a silver rosette for his D.S.O.

Paterson tried to forget MacClintock, and put in some minutes studying the landscape below. It was all strange, alien, and equally as bewildering as the mottled ground models he had "bombed" or "reconnoitered" from the instruction tower at Cranwell. None of those visual aids had improved his scouting ability, and he wondered if he would ever be able to produce a ground report that could be relied on. He pondered on the activities of the Germans below, what they were doing, and if they actually were preparing for some wholesale onslaught in the hope of bringing victory to their arms. Nothing below in that camouflage of turned earth, burned foliage, battered masonry, or the man-made tracks, trails, pathways, ditches, trenches, roads, or the lunar photo designs created by shell explosions made any particular sense to him. That was the war down there, and how anyone could read its daily story, interpret its hourly changes, or determine what that new digging, or that hairline streak winding through field, plowing, copse, and at times through ancient graveyards, indicated was beyond the imagination.

The formation turned once more, and flew the Archie course as far as the outskirts of Cambrai. Then Hoyt pulled a sharp climbing turn that headed them for the British lines almost opposite Arras. In just over a quarter of an hour they were down safely and taxiing up to the hangar.

The Camels were ranked where they had been started prior to the patrol, but Trent, who apparently had had some trouble, watched a group of mechanics haul his bus into the hangar. Hoyt stood off, unwrapping a long scarf from his throat and checking the time with his wrist watch. The fitter and rigger who had been assigned to MacClintock's Camel remained apart; no one went anywhere near them, and when only four Camels came up out of the gathering mist, they picked up their tools, prop-blade covers, and other impedimenta and went back to the tarmac in front of the hangar.

"Everything all right with your bus?" Hoyt remarked offhandedly to Paterson.

"I think I might have a spot of engine trouble."

"What's wrong? That's a good Clerget, as I remember."

"It smells. Seems to run hot and stinking every so often."

"Hot? If you've been running a hot engine, you may have burned it up. That can happen, you know."

"It came on about four times. Then it would ease off, which is a funny thing. If there was anything getting tight inside, it wouldn't repeat, would it? It would just freeze, and that would be that."

"I don't understand. What do you mean, four times?" Hoyt demanded.

"Just that. Every time we went through that Archie fire I don't suppose it could be the concussion affecting the carburetor, could it?"

Hoyt smiled and wagged his head. "What did it smell like?"

"It's a hot stench—a real stinker—like the inside of an old sock."

"Well, don't order the flight sergeant to give your engine an overhaul. That was just Archie smoke. It does pong, early in the morning."

"Oh, I see. I suppose I'll learn all these things, in time," Paterson muttered, disgusted with himself.

"Think nothing of it. You did bloody well for your first job. You just stay with me, and you'll keep out of trouble. We'll make out our reports in the hangar office. Come along."

"Is that all?"

"That's enough for you, for your first day, if that's what you mean."

"But what about MacClintock?"

"What about him?"

"The balloon-cable business."

"We'll discuss that later. Our ground reports come first. They're important."

When they arrived in the hangar office Trent was filling

out a buff form he held up against the side wall. When Hoyt walked in and sat down at the desk, Trent said over his shoulder, "That balloon was just half a mile southeast from the railway junction at Beaumont, I'd say."

"The one MacClintock . . ." young Paterson broke in.

"One thing at a time, Paterson," Hoyt snapped, tossing his helmet to the back of the desk.

Trent continued. "It was a pity when the junction went. That system was put in properly. It was small, but it was beautifully designed. The French usually squeeze in marshaling yards anywhere they have space, but they shouldn't. Marshaling yards are as important as a main line. They ought to be plotted and laid out carefully."

"Right. I'd say about a half mile southeast," Hoyt agreed as he grabbed a report form. He snatched at a pencil, turned and looked back at Paterson who stood fumbling with his helmet, uncertain, remote. His hair was damp, matted, and ruffled. There were patches of oil on his cheeks. Hoyt handed him one of the buff forms and said, "Fill that out, Paterson. It's self-explanatory, I think. Under 'enemy troop movement' you can leave that part blank. I'll take care of that Courcelles business in my own report. We are logging the take-off time at 5:20 and washing out at 7:10, and you can add five minutes to that bracket if you wish. I want you to watch that depression on the east side of the aerodrome when you've got a west wind. We don't crack undercarriage legs and props out here."

"What do you mean, the Courcelles business?" Paterson looked over the report form.

Hoyt smiled condescendingly. "We're not quite sure, but it looks like a new dump going in there."

"There were two narrow-gauge lines pushed down almost to the canal bank. They weren't there the day before yesterday. They've got them just inside the old embankment, but it doesn't throw a shadow across them that early in the morning," Trent said, sucking on a short length of pencil.

"Good. I want you to make that damned explicit, Trent." Hoyt nodded toward Trent's report.

"I bloody well have."

Phelps-Barrington wandered in from the tarmac entrance looking bleak, morose, and bloody tired. He scotched one rump on the end of Hoyt's desk and fumbled with one of the buff forms, twirling it into a cornucopia, pinching the end, and shooting it like a dart at the wastebasket. Then he stared into space until the office clerk appeared with an ammunition box of squadron mail.

"Are you the orderly officer, sir?" he inquired of Phelps-Barrington.

"It's quite possible."

The clerk set the box of letters at P-B's feet and departed.

Hoyt yelled toward the door that led into the hangar, "Sergeant Opperdyke!"

The NCO appeared as if by magic. "Sir?"

"Front spar, lower left wing, Mr. Trent's bus, stopped a chunk of shrapnel. That must be replaced. One elevator cable on my bus is frayed near the kingpost. Please replace that."

"Yes, sir. Depot got through about twenty minutes before you got back, sir. They're flying the new Camel down themselves."

"Good. I suppose someone will still have to identify Mr. Slyne."

"That has been arranged, sir. Now about those two men for orderly room, sir. When will you want them?"

"I damned well don't want them at all. What was the charge? Something about issue petrol?"

"Yes, sir. Washing their shirts in it, and it's the second

time for both of them. 'While on active service, misuse of government property,' sir."

"What kind of workmen are they, Sergeant?"

"They're good workmen, sir, when you watch 'em."

"If you make it 'misuse' it can go to Wing, you know, and you'll spend half a day marching about with an escort and clicking heels."

"I know, sir, but misuse of petrol is serious."

"I'm not in the mood for formalities. Bring them both to that door."

"Yes, sir," Sergeant Opperdyke snapped, and disappeared.

Phelps-Barrington came out of his reverie and asked, "Who has the Red Cross shacks at Harnes? And who got the chalk streak at Drocourt?"

Trent nodded. "That was brand new, wasn't it? The chalk."

"Brand new," Hoyt agreed. "That's a whole new communication trench going in."

"Bloody hard digging in January."

"It *is* early. Damned early for a system as large as that looked."

Phelps-Barrington slitted his slightly popped eyes. "Let's worry somebody about it. Let's bear down hard on the spring offensive, boys. Let's get more balloons up. Let's get the air thick with them. Let's get so many stinking balloons up, it'll look like Bank Holiday at Blackpool. Let's have 'em all different colors. Let's have 'em all on different lengths of steel cable."

"Easy . . . Easy," Hoyt said quietly. "What about the Red Cross huts at Harnes?"

"Thank you," P-B said and bowed. "Sometimes I know you're the greatest skipper on the front."

"What about those huts?" asked Trent.

"Wasn't that Harnes where we got the first Archie?" Paterson put in.

Hoyt turned and raised his eyebrows. "That's not bad. What do you think of that for a first patrol?"

Phelps-Barrington lowered his head over another form. "They didn't want us to see Harnes, but those are *my* huts. They're the same huts they left behind when I was up there with the Lancasters, or at least the same kind. They're sectional, and they are the only worth-while sectional huts between here and the Vosges. What'll we do, gentlemen? Flip a coin to decide which way they're going to move them—up or back?"

Sergeant Opperdyke appeared at the doorway again. "I have Izzard and Featherstone, sir."

Hoyt turned and frowned at two very frightened, peaked air mechanics who appeared to be all eyebrows and issue boots. One of them was hurriedly buttoning the last button on his tunic. "Very good, Sergeant. Don't parade them. You . . . What's your name?"

"I'm Izzard, sir."

"And you?"

"Featherstone, sir. It's just that I carn't stand being lousy, sir."

"Silence!" Opperdyke bellowed.

"You, Izzard, stand over there, and you . . . the other one over there. Stand 'shun."

Opperdyke poked and prodded until the two culprits were where Hoyt wanted them, while under his breath he was saying, "Hands in line with the seam of the trousers, there. Heels together. Heads up. Smartly now. Ah, that's it. Hats orf!"

When this judicature had been set up, Hoyt began, "Do you know where Texas is?"

"No-o-o-o-o, sir," Izzard and Featherstone responded.

"It's about five thousand miles from Galveston to Liverpool. And from what I read in the papers, there's a German submarine patrolling every mile. There are eighteen petrol concentration depots in England. Any one of them may go sky-high any night a Hun bomb finds it. Any petrol that isn't torpedoed or bombed, finally dribbles across the English Channel to be blown up at our bases out here. If by some miracle, a gallon or two happens to get up here to be used in keeping British planes flying back and forth over the lines, is it fair, may I ask you, for you two worthies to use it to remove lice from your shirts?"

"No-o-o-o, sir," Izzard and Featherstone agreed in chorus.

"Let's put it another way. I have heard it said that there's a war on. Has the rumor reached the men's mess?"

"Ye-e-e-e-s, sir."

"Something's going to win this war. You men would like to be on the side that wins, wouldn't you? You'd like to be able to cheer when it's all over, wouldn't you?"

"Ye-e-e-es, sir."

"Do you know what that something may be?"

"No-o-o-o-o, sir."

Hoyt leaned toward them to make his point. "It might be one gallon of petrol."

"Ye-e-e-es, sir."

"In which case, will you kindly go lousy from now on?"

"Ye-e-e-es, sir."

"Thank you," Hoyt closed ceremoniously, and nodded to Opperdyke to take them away.

Bellowing at the top of his voice, although his victims were less than a yard from his chest, the NCO took over: "Hats on! Right turn! Quick march!" There was a double-shuffle tangle at the door, but all three eventually managed to escape to the refuge of the hangar.

Straining to produce some degree of regimental solemnity, Paterson stood staring at his patrol report. Trent came to his rescue. "You put it in that box for the adjutant. He will delay everything for an hour or so. After that it goes up to Wing where the colonel's batman will probably use it to chink up drafty slits in his Nissen hut. This is a remarkable system, for it sometimes works."

Phelps-Barrington considered that, and tossed his in too, and then turned to hoist the box of squadron mail to Hoyt's desk. Trent hurried toward the door that led to the hangar, and almost immediately could be heard bellowing, "No you don't, Opperdyke. I'm not going to take that wing panel you pulled off Mallory's bus. I want a brand new one from Stores, and I want to inspect it before you draw it."

Hoyt moved away to permit Phelps-Barrington to spread out his work. "I'll be out for about ten minutes. I'm rather expecting the CO to call me on the phone. Will you tell him I'll call him back directly?"

Phelps-Barrington nodded, and flipped the flap of the first envelope. Paterson stood watching the operation, and then looked over the thin pile of patrol reports.

"Is this all that happens?" he said to P-B. "No one seems to have mentioned MacClintock."

"Just what would you suggest? The curtain coming down slowly, and the orchestra playing *God Save the King*, all the little children blubbering openly, and the men looking fierce, stalwart, and brave?"

"But, good Lord, didn't he see that cable? I saw it."

"Law of compensation. You *didn't* hit it."

"There wasn't a chance of *my* hitting it. I was off to the left of Hoyt's tail. It was horrible. I saw him heading straight into it, and the next thing, he was spinning round and round . . . like a . . . like a . . ."

Phelps-Barrington spun in the rickety chair. "Do you have to do this?"

"No. I don't suppose I do. Back here it doesn't seem

real. I can't believe it happened, but he went around that balloon cable so fast, there were just four flat turns. The light flashing off the wings as he went around until he wound up with a burst of fire on the winch lorry below. But I also remember two balloon observers coming down in parachutes from the basket."

"And wouldn't you like to say a few words about somebody poking a rifle into the flames and pulling the trigger until Mac stopped screaming?" Phelps-Barrington was icily calm.

"I'm not trying to make it real," Paterson pleaded. "It isn't real. It's absolutely unreal."

"Suppose we leave it unreal, then. Suppose we put it in the box with the patrol reports. Suppose we let it go to Wing and never bother ourselves with it any more."

"I'm damned sorry, old man," the youthful pilot said quietly, fumbling with the strap and buckle of his goggles.

"You don't have to be sorry."

"I should like you to know that I am."

"Why?"

"Because MacClintock was your hut mate . . . your friend."

"That's *my* weakness, and I won't have you apologizing to me for my weakness. But let this be a lesson. Never make a friend on the front. He'll take the strength out of your soul when he goes."

"That's . . ."

Phelps-Barrington snapped to his feet. "Christ! . . . That's what?"

"Nothing."

P-B poked a finger at the pile of letters on the desk. "This is the correspondence our enlisted personnel perennially carries on with the objects of its collective amatory desires. MacClintock was orderly officer for today. Now you're orderly officer. Sit down to this muck and blue-

pencil it. Nothing goes through about the squadron's operations. Nothing goes through about new or old equipment.
No geographical reference to this, or any other part of
France goes through, but don't take all the fire out of their
love lives."

The telephone jangled and Paterson instinctively took
over and grabbed the receiver. Phelps-Barrington began to
bundle up his helmet, scarf, gloves and goggles. " 'C'
Flight officer, Mr. Paterson, speaking . . . Yes sir . . ."
He turned and yelled toward the door into the hangar,
"Sergeant Opperdyke!"

Phelps-Barrington paused at the outer door and gave
Paterson a smile. "And when you are through, I'll see you
in the mess, and I'll buy you a very long, fulsome, double
brandy."

Paterson looked around from the telephone and returned the smile.

BOOK TWO

REALIZATION

February 1918

☐ The ensuing weather forbade a continued program of patrols, and during Paterson's second week with 44 Squadron 'C' Flight left the ground only twice. Rain, snow, fog, and inclement conditions kept the Camels under canvas, thereby affording the maintenance men some much-needed time to catch up on a half-a-hundred odd jobs and repairs that had been put aside for more immediate requirements. The weather also gave Captain Hoyt opportunity to advise the newcomer on the dangers of tactical bombing aboard such a gadfly aircraft.

Paterson was instructed in the physical details of the twenty-five-pound Cooper bomb, its nose cap, the workings of the bomb-rack mechanism, and how to get the most out of the primary bombsight.

Whenever the weather permitted, Hoyt sent Paterson aloft to practice ground-strafing, and the youthful pilot used belt after belt, peppering simulated M.G. pits, sap-heads, and advanced communications centers. During one of these periods he allowed his interrupter-gear hydraulic pressure to go down, and he returned with three bullet holes in his propeller. The mechanism had lagged, and correct synchronization was impossible. The prop had to be replaced and his skipper warned him. "You were damned careless. That could have happened half a dozen miles over the line and you would have been lucky to have gotten back. We've had props break up under those conditions. Keep that damned C.C. gear handle up!"

Late one afternoon, well into February, 'C' Flight was slated for a low-level bombing show, another of those hackle-raising escapades that were driving all Camel pilots insane. Hoyt was still short-handed although Lieutenant Rupert Yardley, a replacement, had reported in from the Pool, but the captain was keeping him on the field until he could make up for the training he had missed at London Colney. Apparently the instruction staff there could not decide whether Yardley, a great galumphing country boy, was more suitable for Camel or S.E.5 operations, with the result he was equipped for neither, but he had enough boyish ginger and ambition to satisfy half a dozen flight commanders.

"We'll be working along both sides of the Bapaume–Cambrai road, and this will be a bit of a rasper," Hoyt warned as he pointed out the area to be strafed on the hangar-office map. "We'll try to keep as tight a formation as possible, but we may become spread out if we all spot different targets. But you, Paterson, I want you to stay as close to me as you possibly can. You're not ready for any lone-wolf forays yet. You're a good man when you play the team game, and I know I can rely on you, but if you lose track of me, tag on to Phelps-Barrington: he has a single streamer, remember."

Inwardly, Hoyt wondered why he had such a brotherly interest in Paterson, but he realized that the objects one has known in better days are the main props that sustain one's affections and give strength to await one's future; in that lay the nubbin of his concern for the young American. As long as he had Paterson to care for, he would have a goal that could contribute to his own safety and see him through.

"From the details of this caper," P-B mooned, "it looks

as though we've got about twenty miles of machine-gun defenses to skim through—and the same distance back. And if Trent hasn't spotted enough new railway lines, we're likely to go back and do it all over again. You know, this would be a lovely war if it weren't for machine guns. It must have been fun out here in 1914, flying some pre-Piltdown device, exchanging courtesies with the Huns with crossbows amid the fleecy pathways of the sky."

Hoyt smiled reflectively. "Remember the London-to-Manchester race in 1910 when Louis Paulhan just beat Claude Grahame-White for the *Daily Mail* prize? Actually racing with those old box-kites. What fun that was. No one in England slept for the four days it took to cover the distance."

"And neither one of them would have made it if it hadn't been for the railway lines," Trent said with pride. "They never would have found Manchester without the L.N.E. lines. As a matter of fact, that was how Paulhan won. He went from London to Lichfield, flying only a few feet above the metals."

"Toot! Toot!" cried Phelps-Barrington. "All aboard!"

"You can laugh all you like," replied Trent, "but you'll never replace railway lines. They're the nerves and sinew of our whole bloody civilization."

P-B went on. "Bloody machine guns took all the fun and glamour out of war years ago. Machine guns and barbed wire. I wonder what savage swine invented barbed wire."

"A gentleman by the name of Joseph F. Glidden of De Kalb, Illinois," offered Paterson. "Illinois, in case you don't know, is in the Midwest of the United States. For that, I went to Hotchkiss."

"Americans go out of their way to spoil wars," Phelps-Barrington continued. "Let's see, wasn't it an American who invented the Gatling gun?"

Paterson smiled sheepishly. "Richard Jordan Gatling of North Carolina, I believe."

"And Hiram Maxim, another Yankee, contributed to the carnage, so much so, the British government adopted him and made him a knight. We have cruel ways of getting even with our American cousins," P-B added.

"The Lewis gun was invented by a Colonel Isaac Newton Lewis, another American who had to go to Belgium to make any money out of it. The Hotchkiss gun was also an American invention that was picked up by the French," Hoyt mused, "and the bloody Germans coppered the lot, and probably improved on them, which accounts for our having to act offensive this lovely afternoon."

"Americans will bugger up this war too. You wait and see," warned P-B.

"Well, let's hope they bugger it up enough to make the Jerries so bewildered they won't know how to win it."

"Machine guns!" Phelps-Barrington spat out. "We haven't had a decent war since Arthur took to his barge and floated off into the Vale of Avalon."

'C' Flight staged a formation take-off that went very well. Hoyt dispensed with any altitude-gathering over the field and headed straight for the line. He played it safe by getting to twenty-five hundred feet until they had cleared both balloon lines, and then nosed down suddenly and leveled off at five hundred feet. Turning back for the churned-up war area, he zigzagged, back and forth, apparently looking for a target. To Paterson, the ground below looked completely deserted, and had it not been for the machine-gun fire and sporadic puffs of howitzer shelling, they might have been flying over some prehistoric barrows that had recently been turned over in the cause of archaeology. The sun, having passed its apogee, was laying foreshortened shadows with directional spires pointing toward the east, lighting the few clouds, and producing segments of glare from varnished struts, Raf wires, and the whirling blades of the props. A few Archie shots were bursting high above, probably probing for a few safe-level S.E.5s, or perhaps a gaggle of back-staggered Dolphins working out their patrol time.

Hoyt was still darting about like some frantic water beetle, and it was impossible to keep any routine formation. Trent was so engrossed in his study of the landscape below, he was a nuisance, and Paterson decided to draw back and ease wider, hoping that Phelps-Barrington would make it a twosome.

After what seemed like twenty minutes of pointless inspection, Hoyt abruptly nosed down at a patch of ruins and pooped off a few short bursts at nothing in particular. Trent went in too, and fired one long burst at a yellow splotch that was daubed in near a crossroad. He turned and looked at P-B who was watching a small packet of tracer stuff twirling like a puny firework display. Paterson wondered where they had come from. If there were Huns in the area, what the devil was Hoyt doing down here pottering about like some fool botany professor with a butterfly net and specimen jar?

They headed north for a time and Paterson fretted about balloon cables, for they seemed to be cruising along over the Jerry support lines. He could not see any balloons, but that did not mean they weren't aloft. He swiveled his head from side to side until he saw that the loose formation was turning south again and diving even lower. He looked over at Phelps-Barrington who had his left arm outside the cockpit with his hand clenched, as he pantomined the pulling of bomb toggles.

He watched Hoyt as the two-streamered boss nosed down for a complex of trenches, saps, communication earthworks, and pocked ground of some front-line sector.

The youthful pilot reached for his toggle handle and put his open sight on what he believed to be an M.G. post, since it was a single-track depression that ended in a rounded hole bolstered by sandbags. He felt himself rammed against the back of his wicker bucket seat, and was almost standing on his rudder bar. The earthwork was in line with the red tip of his sight, and as the design below came up, as though brought into focus by some high-speed binocular mechanism, he yanked on the bomb toggle.

He grinned as he felt the Camel respond to the release of the Cooper weight. He hoicked out and followed Hoyt who was climbing fast but adding a touch of zigzag to evade the machine-gun hornets zipping up from below. There was some slight pinging, indicating that taut linen was being punctured with slugs, but, thankfully, nothing more savage or definitive to worry about.

After the delivery of the bombs, the formation tightened up, and Hoyt settled down once more to study the desolation spread across the sodden area below. Here and there a spectral design of smoke trickled off to wrap a shroud over the waterlogged shell holes. Here and there the solid browns and blacks became patterns of yellow and gray, but, except for these revenant twirls, nothing moved. Everything appeared unclean and decayed. Only the ghosts of a former carnage crept about to remind those who had lived through these almost-forgotten actions, that they still sought release from their bondage.

Finally, Paterson recognized Villers-Bretonneux which was again being battered by long-range shells, and, once more spurting columns of smoke, interlaced with debris, stood like mute statues for several seconds, then collapsed and floated away. New offerings of antiaircraft puffs seemed to attract more formations of British aircraft; bombers, artillery observation buses, R.E.8s doing photography, and Ack-Ws tootling about, burdened with aerial traffic control of some mysterious order. All this made up the aerial defense being flown to save Amiens.

"It was real fun," Paterson remarked when they got back, "but what was all that low-level business about?"

"We don't know. We just go and do it—and hope," Hoyt muttered, as he handed out the report forms. "We've got to stop them from getting into Amiens, if the spring offensive ever gets under way."

"But there's never time to see what we hit, once we let the Coopers go," Paterson went on. "At least I have never seen where mine go. I do hope . . ."

"Just be satisfied you're not on the other end," Phelps-Barrington added pointedly. "After all, you must have some idea how far it is from Galveston to Liverpool."

"We go out and when we come back all we have to report is that we fired so many rounds of ammunition and released half a dozen bombs. I haven't the slightest idea what we were banging at. Can you tell me, Skipper?"

Hoyt turned around from his desk. "I'd give a month's pay for your receptive viewpoint, Paterson. It must be wonderful to come into a ready-made war and take part in the proceedings with such schoolboy enthusiasm." He halted at that, turned back and stared at his patrol report, then he reached out and gripped Paterson's forearm. "Forgive me. I'm a bit off my feed. But for your information we were blasting at a brand-new M.G. concentration area. The Germans were digging new communication trenches, widening a concentration sector, and putting in several new dugouts that could be turned into advance headquarters . . . if they ever start a new advance."

Trent said, "You must learn to look for tracks made by small parties of men who are probably stringing in new wire for communications. They use certain types of flags for signal headquarters, and others for points where headquarters can be put in quickly. Some tracks can be seen only when the sun is low, others when it is up. Some show up when there's dew on the ground. They can't camouflage tracks through the dew any more than they can cover up tracks through the snow. But we can't rely on this bloody French weather, and we're never really sure of what's going on, so we take no chances and blast everything to hell."

"It must be rare fun for the S.E.5 boys. All they have to worry about are Jerry Fokkers and Albatri," Paterson said. "Don't those Huns ever come down to our level?"

"I warn you," Hoyt said with a frown, "they're damned better shots than those fat, contented Saxons on the ground. Fokker blokes play for keeps. The Jerries on the ground shoot to satisfy some inner dread. They just huddle behind the noise."

"Not only that," P-B crowed, "but the bloody fools seem to fire on tracers—when they have any."

"What do you mean?" Paterson looked puzzled.

"I mean that they don't bother to use their sights and lay off for the movement and speed of the target. Good God! Weren't you taught that at Frieston . . . or at whatever school you matriculated?"

Paterson appealed to Hoyt. "What's he going on about, Skipper?"

"Simply this—and I hope you never try messing about with a Hun Fokker if you shoot on tracer—tracers are pretty to watch and make a lovely display, but they're not going anywhere once they get a few yards from the muzzle of your guns. The instant they start burning—to trace— they lose their original bullet form and begin going off in all directions. Too many pilots are too slack to bother with the Aldis sight, and trust in the tracers. The result is that the armor-piercing and regular rounds are being fired at anything but the actual target. In other words you are wasting two-thirds of your ammunition."

"We weren't told that at flying school," Paterson said disconsolately.

"The aerial gunners with the two-seater fighter squadrons taught us that," P-B explained.

"Gunners like Portwine?"

"Chaps like Portwine. P.B.O.'s, Poor Bloody Observers," Hoyt concluded, and turned back to his patrol report. "And by the way, Paterson, those front line points we were battering were just this side of Le Catelet."

2

When the afternoon patrol had been suitably recorded and the results turned over to Wing, Hoyt decided that the likelihood of an early morning patrol was negligible. A cold wind came up and murky clouds followed in its wake. A call to Squadron indicated that some dreary weather was on the way. Although the morning show could not be washed out this early, there was a good possibility that it would be.

"What about Amiens, Skipper?" Phelps-Barrington inquired as he toasted a slice of bread that was speared on a blackened bayonet held over the fire of the stove. "We would like to broaden young Paterson's mind by showing him the Cathedral of Notre Dame."

"You mean the one on the Street of the Three Pebbles," Hoyt snorted.

"I'm ashamed of you, sir! I was referring to the Gothic structure planned by Robert de Luzarches, and erected between 1220–88. It consists of a nave nearly 140 feet in width, with aisles and lateral chapels, a transept with aisles, and a choir ending in an apse surrounded by chapels. Chartres, of course, has much better stained glass."

Hoyt snickered and opened a can of sardines. "Where the hell did you pick up that line? For a minute you almost had me convinced."

"He used to drive a sightseeing bus in Glastonbury," Trent added, hacking at a chunk of cheese.

"I'm just trying to prove my fidelity," P-B said with a pained expression.

"You know," Paterson chimed in, "I've never been into Amiens since the day I came through from Pool. Someone told me there's an American Y.M.C.A there now where you can get Camel cigarettes . . . and tooth paste . . ."

"And chewing gum," interrupted Phelps-Barrington. "Don't forget that bloody awful chewing gum."

"Cigarettes called Camels?" Hoyt mused. "Well, I suppose that's excuse enough. If we can get a tender, I should think that you, Trent, and Paterson might run in for the night."

"What about Mr. Yardley? I think he'd like to go."

"Oh no. Yardley stays here. I'm not through with his novitiate. Once these youngsters are exposed to the back streets of Amiens, they can be taught nothing. He's difficult enough as it is. I wouldn't trust that boy in the Cathedral of Notre Dame. He'd do more damage than all the Jerry shelling."

"The more valuable sections are covered with sandbags, Skipper," Phelps-Barrington explained.

Hoyt wagged his head. "Our Mr. Yardley was reared amid packs of shire horses, those big devils that draw brewery wagons. It seems his father breeds Clydesdales for shows and heavy transport, and young Yardley was raised to push them about. He not only looks like a horse, but I'll bet if he ever takes off his puttees we'll see that he has grown 'bags of feather'—as he terms the hairy growth associated with Percherons and Clydesdales—around his ankles. Why the hell he was picked to fly Camels is beyond me."

"Oh, I agree," Phelps-Barrington said, "and he eats like a horse. He doesn't slice a loaf of bread, he simply devours it, beginning at one end."

"He's quite a boy, Mr. Yardley. This afternoon he tipped over the generator lorry. I have no idea how he managed that, but he was looking for something under the rear wheels."

"You may be right," P-B said, "it might be too much escorting *two* modern schoolboys along the Rue des Trois-Cailloux."

Amiens, not Paris, was the true capital of the war. This ancient city of Samarobriva lies on the Somme, and its affluents the Arve and Selle. Its original ramparts are buried under a complex of modern boulevards, and a patchwork of suburbs provides the habitations and elbowroom for the people who carry on its trade and business in the old town. The busiest area lies between the river and the railroad, and the older quarter is situated directly on the Somme. The original site was the ancient capital of the Ambiani, and Christianity was preached there as early as the fourth century by St. Firmin, its first bishop. Early in the twelfth century the territory had become the countship of Amiènois for which the citizens obtained a charter of enfranchisement. This fief became a dependency of the French Crown in 1185, but wars and treaties brought it under the Duke of Burgundy until 1477. It was captured by the Spaniards in 1597, and recaptured by Henry IV after a long siege. It remained the capital of Picardy until 1790. In the Franco-German War Amiens fell into the hands of the Prussians on November 28, 1870.

Amiens had been the true heart of the Western Front all through the Great War. The city had been taken by the

Germans on August 30, 1914, but with their defeat in the First Battle of the Marne, they were driven back to establish a new front twenty miles to the eastward, where it remained until the March push of 1918. At the peak of this desperate advance the Germans were able to bring their guns to within eight miles of the city; in fact close enough to fire and scatter high-velocity shells and shrapnel through the homes, stores, shops, and warehouses. The determination and impact of the British counterattack saved Amiens, and the few people who refused to be evacuated, came up from their cellars chanting the defiance born at Verdun: *"Ils ne passeront pas!"* But it usually was the women and girls who displayed this indomitable spirit, and when they crept cautiously to the edge of the city and stared toward the east, they looked over the broad graveyards of British youth.

Prior to the March push, Amiens was a lorry-jump from the front lines, and the old capital of Picardy was often crowded with fighting men who had gleaned a few hours of respite from the death of the ditches and the shattering shellfire to seek this civilized paradise where one could get a bath, a bed, and, best of all, a *friction d'eau de quinine* in a barber shop that gave a rewarding sense of cleanliness after the rot and filth of Pozèires or Bullecourt. The streets were straight, cobbled, and decorated with shops and gleaming windows. Available, too, were welcome doorways, flower shops, wine sellers, and here and there a milliner's. Even more surprising were the well-dressed women and laughing children, and had it not been for the language, one could have imagined he was strolling Oxford's High Street or Trinity Street in Cambridge. It was a heart-warming delight to shop, to spend some of the money accumulating in Bedford-cord breeches' pockets. Whether it was the stock available, or the social intercourse with the salesgirls who did their best to interpret the trench-French of the visitors that provided the greatest reward, will never be known, for so few of the patrons lived to explain the lure of Amiens' attractions.

The buyer's routine was always the same. First, three cakes of scented soap, a packet of stationery, and some frilly sachet that was embroidered with what purported to be some famous regimental or service badge. Next came perfumed hair oil, notebooks, an envelope of Kirchner-girl prints, and, whenever possible, two or three phonograph records. Any funds left over were squandered on English magazines, *La Vie Parisienne,* flea powder, and blue ointment.

The girls, whose sweethearts were perhaps in the Vosges sector or had been buried at Verdun, played their roles to perfection. Although they laughed and tried to interpret Scottish or Australian accents, they were under no illusion. It was their job to charge twice the price for a bottle of eau de cologne or a satin handkerchief case, but they made up for it with a standard retort in some gay sentiment whether the patron was a staff captain or a tongue-tied lance corporal. They had lived too long in the war zone not to recognize the realities. Transient love was not for them, and in most instances their virtue was high above reproach. They left the commerce of passion to others more adapted to the profession—the women who walked the side streets, women whose papers usually were in order and up-to-date with a doctor's signature.

The Street of the Three Pebbles, which is the continuation of Rue de Noyon running up from the station, courses through the heart of Amiens, and is unquestionably the chief thoroughfare of the city. If one halts at its eastern end he will quickly spot the Cathedral of Notre Dame by looking up the Rue Victor-Hugo. Along this gay boulevard could be seen all breeds of Allied soldiers, weaving in and out of Charlie's Bar, the Cathedrale Restaurant, the

Hotel du Rhin, or the Godebert. Some were all merry and bright, some moody and suspicious, some were maudlin, some were trying to make the best of it, and to hell with the price. There were English, Scots, Canadians, Irish, Welsh, Australians, New Zealanders, and a few Portuguese dressed in their frayed, cheap, sky-blue uniforms that were more suitable for some desert campaign than the winter conditions on the Somme.

By now, too, one could spot a few Americans who were immediately marked by their devotion to the steel helmet, and a total inability to cope with spiral puttees. They also wore brown, toe-capped shoes, and were already flaunting the ribbon of the Overseas Service medal, sewn on their overcoats. Strange, incongruous men, but those who knew them had high regard for their capabilities. Give any American a revolver or an automatic and he's instantly transformed into a real fighting man; he acts and moves as one born with a brace of small arms in his hands—but turn him loose on leave and he looks and behaves like an operatic spear-carrier who is suddenly assigned a role as a chariot driver in a *Ben-Hur* production. He's a fighting man, not a boulevard soldier.

Charlie's Bar at night: A conglomerate mass of trench-coated, field-booted men jostling and crowding a long, mahogany-and-brass bar, each defending his off-duty hiatus with as much determination as he had held a saphead. A few of them wore red tabs, one or two green. There were Brass Hats, and chalk-smeared tin hats only a few hours away from Pozières. Engineers, Royal Field Artillery, Anzacs, Yeomanry, and every branch of the Infantry. Here and there small, boisterous groups of Royal Flying Corps men, the stiffness of the tender still in their limbs, clamored for attention, drinks, or appeals for recognition.

Many who had stood in their places the night before were now dead somewhere near Warlencourt.

Charlie was one of those cosmopolitan characters who are as much a part of the popular bar as the till, the cork screw, the mirror, the cocktail shaker, the rows of bottles, and the pharmacopoeia of the profession. His nationality was unknown, but he could associate himself with an adjutant of Chasseurs Alpins, a second lieutenant of the Black Watch, or a captain of the Coldstream Guards, and give the impression that he was unquestionably of their blood line. While developing this relationship he would cheerfully cash checks at usurious discount, and suggest a visit to some nearby house of purple passion—all quite fraternal and above board, of course.

This host was a man of medium height, bland, clean-shaven, with cheeks tinged with the mortuary gray of years devoid of sunshine and fresh air. He walked stiffly erect on bowed legs to support a generous paunch which resulted in flat feet and no buttocks to speak of. He was as strong as a bull, and exuded an air of fake intelligence and wide knowledge. As a purveyor of war news he had no equal. He knew every general on the front by his first name and could predict every push, assault, withdrawal and defeat within twenty-four hours. He could spot a cap badge at twenty paces and docket its owner's division, corps, or brigade while drawing a glass of lager.

During the March push Charlie's was wrecked by shellfire, but with the patience and sagacity of his breed he moved up to Abbeville on the Channel and put up a very pretentious establishment, but by this time his luck had run out. A Hun air raid, one of the enemy's final gestures of desperation, flattened the building before the first platoon of customers had tramped over his threshold.

There always was music at Charlie's. Where it came

from no one knew or cared. It may have jangled off a large upright music box, the kind that provided discordant marches and Strauss waltzes from a gleaming disc of metal that turned against a nickel-plated harmonics comb. It may have come from some hidden phonograph, or a mechanical piano. No one bothered to inquire. One and all were satisfied to hum or nod in rhythm to the strains of *Give Me the Moonlight, Show Me the Girl and Leave the Rest to Me . . . Beware of Chu-Chin-Chow . . . I Know Where the Flies Go in the Wintertime . . . What Do You Want to Make Those Eyes at Me For? . . . She Had a Hole in Her Stocking . . . Goodbye-e-e-e, Don't Sigh-e-e-e, Wipe the Tear Baby Dear From Your Eye-e-e!* Broadway had not as yet taken over on the Picardy front, and Shaftesbury Avenue was still in command.

The redolence of Hollands gin, leather polish, cheap champagne, pomade, stale beer, Castrol, juniper, and to-bacco filled the long room which resounded with harsh fragments of talk, deep-rooted coughs, and hysterical laughter of men teetering on the brink of shell shock. There were mutters and whispers, some definite talk, but all on the same subject—the spring offensive.

"What does Charlie say?"

"The blighter guesses, and I wouldn't trust him."

"I hear the top staff blokes won't listen to a word about it."

"The staff is still working on the relief of Mafeking, and Jerry might be banging away at Villers Bretonneux by now."

"By the way, what's a bronx cocktail?"

"I had a flapper out last time I was home on leave, and offhandedly I asked her if she liked cocktails. Do you know what the silly little kipper said? Oh, I love them. Tell me one!' "

3

Phelps-Barrington, Trent, and Paterson disembarked from the tender in front of the Palais de Justice and wandered along a side street until they came out on the Rue des Trois-Cailloux. They peered into the misty window of an old bookshop, and passed along to the Arcade where they were drawn by the perfume of a flower stall, gay with posies. Trent wondered if it would be a good idea to buy a bunch or two to take back to their mess.

"They're very nice," P-B agreed, "but we have a long night before us . . ."

"And what flowers might evade tonight's Battle of Amiens perhaps would get back to 'C' Flight, only to be eaten by Mr. Yardley," Paterson chimed in, paraphrasing Hoyt's dissertation on the importance of petrol.

Trent and P-B exchanged knowing glances, and Phelps-Barrington observed, "This young gentleman is taking his growing pains very well."

In a general emporium they purchased, and stuffed into their trench-coat pockets, soap, tooth powder, shaving soap, boot laces, and khaki handkerchiefs. Thus supplied, they went on to a wine seller's, chiefly to study the market and learn what was available in case any of them was appointed mess secretary some dud day.

"Looking at all this reminds me that so far we have not, shall I say, wet our whistles. Shall we gorge ourselves on a dinner *avec* table wines, or should we avoid temptation and turn our fullest attention to the joys of *spiritus frumenti*—Charlie's Bar?"

"I'm ravenous," intruded Paterson.

"You're always ravenous," Phelps-Barrington cried in mock outrage.

Trent broke in to assuage both sides, "Look here, you

go gorge yourself at the Rhin or the Godebert, and pick us up later at Charlie's . . . just up the street here. If we should become completely displaced, remember we arranged to have the tender pick us up at the cathedral, near the front door."

"Eleven o'clock?"

"No later. The driver's pass is made out for midnight."

"I'll see you at Charlie's." Young Paterson beamed and hurried off to see Amiens through his own eyes.

Perhaps by youthful instinct, he turned down a side street and headed back toward the river. There was no moon but a luminescence from the water enabled him to walk along the quayside, pondering on the vast complex of cranes, warehouses, and the latticed paraphernalia of waterborne commerce. The sky to the north and the east shuddered and gasped white lights; at intervals a shaft of heated red daubed its raddled brush against fringy clouds, leaving a fleeting bouquet of artificial flowers. Larger blossoms marked the destruction of an enemy dump, or perhaps one belonging to the French. There was the rumble of guns, ugly and menacing, a drum roll that had been supporting the martial air for more than three years.

Enticed by the comparative quiet, Paterson sat on a dockside bollard and considered this tangled skein of war. His mind went back to the afternoon's patrol, to other days of flight and fright behind Hoyt's two streamers. His eyes turned and took in the sable scope of the wide battleground, and for the first time he considered the immensity of the war, the stupendous price of the massacre. In his mind's eye he arched across the Amiens night and focused on the map tacked up in 'C' Flight's hangar office, and brought to his vision the network of roads cluttered with endless trucks of wounded, the quilting of white crosses, and the never-ending streams of human energy being kept in motion along all the roads between Nieuport and Pontà-Mousson. Beyond that the Vosges applied a ribbed stopper to the carnage, and weary men thankfully huddled in that sylvan sanctuary and made the most of the respite.

Between Boulogne and Péronne convoys of lorries hauled food and ammunition for British troops. What trains that would run, and were available, carried more food, more men, and more shells to destroy the food and men of the enemy. And to pay for these attacks, ambulance trains and canvas-covered vehicles daubed with red crosses, crowded with the maimed and wounded, wound their way back to the casualty clearing stations, the hospitals, and perhaps home. The machinery and materials of slaughter passed back and forth inexorably; the figures, charts, graphs, and accounting staggered the imagination.

"I suppose it's the same down on the French front," he reflected with some awe, and rubbed his palms against the knees of his breeches. "It's the same in Italy, Salonika, Mesopotamia, and Egypt. At times it seems damned senseless, futile, wasteful. What am I contributing? What have I been trained for? I do nothing but book flight time. I take out racks of Cooper bombs, two belts of ammunition, and distribute them where they will do the most good. But wouldn't it be more rewarding to fight the Jerries in the air . . . and clean them out of the sky? As Hoyt says, 'It's all poohbah!' "

Paterson wound his way back to the center of the town, weaving through the dim electric torch lights that were flicked on and off by other pedestrians. Now and then a husky-voiced crone would croak her solicitation, but Paterson ignored the message, and continued on, quietly reveling in his personal salubrity.

"Not tonight, Josephine," he chided one particularly aggressive Suzanne.

"You no got five francs, eh?"

"Naughty! Naughty!" Paterson laughed at her.

As he strolled through the crowds he came to a lively looking restaurant, and he studied the clientele through a slit scraped in the blackout paint. Inside, there were a number of lanky Australians, glowing in brand-new Sam Browne belts and Digger hats. Among them were two colonels who had been privates before the Gallipoli landing. There were a few stocky Canadians with the whiff of horse dung and amatol on them, testifying that they were gunners—probably in from Combles. Some Americans with razor-blued chins, gaudy divisional patches, and an instinctive dislike for the Aussies and their big hats, were grouped in determined isolation. There were men with tired eyes and flecks of silver around their ears, who had no need to put up campaign ribbons or blue service chevrons; the long stain of war was on them. They were marked by their neat, oft-brushed tunics, and Sam Brownes that now were ruby-red with years of Kiwi polish. The blue and white Military Cross ribbons they had been awarded at Neuve-Chapelle in 1915 had frayed out months before, and had not been replaced, but the half-effaced oblong of unfaded serge where they had once gleamed, proclaimed the honor and service.

A greasy-fronted waiter snatched at Paterson's arm. "You are alone, sir? I take you at my table, eh?"

"Anywhere. You look crowded."

"Crowded? Yes, but I have a place wis another gentleman, an h'officer, sir . . . like you. You do not mind, eh?"

"Not at all, if he'll have me," Paterson said, and shucked out of his trench coat.

"He not mind, sir. He's a fine gentleman. He come to my table every night. You will find him . . . interesting, maybe."

"Just as long as I am not intruding."

"You not intrude. This way, sir."

The table was the last one along the side of the boxy

room, and a thin, emaciated man with the talc of war exhaustion on his face sat with his back to the angled wall.
His sparse amber hair was brushed down tightly over a
vein-knotted scalp; coal black eyes were sunk deep on
each side of a prominent, wedge-thin nose, and a neatly
trimmed mustache arched over a pair of scab-encrusted
lips. His long thin hands dithered uncertainly with the cutlery, and then reached up, seemingly to steady his loosely
hung chin.

"Ah, good evening, Flying Corps," he greeted with
some faint warmth. "Do sit down."

"I'm not intruding, am I? It's not a very roomy table,"
Paterson observed, hoping the waiter would agree and
guide him to a livelier companion.

"You not intrude," the waiter insisted, flicking at the tablecloth with his napkin, "the captain will be glad to have
you, sir."

"I suggest the rack of lamb," the specimen of the morti-
cian's art said hollowly, "and they have a very good Chauvenet available. You could try a spot of mine before
ordering."

"Chauvenet? I take it that's a French wine."

"A sparkling wine. Goes well with the mint sauce."

Paterson nodded to the waiter. "The rack of lamb *and* a
small bottle of Chauvenet."

"Good! Jolly good!" The man opposite him beamed.
"You'll enjoy them both I'm quite sure."

"It's very good of you to have me, sir," Paterson said,
feeling he was intruding on stark tragedy, and he tried to
avoid the piercing eyes set beneath the feminine curves of
the eyebrows. He steadied a rising concern for the ghostly
head precariously mounted on a frail neck swathed in an
oversize shirt collar.

"A good wine is so important to a meal these days," his
companion said, and Paterson took time to vet the

wretched figure while shaking out his napkin. A pallid, weak-chinned tailor's dummy that had been decked out in a new tunic with some indeterminate badges but it bore no decorations, wound stripes, or service chevrons. His hands, now resting lightly on the table, had once been fine, but today were hardly capable of the violent action of military service. Paterson came to the conclusion that the poor devil had been called up—presumably from a nursing home—to assume some unimportant administrative post, and was now tucked away in one of the many funk holes provided by the General Staff, a job that already was proving physically difficult.

"Jolly interesting work in your lot, I suppose," the frail man said and coughed. His words, low and halting, were spoken with that kindly depth of appeal the cultured Briton inherits and which no foreigner can ever imitate.

"Well, it is at times," Paterson agreed, "but we have our dud days the same as anyone else." He knew exactly how this poor devil must feel, propped up in a corner trying to avoid the contemptuous glances of real servicemen.

"Do you fly every day?"

"When the weather permits, and now and then when it's absolutely dud. But even then it's not too bad."

"Must be glorious. Have you had any good fights in the air?"

"Not yet," Paterson said, and felt he was operating under false pretenses. "We do low-altitude jobs, bombing and strafing enemy trenches, work of that sort. We don't get much chance to engage enemy aircraft down that low."

"How exciting! I've heard about that type of work. And you do that every day? It must be very encouraging to the ground troops. Poor devils, they need all they can get."

"They need all they can get? I really don't know what they need. We are supposed to provide what is called air support. How much the troops appreciate it or even know what's going on, I've never been able to find out."

"Oh, I see."

"It's a bit frustrating, in a way," the youthful pilot went on. "I fully expected to join a fighter squadron . . . that is, scout fighters, and get a lot of air fighting, but it seems that certain squadrons, those flying Sopwith Camels, have been assigned to this new low-altitude program. I'd rather be higher upstairs, fighting."

The thin man twirled his Chauvenet and considered the situation. "I see, I see."

Paterson decided to level the score, and asked, "Have you been up the line lately? I mean, you may have seen some of our chaps strafing the enemy trenches."

"Er . . . no. That is, unless you were in the Ypres show."

"Ypres? Which particular Ypres show?"

"The 1915 one when Jerry staged the first gas attack."

Ypres—1915! Paterson had to think that one out. Ypres—1915 sounded a bit like ancient history—Alexander the Great—chariots with knives on the wheels. "I'm afraid Ypres, 1915, was a bit before my time. Were you gassed at Ypres?"

"Gassed and captured," his companion said, and sat back while the waiter laid out Paterson's meal. "I'm sure you will like the Chauvenet. Watch the corkage Louis."

During the wine ceremony Paterson came to the conclusion that his host had indeed been through that dreadful period, and had gotten back somehow. No wonder he looked so peaked.

"Am I to understand that you were captured in 1915, and managed to get away . . . and are now back in harness?"

"Proper mess, Ypres. I was knocked out, you see, and

didn't quite know what was going on. I seem to have come to in a Jerry hospital at Tournai."

"And you recently escaped?"

"Yes, but I was a rotten long time managing it. Let's see, it's late February of 1918 now, isn't it? I mean, I missed the Somme show, didn't I?"

"But you were lucky to get out," Paterson retorted, and tried the wine. "This is very good, sir. I must remember it."

"I took a blasted long time, didn't I?"

"But most of the poor devils never make it," reflected Paterson. "I'd hate to be taken prisoner. I . . . I think I'd rather be killed outright than fall into the hands of the Hun."

The thin man leaned forward with a flash of enthusiasm that lit up his waxen features. "That's exactly how I felt. I felt dirty—as a prisoner—as though I had fallen into something foul. It was the Germans. I couldn't stand their touching me, not even the doctors and nurses. Night after night I begged for hot water to wash away the foulness of them."

Paterson nodded gloomily. "I don't think they'd hold me, if I was not too badly hurt." He retrieved his smile, and asked, "By the way, how did you get away . . . escape?"

"It's quite a long story," the emaciated one muttered, and stared at his savory. "Breaking out was not too bad, in spite of my . . . general condition, but I started off in the wrong direction. Instead of heading for Holland, I got turned around somehow and had to crawl over the Alps from down near München. I ran into a lot of cold and snow down that way."

"Then you crossed into Switzerland!"

"Over the Alps, yes. I presume it was Switzerland. There was so much snow and cold. This was last winter, remember. About a year ago. I was knocked about, rather, and have been in and out of dock ever since. You do understand, of course."

"You must have gone through a very bad time," Paterson agreed, "but how did you wind up here in Amiens? I should have thought you would have been sent straight home."

"Up to now that part is not very clear. I seem to have been passed from hospital to hospital until I arrived here. The Intelligence people have been giving me a proper going over, trying to get the story out of me so they can improve the How-to-Escape booklets, I suppose. I wasn't much help to them since I took so long. I think they prefer a more efficient job."

"Well, here you are, safe and sound." The young pilot smiled. "What happens now?"

"Well, I have been fixed up with a new uniform of sorts, and given a few days to get myself together. Now I'm waiting for a chance to get up to Boulogne or Le Havre. After that, home, I suppose."

"Let's hope you'll be able to make up for lost time." Paterson grinned. "Do you have any special plans?"

"Nothing particular." His companion drained his glass. "I do want to get over to Ireland and get in some riding. I used to keep a couple of nice hunters there before the war. Have you ever followed the hounds?"

"No. I'm afraid that was a bit beyond my allowance. A push-bike, and then just before I joined up, I did manage an Indian motorcycle."

"Not exactly the same thing, eh?" the ex-prisoner agreed. "Then I want to get back into tennis. I used to play a bit at Wimbledon. I think I might have reached a fair ranking, had it not . . ."

"Tennis! Now that's more in my line," Paterson boomed.

"And I'd even like to go back to Switzerland," the thin man mused, and stared into space.

"I should have thought you'd had enough of Switzerland."

"Ah, but the skiing there. Nothing to compare with it."

Paterson felt a new concern for this man. "Don't you think you'd better wait to get a little flesh on you, and . . . well, some rest and a few wholesome meals? You seem to be booking quite an active program."

"Oh, I'll be all right," the man protested. "Of course I shall have to take it easy at the start, but there's so much time to catch up. I was taken in '15, remember. Have you done any mountain climbing?"

Paterson capitulated at that. "You must be quite an athlete," he said, slowly savoring the thought. "You make me feel a pretty sedentary character. A bit of hockey in school, tennis with my sister's tomboy pals, and a run now and then with the cross-country team. No, I've never climbed a real mountain. I can't say that I've ever seen one, except in geography books."

"Ah, well." His new friend smiled. "You have a lot of years ahead of you, and you've done some flying. Now, I've never been off the ground, not even in a balloon."

"I can't quite believe that," Paterson said with an acidulous tinge in his voice, "you seem to have done everything else."

"I'd give a packet," the thin man said, "to go up . . . just once and have a shot at some Hun . . . and watch him go down in flames."

Paterson tried to find the secret of the man's bitterness by searching his eyes. "Who knows?" he said. "Perhaps you will if the war lasts long enough. I'm afraid I never shall as long as I'm on low-flying Camels."

"Flame is a great cleanser," the ex-prisoner said thoughtfully, and spread his thin hands on the table and raised a new smile. "Well, I suppose I shall have to be toddling. It has been very pleasant talking with you. I do hope you liked the Chauvenet . . . and, good luck!"

Paterson sat with his knife and fork poised over his lamb, then nodded, and watched his companion painfully force himself from his chair. The effort involved a slow, mechanical movement that held the pilot's eyes He started to offer some assistance, but the coal-black eyes flashed determination, and he was ordered to remain seated.

"Please don't bother," the man said with authority, and with that admonition he retrieved two walking sticks from behind his chair, fumbled unsteadily, finally propped them before him, then hobbled painfully through the gymkhana-maze of the tables—on two artificial legs

As Paterson watched the crippled man, he remembered his saying, "I ran into a lot of snow and cold down that way." He took short sips of wine as he considered that tragic journey to freedom.

4

The Chauvenet had body, bouquet, benevolence, and Paterson was pleasantly relaxed after his meal He left the restaurant, and after checking the time, decided to look for Trent and Phelps-Barrington At Charlie's they were nowhere to be seen, although he added two whiskies to his cargo. He talked with a captain of the sappers who had been in the Messines show, and then decided that his flight pals probably had gone on to the cathedral where they might be waiting for him in the shelter of the drafty tender.

"Good night, sir." Paterson said to the engineer bloke. "Nice talking to you. Next time I'll try to have a bloody good air fight for you."

"Take care of yourself, young fellow."

There was no trace of either Trent or Phelps-Barrington at the cathedral, and the tender was nowhere in sight. The young pilot sat down on the steps with his back to the built-up sandbag protection to the left of the sacristy door. He buttoned his trench-coat collar against the cold, and tried to remember the name of the wine the ex-prisoner had recommended. Then he was positive he could hear familiar voices.

"Trent? Is that you, Trent?" he called.

"Hello-o-o! Is that the tender?" Trent's voice came from somewhere above.

"No. It's Paterson. Where the devil are you?"

"Up here . . . a high-altitude show. Come on up."

From the flat space on top of the sandbags, Phelps-Barrington added, "We have Mr. Farquharson here, Mr. Paterson. Won't you join us?"

A puzzled Paterson climbed up the notched corner of the sandbag protection, and some fifteen feet above found Trent and P-B sitting with a third officer who was well potted. In fact, all three were well along, but Mr. Farquharson proved to be one of those precious toffs whose masticated accent at the best of times was almost unintelligible. In his cups he was beyond compare. He was saying, "As a matter of fact we haven't been in Amiens in one hundred and sixteen years."

"What's he say?" Paterson asked, wondering if he should have taken those two whiskies.

"He says they haven't been in Amiens in one hundred and sixteen years."

"Who?"

"His regiment."

Trent attempted to clarify this. "They wear tin things up here, long white plumes in their helmets . . . and they clank."

"Sounds interesting. How do they like it?"

"Apparently they're very fond of it," Phelps-Barrington added from the human pile.

"And when I say Amiens," Mr. Farquharson bumbled on, "the records aren't quite clear whether or not we passed *through* Amiens, or about eight miles south. We were chasing Ney's rear guard, y'know."

"He can't be that befuddled," Paterson said with some concern.

"This is nothing. He's not sure he was in Amiens, even then," P-B explained.

· "And they ride white horses," Trent broke in, trying to light a cigarette. "Charles the Second made them ride white horses."

Farquharson snuffled into the scene again. "And I assure you there's a very good reason to believe that wasn't the first time either, because I'm positive the regiment was raised as a private body of retainers for His Grace the Duke of Slough, and the Duke of Slough let them out as mercenaries to serve with the Spanish in Alva's train, somewhere around 1552."

"The date could be right, but I'm getting bewildered again," argued Paterson, and sat on the edge of the sand-bag pile.

"Of course the date is right, but he said they were in Amiens before that."

Trent barked, "Be quiet. He's trying to think."

"The important thing about the whole thing seems to be that if a regiment is worth a gentleman's attention at all, it's been almost everywhere before you join it," Farquharson muttered, "and there's not the slightest use in worrying about where it is, or where it's going next."

"Oh, quite, quite!" seconded Phelps-Barrington.

"Now what is *he* saying?" Farquharson rose to his elbows.

"There's nothing to it, really," P-B continued, "but tell Mr. Paterson about the *pot de chambre*."

"Oh, you must hear about that," Trent said solicitously.

"The *pot de chambre?*" Paterson said. "Are we still with his regiment?"

"Of course. Mr. Farquharson has been wounded five times."

"Is that possible?"

"Oh absolutely," Trent persisted, and explained, "Once at Namur where the regiment was in 1815, three times at Mons where Alva was in 1572, and he was shot off the latrines at Dunkirk—right into the chloride of lime. No man would admit that if it wasn't so."

Farquharson elbowed his way to a sitting position. "You see, Napoleon got out of his carriage at Quatre Bras, and then had a horse sent for, and he got on the ruddy horse, and then the carriage ran away, and it ran right into a patrol of our chaps, only they headed it off, and chased it down toward the sunken road. It was there the damned thing tipped over, and everything fell out—including the *pot de chambre*. Well, you can imagine the situation, eh? Our chappie who was in command there, grabbed the piece of crockery and yelled, 'Yoicks!' or 'Tally-ho!' or some such hunting nonsense. I don't go in for that sort of thing myself. I'd rather shoot grouse."

"None of this makes much sense to me," Paterson said.

"It's simple. He says he prefers to shoot grouse."

"But what about the . . . er . . . *pot de chambre?*"

"Don't be so damned impatient. It was Napoleon's piss pot, and it had an 'N' and crown inscribed on it," P-B explained.

"Oh, bloody funny, eh?" Paterson cried, finally getting the drift of the conversation.

Farquharson beamed, nodded, and said, "And when we get a civilian in the mess, we sconce him with it."

"A nice touch, that," P-B added. "That's how you build up regimental tradition. All you need is a piss pot."

A hoarse voice cried out from the steps below. "Forty-four Squadron tender here. Any officers up there on the sandbags, please?"

Phelps-Barrington cupped his hands and answered, "Three of us, driver, and one man just getting back from fighting Napoleon at Waterloo. May we bring him? He'd like to go as far as Albert with us."

"Right you are, sir. Bring him along. Plenty of room."

"He's from a very good regiment, driver."

"That's quite all right, sir."

"Thank you. Please come up and get us."

5

Early the next morning when the weather kept the war birds in their hangars, there was time for rest and reflection. In the cookhouse adjoining the officers' mess, Shuffling Joe and Shuffling Wally sat on a brace of engine-oil boxes peeling potatoes. In the faint glow of a service range nearby, a very thin, cadaverous corporal-cook was stirring a tureen of gray-flannel oatmeal. Corporal Fairbrother was monarch of all he surveyed in this foul, disordered cavern.

"Wot I say," Shuffling Wally contributed, as Fairbrother guzzled a small basin of tea, "is that Mr. 'Oyt likes to strut 'imself mentally, that is. That's wot keeps 'im going. 'E'd go out of 'is way to 'elp a man, if 'e thought 'e could do it without much show; just so that other man could say Mr. 'Oyt *ad* done it. 'E's always meeting 'imself 'alfway round."

Shuffling Joe had another viewpoint. "That ain't the way to say it. Mr. 'Oyt is like something you read in books. 'E's like them knights wot lays on tops of their own coffins in Windsor Castle. 'E's real, 'is Mr. 'Oyt."

"Capting Hoyt!" Corporal Fairbrother corrected, waving his ladle.

"Well, 'e was Mr. 'Oyt not so many days back."

"I'm a man for h'etiquette, I am," Fairbrother said pointedly.

"An' then there's Mr. Phelps-Barrington wiv 'is women," went on Shuffling Wally. "That's wot keeps *'im* alive. 'E ain't got all them women. 'E's got one woman—somewhere."

"Right! 'E's got one woman somewhere, an' 'e makes every other woman in the world look like 'er," Shuffling Joe said and stared at the dusty eye of a large spud.

"Then there's Mr. Trent an' 'is bleedin' railways. It ain't a railway wot keeps Mr. Trent goin'. It's system. Doin' *this* on time and *that* on time, and goin' to the W.C. on time, an' 'ow much 'e does, and 'ow much 'e doesn't do. Is 'e turnin' in an accurate report? That's wot keeps Mr. Trent goin'," said Shuffling Wally, poking a finger at his audience.

"Mr. Trent's afraid," Shuffling Joe muttered.

"Of course Mr. Trent's afraid. 'E's so afraid that if 'e didn't keep on time, 'e'd bolt! An' take young Mr. Paterson. If Mr. Paterson didn't believe that Captain 'Oyt and Mr. P-B were the greatest pilots on the front, 'e'd bolt too!"

Corporal Fairbrother stood with his hands on his thin hips. "An' where would they bolt to, may I ask?"

Shuffling Joe put on a wrinkled frown and bored in, "Do you know 'ow easy it is for a pilot to bolt this game? It's easier for them than it is for us. Did it ever occur to you 'ow close Germany is? I don't mean the real Germany. I mean the h'occupied area. For instance, if a pilot really wanted to bolt, all 'e'd 'ave to do would be to pick the right morning, and the right engine trouble."

"Very interesting. An' wot would 'e do then?" Shuffling Wally inquired as he cleaned his fingernails.

"Ignition trouble, my lad," said Shuffling Joe with the professional touch. "First you pulls the throttle back, flood 'er wiv a very 'eavy mixture, which gives you a beautiful blue plume of smoke. You 'ave to cut the ignition, you see. Anyone lookin' at you would think you 'ave a very bad case of engine trouble. Then wot do you do? You poke your stick slightly forward, an' then to the right, an' that makes your nose *and* your right wing go down . . . an' you start to slip. You give yourself a slow count of 'ten' and you pulls the stick back hard . . . an' to the left, and then wot 'appens? I'll tell you wot 'appens. You almost goes over on yer back. But mind you, you've got to keep the rudder bar steady, else they'll know wot yer up to; because if you're really 'it, your feet will be froze, side by side. *Rigor mortis* could 'ave set in. So now yer slippin' orf to the left, an' they've all seen you actin' erratic—and the smoke, so in their minds, yer 'it, and yer a casualty, an' all you 'ave to do from then on is to flop down into Germany, an' yer out of the fight, an' yer out of the war, an' yer an 'ero."

" 'Ow simple," Corporal Fairbrother agreed.

From the area of the mess beyond came two quick bongs on the dinner-gong cylinder, followed by a space, and two more quick bongs.

"That'll be a double whisky and soda," observed Shuffling Wally.

Three bongs followed the last two.

"That'll be a Special Reserve whisky," said Shuffling Wally. "They're startin' in early today."

"That's for Mr. MacClintock," Shuffling Joe said.

"Mr. MacClintock's bin dead several weeks. Where's yer mind, anyhow? It's only Mr 'Arboard takes the Special now. The rest drinks any muck."

Paterson was at loose ends, and somewhat thoughtful over his late breakfast as he sorted out the indistinct memories of the night before. He could still savor the wine and the glucose confection of the dessert as he reviewed the escapades of Mr. Farquharson and his mysterious regiment. But it was the strange, courageous man with the artificial legs who centralized his interest. Why had he been so intrigued with air fights and concerned about shooting down Huns—in flames? What a rare personality! one to be admired, and yet, they were all the same. The instant they spotted a Flying Corps chap, their instincts were to go aloft and joust with enemy airmen. How many Huns have you shot down? What is it like to get into a fight up there? That sapper bloke from Messines had asked the same questions, and he hadn't been able to explain any of it; might just as well be back home teaching Quirks to make three-point landings.

He thought they were quite right in their assumption that a flying man should be fighting the enemy high in the sky. Anyone who swanked about with wings on his jacket, drawing flying pay as well as his rank money, ought to do something to earn it. Just messing about down low trying to pitch Coopers into enemy trenches wasn't really in the category of air action. Couldn't the artillery do that ten times better? They could, if some old B.E.s or R.E.8s were in the air to register the shoot for them, and *they* could spot for the guns only if some bloke in a Camel or an S.E.5 would shoot the Huns off their tails while they tootled about down low, doing the Eyes-of-the-Army act. But someone *had* to be up there to take care of the artillery spotters and the poor bloody photo-reconnaissance chaps. It stood to reason.

Paterson stared about the room while he tried to put a vague plan of action into some workable format. Mr. Yardley, the gigantic rustic, was pawing with the phonograph trying to make it work, but he produced only harsh scratches, moans, discordant tympany, and strange guttural phrases. Mr. Harboard sat on the front edge of a rickety wicker chair opening and reading a number of letters, all written on beautiful cream paper, and drawn from expensive, gaudily crested envelopes. Trent was partly hidden behind a two-week-old copy of the *Devon Morning News,* digesting the details of the Sidmouth Assize Court. P-B was stretched out on two old chairs, a steaming cup of tea in his hands, and a look of aristocratic resignation on his countenance.

Outside, the last signs of winter were sparkling on the tawny grass; every twig and small branch on the few bare trees was silvered with thin, icy armor; diamond pendants were strung from hapless bushes, and light brushings of frost left indefinite designs on the hangar canvas. Yet there was a promise of spring, for with the coming rains there would be an early peep of blossoms and vernal melodies from earth and sky. Winter would soon pass, and the wrecks of her storms would decay to feed the expanding leaves and bright blossoms to set an incongruous backdrop for man's battles to come.

"Good morning, Paterson." Captain Hoyt broke into the youth's reverie. "Have a good time last night?"

"Well, it was a change, sir."

"I hope Trent and P-B didn't get you potted. We may get a special job later this afternoon."

"Oh. How late?"

"In time to get back before dark . . . if the weather holds.

"Special? In what way? We're always getting specials, but they always turn out to be the same damn thing. Using up good gasoline to fire belts of ammunition and dump racks of Coopers on the same old trenches. What's special about that?"

"There's a big Hun push coming up. I presume you have heard something about that. The men who will make the attack will be in those trenches, awaiting the word. Anything we can do should make it all the harder for them. I don't want you to forget that."

"This special, this afternoon . . . the whole flight will go?"

Hoyt allowed Shuffling Wally to set out a plate of bacon and eggs, a bowl of the gray porridge, a large mug of steaming tea, and two thick slices of toast. Once the breakfast was arranged, Hoyt said, "All of us . . . Yardley included. He should be about ready now, and you know, we have Mr. Mallory again, and though I had intended to work him back in gradually, I may have to include him. His punctures healed nicely, and he's really entitled to some leave, but he insisted on coming back here instead of going all through the Pool routine and winding up, God knows where."

"But if he had gone on leave, passed his medical in London and was declared fit, wouldn't he have been promoted and given a flight in some other squadron?" protested Paterson.

"One hundred to one, but that's Mallory. He doesn't want a flight. He insisted on coming back here to his old job."

"I must say that's a rare compliment to you, sir But I hope you aren't rushing him."

"I wish he would take some leave, but Mallory has other ideas," Hoyt explained dawdling with his porridge. "Frankly, I don't believe he has a home to go to."

Paterson looked troubled at the remark.

"I have an idea Mallory's home is somewhere in Canada. He seems to have bought his way over to join up in 1915. The family is English, of course, but he doesn't seem to have anyone he cares for in Blighty . . . so leave there doesn't mean much to him."

"It's very hard to picture a situation like that," Paterson said slowly. "Imagine no one to go home to."

"He's like so many of us," Hoyt went on in a confessional tone. "The war set up a new world, a new life, a new group of friends and acquaintances. A lot of us came up from the gutter and the war has cloaked us with a temporary social standing, and our former life is something we're trying to live down."

"You're still talking about Mallory, of course," Paterson probed.

Hoyt searched the young pilot's face—and decided to go on. "You take a kid who joined up just before the war. Let's say he went into the Territorials to get away from a slatternly home, a dreary job in a factory, to enjoy a few weekends in the fresh air, or a summer respite from the murk and rut of civilian life."

"I know one or two like that," Paterson said thoughtfully.

"But a war broke out and caught these kids up in its net. They were sent out here to fight, and if they lived long enough or went through one big show, they probably picked up a couple of stripes. One or two may have won decorations and before they realized what was happening to them they were commissioned in the field, and found themselves suddenly bundled into a new level of society. The officer class."

"But, of course, it won't last long."

"Impermanent, temporary, I agree, but you must remember that this war has been on for nearly four years, and for many of them this new level of society now seems regulation. Most of them like it, and have gradually worked into the new life, aping all the mannerisms, speech, conversation, and what goes for social graces in this new order. Then one day they learn that leave has been granted, and they find themselves being sent home, dressed as officers, and they realize they will have to mingle with the lower orders they grew up with, and face an environment that is now repellent to them. They simply cannot go through with it. I think Mallory comes in this class. I have never found out where he went to school, where he was brought up, or what he did before the war. He always manages to evade every question: you can't drag any of his past out of him."

"In other words," Paterson said, as he rubbed his peach-fuzz cheek, "this war isn't changing the social order. It is just shuffling it about, and it will end with all sorts of people on top who will spend the next few years scrambling to hold on to what they have attained. It doesn't speak too well for the prospects of peace, does it, Skipper?"

"A lot of the Mallorys will hope it never ends," Hoyt said sadly, "especially those jossers in the staff jobs. They've never been so well off in their lives. They live high, get better-than-average pay, enjoy a social standing they've never deserved, and seldom have to take any risk greater than a tin of spoiled salmon. But what is there for them to go home to? Most of them were seedy solicitor's clerks before the war, one or two perhaps were Yeomanry blokes who, instead of riding to hounds, did two weeks in the summer having their boots polished, their saddlery cleaned, and their clothes brushed while a few old-sweat sergeants tried to teach the rustics how to do dismounted action. When trench warfare broke out there was nothing for the horse soldiers to do, so many of their officers were given a pair of red tabs and made staff officers. No wonder we can't win the war."

Paterson missed most of this diatribe; he was trying in his mind to justify himself before the man with the artificial legs. But he was still under hypnotic spell of his skipper, and to continue this cozy interlude he suddenly asked, "What did you do before the war, sir?"

Hoyt thought the question over, as he watched Yardley enjoying the fruits of his all-thumbs' effort to get the phonograph to play.

"Me? I suppose I'm another Mallory. I have little idea how I got here, but there ain't many who do. The war at least created a goal. I had none before 1914. I was burdened with an unco-ordinated education that wasn't worth a damn. It fitted me for nothing because it was designed for nothing, but to keep a handful of unworthy teachers in a job. When they were through with me I had little more than a middle-class attitude of snobbery for anyone who hadn't reached the same form."

"What about your parents?"

"My father was a reformed burglar, not a particularly good one, either. He became a locksmith, a general tinkerer, and a mender of umbrellas."

"Oh, I say, you're kidding me," Paterson objected.

"You asked me, and I'm telling you. My dad was fairly clever with locks and he was not too particular whose locks he picked until the police took him in hand and showed him how he could put his skill to better use. He opened a shop, took on all sorts of odd jobs, and when he picked up umbrella repairing, he gradually worked up a tidy little business. Umbrellas are big money in England, you know. I think he did very well for a time, and Mother who had been on the repertory stage in a few supporting roles, was glad to retire and become 'respectable.' All this took place in Birmingham."

"But where did you go to school?"

"School? Oh, now you have me. I dawdled through the local Board schools with no particular honors. I loved history, geography, and anything about the coal-mining trade of Britain. I was no good at arithmetic, drawing, or music —and even worse at sports. I was the basher type, banging or thrusting wildly at everything, and displaying no skill of any kind. Queer, too, because I always wanted to be a champion at something so that I could wear a distinctive blazer, cap, or medallion."

"What about your rugby football? You ought to be good at that if you're such a charger."

"I was hopeless. Any mug could evade me. I was always bashing about in all directions. At soccer, I was even worse!"

"But you don't behave that way in the air—over the line."

"I've learned a lot of lessons out here in France. It takes a war to knock sense into most of us."

"Funny thing. I'd have taken you for a university man, Skipper."

"Well, I'm not. There was a time when Mother decided that they could afford to put me in a small preparatory school, hoping the advertised individual attention would bring out the best in me. I must admit that it did, for a year or two, and I was really in my element, but the money dropped off, and I had to go back home and see what could be done next."

"That was tough, sir."

'But those two years had planted a seed. I had met first-class chaps who inspired me, and I suppose I might have become someone had I been able to stay. However, I had seen what I wasn't, and I began to get some sense and ambition. I mimicked everything I admired. I did my best to obtain and read good books. I tried to behave and speak like a university man—a product of Eton or Harrow; but I must confess I'm really a graduate of Mr. Andrew Carnegie's free public libraries. Mother next got me a post with a good bank in London, but at that point Dad went off the rails again and wound up in Pentonville Jail, after a particularly juicy trial that appeared on the front pages of the *News of the World* for three straight weeks. I must say Dad went out in a blaze of glory, and I was politely asked to resign from the bank. Fortunately for me, the Kaiser decided to rape poor little Belgium, and I, 'aflame with patriotic fervor,' as they say on the war memorials, sacrificed my doubtful future and enlisted."

"You said you came out with some cavalry regiment," Paterson said eagerly.

Hoyt looked sheepish. "That wasn't true. That's what I told you when you arrived here. It's an old habit of mine. Actually, I first enlisted in the Army Service Corps, for somewhere along the line I had learned to drive a Leyland lorry. So I began my service at six shillings a day, whereas most other poor devils had joined up in the infantry where they were paid only one and six a day."

Paterson looked woebegone, but managed to ask, "Why didn't you stay in the A.S.C.?"

"Why didn't you stay at er, Yale?"

"I didn't like being out of uniform."

"And I didn't like getting six shillings a day for driving a supply lorry in comparative safety behind the lines when other men were being wiped out for eighteen pence a day. Neither of us makes the slightest bit of sense, but there it is, and let the bloody historians and psychologists figure it out. They'll have some cockeyed answer by the late nineteen twenties."

Paterson mulled that one over, and then said, "Have you ever told all this to anyone here before, Skipper?"

"No. No one ever asked me before."

"Would you do me a favor? Would you give me what the journalists call an 'exclusive' on the story?" the youngster asked with simplicity.

"Thanks. That's one of the nicest requests I've had in years," Hoyt said, staring at his cold egg. "I feel as if I had suddenly come across my name in a prominent position in the Military Gazette."

Yardley's record ground to an asthmatic halt and the big boy leaped to his feet to feed another disc to the machine: *Beware of Chu-Chin-Chow*.

Whether it was because of Hoyt's few minutes of confidential disclosure which he felt gave him some license, or whether he had decided that the time was ripe to put a gnawing idea into action, Paterson was not certain, but he said, "By the way, Skipper, if the weather clears a bit, could I do a test flight? I've had my rigger replace the aileron cables on my bus, and I'd like to make sure he has run them in so there's no lag. I hate a soggy aileron control."

Hoyt dropped his knife and fork. "You didn't tell me you had cable trouble. I want to know whenever you have any problems of that kind. I like to keep after Opperdyke on jobs like that. They can get bloody slack, those chaps. However, if you get a chance before this special show, go ahead, but don't stray off too far on your own. Understand?"

"It'll be just a test flight over the field, sir. Nothing more."

Hoyt studied Paterson's eyes and wondered just what he planned, but added pointedly, "Nothing more."

"Thanks, Skipper."

"I can be back in less than an hour," Paterson assured himself when he was back in his cubicle pondering on whether to use only a short leather flying coat or his full-length Sidcot suit. "I just want to try to satisfy myself. There can't be any harm in just going up around Péronne–Cambrai and looking things over with my own eyes. Who knows, I may come across some lumbering old reconnaissance bus doing a photography show over our lines. That would be lovely."

He drew on his trench coat and service cap and sauntered out to the hangar trying to appear nonchalant, but keeping an eye open for any surveillance on the part of Hoyt who had said he had a few letters to write. Sergeant Opperdyke was superintending the opening of a propeller crate and making sure that Izzard was careful in hauling a new, highly polished airscrew from the container.

". . . and I want you to check the bolt holes to make sure this one fits a Clerget boss plate," Opperdyke was saying when Paterson appeared. "Oh, good morning, sir."

"Good morning, Sergeant. Someone else been shooting holes in props?"

"Oh, no, sir. We're just checking stock in Stores—in case we have a quick change to make. We never know what we have until we open the boxes. The Aircraft Park will ship anything out, unless we watch them."

"The farther back, the slacker they get, I suppose."

"That's how it goes . . . yes."

"Oh, by the way, if the weather clears a bit, I'd like to do a fifteen-minute test. I've talked about it to Captain Hoyt, and he said I could if the weather lifts."

"Anything wrong, sir?"

"Nothing particular. But I have noticed that my aileron control has become a bit soggy. We have a special on later this afternoon and I just thought I might make sure it was nothing that couldn't be attended to before we take off later on."

"Of course, sir. I think 'A' Flight across the field is warming up to get away in half an hour. They must know the weather is breaking, somewhere. At any rate, if there's anything requiring my attention, let me know and I'll see to it personally, sir."

"Thank you, Sergeant. Let's run my bus out, take the bombs off for now and have her handy if we get a break, eh?"

"You want the bombs taken off, sir?"

"I don't want to risk a landing with them on, do I?"

"No, sir. Right you are then. I'll have the bombs taken off."

"Only if we look like getting an early break in the weather," Paterson explained, and hurried back to his cubicle. "I don't see anything wrong in just going up and having a look around," he reassured himself for the twentieth time. "I've been out here several weeks now, and I ought to know where I am, and what I am doing."

But reassurance came hard. From some obscure area beyond the walls of the living quarters he could hear the buzz, popping, and high screams of engines being warmed, and with this preparation he twitched with the first twinges of concern. As he walked up and down the limited space, his knees felt slack and shot with indeterminate pain. He looked about the room for a new focal point, and then went over to the framed photograph on the orange-box convenience. There was a leaden fullness in his throat, and something itchy triggered a cough. To the girl in the frame, he confided, "I needn't be gone very long. It'll be something like going back to school for examinations. You don't feel too keen about it, but you know you'll be back within a week, or a few days. I'm probably asking for it, but I've got to go."

He unbuttoned his tunic and took his Sidcot suit from its peg. He retained his service boots and puttees to give credence to the claim that his flight was to be merely a test that would require no great altitude or time. Knowing that

Opperdyke would be in no particular hurry to put a couple of men to hauling his Camel out of the hangar, he sat down on the edge of his cot to stay clear of any possible interception. Once he had heard one of the Camels from the opposite side of the field take off, he planned to saunter out, hoping that no one would question his being in flying kit, or query why a 'C' Flight bus was being warmed up.

As he huddled there with his thoughts, he became sleepy and half-considered a post-breakfast snooze, but feared he might drop off under the spell of some self-hypnosis, so he checked with his watch, and contemplated the possibility of brightening his cell with a few *La Vie Parisienne* pictures, or perhaps a couple of Bruce Bairnsfather's sepia cartoons of Old Bill and Bert cut out of *The Bystander*. His head seemed stuffy, his breathing came in uneven spurts, and he decided that the Sidcot suit was too tight across his chest, so he unbuttoned the flap.

But why this sudden depression, this annoying, inner doubt? He had felt confident while talking to Hoyt at breakfast. Now his mind had wound up into a tangled ball of irrelevant ideas, among which was a sudden recollection of old Magthorpe. He gradually realized that he hadn't seen much of the talkative tender driver since the day the old codger had brought him up from Pilots' Pool. Damned interesting, old Magthorpe and his ghosts from France's former wars. "Good old Agincourt. I must try to get up that way one of these days to see if there's anything left of the two woods at Agincourt and Tramecourt. I'd love to walk through that historic defile:

'For he that today sheds his blood with me
Shall be my brother; be he ne'er so vile,
This day shall gentle his condition:
And gentlemen in England now a-bed

Shall think themselves accurs'd they were not here,
And hold their manhoods cheap while any speaks
That fought with us upon Saint Crispin's day.' "

Paterson smiled to himself. "You're right, Mr. Magthorpe, that was Shakespeare again, putting words into other people's mouths." And with that ancient assurance, he rose to his feet, grabbed his goggles, gloves, and helmet. "Up and at 'em!" he challenged, and went out to the hangar.

6

The Camel marked 'R' was standing alone with Bream, the fitter, leaning against the fuselage near the tail assembly. Sergeant Opperdyke stood in the hangar doorway showing little interest, seemingly engrossed in a wad of indent forms.

"Is she fully fueled?" Paterson asked the mechanic.

"Everything. Petrol, oil, and ammunition, sir. I 'ad 'er ready for this afternoon's patrol. Now I suppose I shall 'ave it all to do again when you come back."

"Sorry. I shan't be long."

"The S'nt said that you said there was something wrong with the aileron cable. I carn't find anything wrong. Are you sure you meant this bus, sir?"

"It's been getting slack for days. I just want to check it. Come on . . . Switch off . . . Petrol on . . ."

The mechanic swung the prop several twirls while Paterson fastened his belt, waggled the joystick, and watched the reaction on the ailerons and elevators.

"Switch on, sir . . . Contact!"

The Clerget opened with a series of loud pops, but continued to twirl. The engine firing smoothed out as Paterson made quick adjustments on the throttle and fine-adjustment lever, and she gradually flowed into a concerted roar of power. He eased back, and allowed the Clerget to warm up, but kept a cautious watch on the hangar opening, half expecting to see Hoyt hurrying out to renew his demand that the test be confined to the area over the field.

Izzard shuffled out to help Bream hold the tail down while the pilot ran the engine up for its final test. She put on well over 1300 rpms, and he signaled to Bream to haul the wheel chocks away.

As he waddled out to the center of the field, checking the wind sock that was fluttering over the hangar, a trace of filtered blue could be seen off to the west, and there was some evidence of a breeze that flattened the hangar canvas against the inner framework. Paterson now wished that he had risked changing into fleece-lined flying boots, for he had not yet been up anywhere near the Camel's ceiling since he had come out to France. It could be damned cold, wearing only military boots and a pair of lightweight socks.

Swinging into the wind, and running his thumb around the belt to smooth out the binding, Paterson finally fulfilled his quaking ambition; he eased up the throttle and went off to the war. The Camel behaved splendidly and climbed well for the first ten minutes. He turned back and circled the field twice, and then put on some evidence of testing out his ailerons by making right and left banks, hoping that Hoyt might be out on the tarmac watching. Then, with that obligation completed, Paterson turned, continued to climb, and headed for the bend of the Somme and the disorder that was Péronne.

"I'll get up to about fourteen thousand and mope about, just to see what goes on. If anything turns up, and I think I have a chance, I'm going to have a crack at him. Perhaps I can join up with some Nieuports or French Spads."

The sky was still leaden, with here and there faint

grayish-blue spots, and far to the north a streak or two of dirty yellow seemed to probe down through the murk and die away in the low-level mist. He circled the old town twice, checked the line and activity of the balloons, and then risked a short intrusion along the Péronne–Saint-Quentin road. There was no particular activity, except a couple of ranging Archie shots, and the young pilot turned once more, took on another five hundred feet and coursed back northwestward. He spotted a formation of Bristol Fighters and tried to join them, but they obviously were intent on escorting a flght of D.H.4s on some bombing mission, and after a few minutes of effort and experimentation with his fine-adjustment control, which in no way improved his speed, he turned back with the intention of patrolling the Péronne–Saint-Quentin road again.

He had hardly settled back with his compass card leveling off when he suddenly caught sight of a German two-seater, one with the modern straight-barred crosses on its wings and fuselage. He tried to identify it, finally settling for a Hannoveraner. It had the typical whale body, splayed center-section struts, and a heavy biplane-type tail assembly. It was daubed in green-and-brown mottled lozenge designs.

"What the devil is he doing up at this height?" Paterson pondered. "That's supposed to be a ground-attack fighter. Probably the pilot wants to make out he's a Bristol Fighter chappie. Well, I might as well have a whack and see what that gunner will do."

A short time before Paterson had encountered his enemy aircraft, Captain Hoyt was interrogating Sergeant Opperdyke in front of 'C' Flight's hangar.

"You check out that aileron cable replacement on Mr. Paterson's bus, Sergeant?" he demanded with a black frown.

"Cable replacement, sir? There has been no cable replacement as yet. Mr. Paterson just went up to check it out, sir."

"He told me he had ordered his rigger to make a cable replacement; that he wanted to do a test flight before this afternoon's patrol. I was under the impression that a replacement had been ordered and made. What the hell is going on?"

"There seems to be some misunderstanding, sir. Mr. Paterson came out and told me he had permission from you to do a fifteen-minute test. Said his aileron control had become a bit soggy—as he put it—and asked me to have her brought out, the bombs taken off, and that was that."

"He said nothing more than that?"

"Nothing, sir. I wasn't on hand when he took off. Bream started him up . . . and off he went," Sergeant Opperdyke explained.

Captain Hoyt stared off to the east, and realized his blackest fear. "He ordered the bombs taken off? But his bus was fueled and ready for this afternoon's show, eh? The bloody fool!" He glanced over his shoulder toward the hangar. "Get my Camel out, Sergeant. Same thing. Take the bombs off, but make certain the tank is full, and that I have some ammunition. Make it fast!"

"Yes, sir. Fast it is."

"Right away!"

"Izzard! Featherstone!" the sergeant bellowed. "Get Captain Hoyt's Camel out . . . fast!"

As Hoyt sprinted for his cubicle to pick up his flying equipment, he yelled over his shoulder, "Warm her up fast, Sergeant!"

In the hutment corridor Hoyt almost bowled over Phelps-Barrington who was just leaving Portwine after some routine order concerning the disposal of his laundry.

"Sorry, P-B. Out of the way. I'm in a bit of a hurry."

"Anything wrong, Skipper?"

"Young Paterson. He's buggered off on a flip into Hunland. He's had it in his mind for days."

"Well, he's picked a sure way to cure that malady. What are you doing in such a bloody rush?"

Hoyt put on a faked look of surprise. "I'm going after him, of course."

"Going after him? You must be wonky!"

"No, it's Paterson who is wonky, the bloody fool!"

P-B leaned against Hoyt's doorway watching the flight commander clambering into his Sidcot suit. "Just what are you planning to do, Skipper?"

"Go over there and bring him back."

"I take it, you know exactly where he is."

"Of course I don't, but he'll be on his own front somewhere."

"You sure he knows where his own front is?"

"Don't act so bloody difficult. I'm responsible for that kid, and I'm going to bring him back and give him a bloody good talking to."

"I hope he'll be alive to hear it."

"Of course he'll be alive," Hoyt ranted. "Don't take that attitude. He's a damn good pilot, is Paterson. I just want to . . . to make sure of him."

"He's not that damn good. None of them are until they've been out here a couple of months. If you're so sure he's a good pilot, he'll come back. If not, nothing you can do will bring him back—unless, of course, you have devised some practical plan of going down and picking him up out of Hunland."

"Don't be an ass!"

"What was it the kettle called the pot?"

"The least I can do is to go over, find him, and order him back . . . and see that he gets back."

"If you do that you have a very bright future with Scotland Yard," Phelps-Barrington said offhandedly, and looked down the corridor. "You haven't the slightest idea where he is. He could have buggered off to see some pal he thinks is up at Doullens, Abbeville, or Saint-Pol."

Hoyt was pulling on his helmet. "He would have asked me if it had been anything as simple as that. He knows I wouldn't have denied him anything like that," he raged.

"So on this basis you have decided that he has gone over the line to have a go on his own. Is that it?"

"You know damn well it is. It's all he has talked about since he arrived here."

"I know that. I've heard him prattle on, too. I'm just surprised he has waited this long."

"Kids like Paterson are like that. I suppose they're the blokes who are going to win the war. They'll never see the end of it, but this is their code."

"Very commendable. Misplaced idealism, of course, but it makes nice history." Phelps-Barrington smirked, and turned back to the corridor. "By the way, would you like me to go along with you?"

The skipper stared at P-B, and then smiled. "No thanks. It's good of you to offer, but someone has to behave rationally. I want you to stand by just in case someone else has to take the late-afternoon show."

"You know, Skipper, it must be very gratifying to have high ideals. But I'll be here."

"Thanks. If you ever think up a new religion, let me know where you're preaching, will you, P-B?"

Paterson began making zigzag passes as he moved closer to the big two-seater. He stalked——or believed he did——watching the leather-shrouded gunner who was keeping the Parabellum machine gun aimed in his general direction. He tried to remember all he had been taught at gunnery school, but none of the classroom dogma would come back. He was tense and uncomfortable; he was gripping the stick so hard the folds of his glove were clamping chunks of his palm until his hand ached.

There was a minute or so of pusillanimity when he wondered who was stalking whom, and he looked back and up, expecting to see a swarm of Albatros scouts drilling down at him. But the sky above was clear, except for several black Archie blobs.

"I wish I could have caught them by surprise," he mumbled to himself, "but the gunner bloke has me spotted already. Now what?" He treadled through the motions of darting back and forth, but the effort was aimless and had no definite goal. He wondered how to go about this quest, now that the road had been opened, but mental effort was beyond him as some ague of the soul tightened a broad band about his chest. The Jerry gunner pooped off a short burst, and several tracers gamboled over the wing of the Camel, making Paterson suck in his breath. He heard mysterious thuds somewhere in the framework, but could see no fabric punctures anywhere, and he hoped nothing serious had occurred.

"Well, what do I do? Here's a big juicy Hun all laid out for me, but just what do I do?"

He darted back and forth once more, and then went in neck-or-nothing. The Hannoveraner continued on its course and was now about fifty feet below the level of the Camel. Paterson made certain his C.C. gear handle was up, and then he rammed his face up against the rubber cup that protected the end of his fixed Aldis sight. His right thumb was spread across the two triggers mounted inside the spade grip of his control stick.

The instant he started down, trying to bring the cockpits of the German two-seater into the Aldis tube, he knew he was making a horrible mistake. "For God's sake, what am I doing?" he cried. "This is a two-seater, and it has a rear gunner." He pressed his triggers and the two Vickers guns began to fire . . . slowly and sluggishly. Paterson, the young Hun-hunter, had forgotten to trigger a few warming bursts before going into action. He was almost colliding with the Parabellum muzzle before his weapons had worked up any real speed; by that time the Jerry had poured a heavy burst full into the oncoming Camel.

There was a series of terrific crashes all around the nose of the single-seater, and Paterson let out a scream, hoicking wildly to get away. He hauled the Camel up hard, and tried to pull into a left-hand climbing turn. At the top of a threatening stall a wild spray of tracers sparkled all around him, and he was positive that every longeron and strut had been hacked in two. He stared about, checking his mount, and saw two short strips of fabric fluttering back from the lower side of his upper wing. Then a clipped flying wire began to flail the lower wing like a savage whiplash.

"What a bloody fool!" Paterson screamed as he fought to bring some response from his elevators. "I should have gone in from below and behind. That damn gunner had a sitting-duck target. The swine!"

The Camel was sideslipping away with very soggy controls until at last Paterson managed to get his nose down and bring some order out of chaos. He had sacrificed more than one thousand feet of altitude, and he saw the Hannoveraner continuing on its course, still heading for the British lines.

"I . . . I thought I poured fifty or sixty rounds into him," Paterson raged to himself. "Why the hell didn't he go down, break up, or make some effort to go back home?

I went all the way in, and practically forked out that gunner with my axle fairing. How do they shoot these bloody things down, anyhow?"

He took a quick look above and behind again and ranted on about the ridiculous manner in which he had tried to attack the two-seater. "Only a real Quirk would have done that. After all I had been told, the first time I tackle a two-seater I dive straight down the gunner's burst of fire. I should have tackled him from underneath and come up from below his tail assembly. He never could have fired at me then."

Paterson wondered what Captain Hoyt would say when he returned with all this damage. He would rag the guts out of him for bashing a good Camel about. He glanced up at the plodding Hannoveraner and wondered if he dared risk another encounter with the enemy gunner.

"Well, he's still heading for our side. At least I can try to harry him off, and with a bit of luck I might send him down. But I'm not taking any more chances with that Hun gunner . . ."

He went into a tight turn, throttled for some power and started to climb while maintaining the same course as the two-seater. He watched the enemy plane flicking its tail back and forth, giving the gunner opportunities to keep his eye on the stalking Camel pilot. This continued for some minutes until Paterson spotted two kite balloons not too far below, and realized that he was somewhere over the enemy back area. Two Archie shots made him jump, and two more bounced the Camel off bolsters of concussion.

"Go ahead. Bang away," Paterson growled. "You're not driving me off. I'm going to get that two-seater bus, if it's the last thing I do."

He worked his way to a position almost dead under the Hannoveraner, checked his C.C. gear once more, fired a test burst, and decided on another neck-or-nothing effort.

He was carefully adjusting for a few more revs when several tracers went streaking over his head. There was a sudden and frightening chain of heavy thuds that made the Camel seem to stumble in its course. Paterson turned his head, and gasped as he saw two German single-seaters boring down on him from tight angles.

"Where the hell . . . ?" he cried, and kicked his rubber hard and snapped the stick over. The Camel went down on one wing, floundered badly, eventually sliding into a sideslip. One of the Albatros fighters roared over Paterson's head, so close he could have reached out and spun one of its wheels. He glanced about and saw more tracers coming from still another direction. The Hannoveraner gunner was sending off long-range shots, enjoying the new twist in the situation.

Paterson tried to maneuver the Camel into a tight right-hand turn. He knew that was his only hope. The Camel could out-turn anything in that direction. If he could make a number of overlapping circles that would finally bring him close enough to his own line to risk a wild dive to safety . . . but in the meantime.

"Where the hell did they come from?" he fretted, and pulled the stick back into his stomach while he held her nose up in the turn with plenty of top rudder. He could see the two Albatros planes curling away in opposite directions, each waiting its chance to nose down and spray bursts of bullets again.

Paterson hung on, his lower lip trembling. While maintaining these tight circuits he realized that now and then his nose passed the Jerry two-seater, and the next time around he decided to chance a wild deflection shot. When he pressed the triggers, nothing happened! He pressed them again for a long burst at an Albatros that was maneuvering for a dive position, but again nothing happened.

"That corks it!" Paterson muttered. "They must have

hit something in the hydraulic system. I have no guns. Plenty of ammo, but no guns. Christ!"

He saw an Albatros, a gaudy devil with green bands painted around a white fuselage, coming down at him. There was nothing he could do but try to keep in the tight circles and trust that such a target was too much for the German. A spatter of slugs went through the top plane, and then the aileron control went out. When he tried to level off to get a bit closer to his own line, the Camel slobbered out of its tight turn and floundered into something resembling a falling-leaf maneuver.

Paterson rammed the stick forward and went into a wild runaway dive, blubbering and sniveling as he watched the Albatros pilots nose down for the chase. Another short burst hammered his right wingtip, and the Camel stumbled once more. Paterson tried in vain to get the wing down so he could haul back into another tight right-hand turn, but all that was over after the loss of aileron control. There was nothing left to do but hope that the two Huns would desist once they reached the British lines, and Paterson had to fall back on a number of sharp dives, and quick changes in direction with his rudder.

"Well, I wanted to see what it was like to fight Huns in the air," he muttered, watching for the concerted attacks of the Jerries. "I'm certainly finding out, but damn it all, this isn't fair. If I had guns and just a wisp of aileron control, it wouldn't be too bad, but as it is I'm Joe Muggings. Those blasted Jerries! Here they come again!"

Paterson was talking to himself somewhat calmly, and with rationality, but his physical reaction was that of a frightened man. He kicked the rudder hard, and let out low cries. He nosed down, blubbering like a baby, and then snatched the stick back again to hold as much altitude as he dared. Now antiaircraft of both sides, black and white, was bursting all around him, and his padded ears could hear the great shapeless chunks of metal screaming past his head. Terror gripped him, until it seemed he would never get his breath, or force his jaws together again. He turned in jerky movements, trying to watch his attackers, and the movements were so incoordinate his feet continued to treadle the rudder bar, making the Camel writhe and plunge, killing much of the speed still available to her.

He went roaring over the top of a grayish kite balloon so close he could note the details of the fabric seams and harness grommets. How he took all that in at a time like this, he had no idea, but it was something he remembered for years; the seams in that balloon fabric and the winking brass grommets. With that, something told him he was inside his own lines, and he looked back to see how many more times the Albatros pilots would come down on him. He snuffled, and wiped his nose on the back of his glove. He pressed the gun triggers on his spade grip for no sane reason. He was drenched with sweat, yet icy cold. His stomach muscles were tied in knots, so tight in fact, he found it difficult to turn and look back over his tail.

Snuffling, blubbering, and swearing whenever he could get his breath, Paterson held to his flat turns, curling through bursts of tracer and armor-piercing slugs while the earth below twirled tauntingly in the opposite direction. He tried to look at his instrument panel, but by now could not decide which was the altimeter and which the rev counter. There was a choking whiff of oil, cordite, and hot metal under the Triplex windscreen. He stared about, still jerking his head from side to side, wondering when the end would come.

It seemed at times that both Albatros scouts were nosing down at him in beautiful alignment, but at others, one or the other was mysteriously missing. There were instants when they obviously were tagging close to the Hannoveraner, and sharp flashes when they seemed to be ignoring him completely. He wondered why they did not concentrate and finish him. He also wondered why there were no other British aircraft in the area. He now was writhing under that virtuous fear that is based on vague faith. "Where the hell is everybody?" he screamed and looked up above. "Where the hell . . . ?"

To his disbelief he saw another Camel riding just above his tail fin. There was something familiar about it, but for the life of him, Paterson could not fathom the connection. It moved up and sw____ out off his right wingtip, and it was at this point tha____ potted its two streamers fluttering from the elevator ____ osts.

"Streamers? . . . ____ treamers on a Camel. Sopwith Camel . . . Hoyt! M____, it's Captain Hoyt. For God's sake . . . where . . .

The Camel pilot wav____ d nodded his head. Paterson had no idea what that ____ t, but what was Hoyt doing out here when he was s____ sed to lead a late-afternoon special show? The frighte____ young man looked back, expecting another concerted ____ st from one of the Albatros pilots, but there was noth____ in sight except the streamered Camel and a few blobs of dissipating Archie smoke.

"Oh God, am I glad to see you, sir. How glad I am . . ."

7

The flight back to the field was a nightmare, for Paterson had to make the best of what he had left on the stick. He eased her around, ruddered his nose down a road that ran toward the west and held here there until familiar fields, villages, and landmarks streaked past his lower leading edge. All the while Hoyt sat above and behind him, flying careful S-turns to stay back with the prodigal until at last Number 44's field suddenly appeared. Hoyt waved as he shot past and went in to land first. Paterson knew why he did that. If he had any trouble putting the Camel down without aileron control, Hoyt would have every man in the flight out ready to come to his aid if he wiped off the undercarriage or stood her on her nose. With no aileron control, an aircraft as sensitive as the Camel, could cause plenty of trouble if the wind veered or acted gusty.

Paterson started his glide well back from the edge of the field and prayed that he could keep her reasonably level when attempting to set her down, and make her behave. He approached the low hedge guarding the long strip of landing turf, and hoped there would be no gusts as he nosed over the low barrier. He was well throttled back and going in as slowly as he dared without risking a stall spin. He cleared the hedge, felt the wingtips start an argumentative flutter, but with a short jab at the throttle she surged on and straightened herself out, and seemingly behaved well until it came time to ease back on the stick to get the tail down. Then she acted fractiously again, and Paterson feared she would dip one side or the other and scrape a wingtip which would snatch him into a dangerous ground loop. That would mean a damaged wingtip, possibly an undercarriage wheel, and unquestionably a prop tip.

But Paterson's gods were good and the devil wasn't looking. He managed to get both wheels and tail-skid down together, and the Camel bounced uncertainly until two mechanics appeared from nowhere and grabbed at the wingtips, hauling her into good behavior, just as a knowing hostler curbs a lively cob for saddling. Bream and Featherstone stayed on the rear struts while Paterson taxied up to the rank where Hoyt, Phelps-Barrington, and Rupert Yardley stood waiting on the tarmac. From his seat he could see the evidence of his damage in the expressions of the two mechanics as they trotted along with him. He knew they were saying, "Coo! What a write-orf!"

Captain Hoyt led the delegation from the hangar front, but Paterson could not raise the strength to unflip his belt and haul himself from the cockpit. He sat watching Hoyt running his hands over the front of the engine cowling, letting his eyes take in the knifelike slashes that enemy bullets had hacked through various panels. He fingered the clipped flying wire, and then saw the four ailerons hanging limp from their hinges.

"You all right?" he asked calmly when he came up to the cockpit.

"No, sir. Frightened to death."

"You did damned well to bring her in like that with no ailerons. Well, climb down. I want to look at you."

Paterson unflipped his belt, managed to get one heel up on the seat cushion and lever himself clear. Hoyt grabbed his elbow as he stepped back off the wing root.

"You're not hit . . . anywhere?" he asked quietly.

"No, sir. I'm just scared stiff."

"Good man. Here, let me clean you up." He unbuckled Paterson's helmet strap and wiped the mucus and slobber from his upper lip and chin with a handkerchief, looking deep into his eyes as he removed the droolings of his trial. "I don't want any remorse about this, remember. I just hope you got it out of your system."

"Where did you come from, sir?"

"We were both lucky. I arrived in time to knock one of those Jerry scouts down. He smoked beautifully, all the way. Didn't you see him going down?"

"No, sir. I was too scared to see anything."

"Ah, well. He probably was faking it. We'll never get a confirmation unless some balloon observer saw it all."

"I'm sorry about the whole mess, sir. Most of all, I'm sorry I lied to you . . ."

"The aileron cable line? Forget it. You've got plenty of aileron trouble now," Hoyt said as a half smile softened his frown. "At least I have to give you credit for a new one. They usually try some sort of engine trouble."

"I just had to try it. I'm very sorry to have made such a mess of it. I won't do it again."

"Don't be sorry. Just be thankful you got away with it. Very few of them do, you know."

"I . . . I did everything wrong, Skipper. I had a Jerry two-seater, but I went about the job all wrong. I should have got him . . . but I forgot all I had been told about two-seaters."

"Then I know what you did. I once did the same bloody thing. Tried to get him from above and behind, instead of going up from under where the gunner couldn't get at me." Hoyt put his arm across Paterson's shoulder. "Well, I assure you, you'll never do *that* again."

"I suppose I've made a proper mess of my bus," Paterson said ruefully, and looked back at the Camel.

"You did a beautiful job. That Jerry gunner almost shot your engine completely out. He made your cowling look like a pepper shaker. How the hell that Clerget kept running all that time, I have no idea. I hope you'll always be this lucky."

"My hydraulic gear went out too. My guns wouldn't fire when those Albatros scouts joined in."

Hoyt grinned, and said, "I can see you've had a lovely afternoon. Well, that's the way it goes sometimes. Just don't try any of this ambitious schoolboy stuff again . . . particularly when we have a special show scheduled. We could use you, but you've written her off properly."

"I'm sorry, sir. Could I go in Yardley's place?"

"No. It's time Yardley did a show. He's been messing about long enough. You're to stay here and watch the mechanics pull your bus to bits, and see just what damage has been done. It's the only way you'll appreciate what it takes to keep six Camels flying. You are not to go back to your bunk, except to kick out of your gear. I don't want you flopping on your bed, reliving all that happened to you. You're to stay out here in the hangar until the dinner gong rings. That clear?"

"Yes, sir."

"Well, wrap up. It's bloody cold."

Captain Hoyt was deeply disturbed by Paterson's hapless revolt; not so much because of his flaunting of discipline, but the fear that the experience might have broken his spirit. He had pinned high hopes on this young man and was certain that he would make a fine front-line pilot. He secretly rejoiced that Paterson had kicked over the traces, and gone off on his own to satisfy himself, and he half wished that he had downed that two-seater. It might have served as a real tonic . . . and yet: "No, if he had shot down that Jerry, that would have been no holding him. He's got to learn to stay in formation and do the important job," Hoyt concluded. "It may have done him a world of good to have taken that beating—and get home again. It's just as I tell them, the important thing is to get home."

He also had the problem of wet-nursing Yardley, the new pilot, through his first patrol, and he was having to take Mallory, who had returned only the day before from a short period of convalescence. It was difficult to decide which of the two needed the more attention. The black-haired Mallory seemed pleased to be back, but he was far from the old, jovial, rollicking character he had been before he had come home with a couple of bullets through his upper arm. However, after a short, reclassification flight and some in-air gunnery against a ground target, he appeared refreshed and willing to take up where he had left off.

"This is the only place to be," he had said, when

Phelps-Barrington remonstrated with him, and suggested that he should have taken at least ten days' leave, once he was considered fit. "What is there to do in Blighty? Ram around all night with a lot of pigs, squandering hard-earned money, and winding up feeling like hell. There's no one in London who speaks your language. The old sweats who have been discharged, or put on light duty, moan and groan because they can't get back and draw flying pay once more. The kids coming out of the flying schools annoy hell out of you with all their silly questions. Don't they teach 'em anything at Frieston or Turnberry? I tell you, this is the only place to be; back with your pals, doing the things you understand, and being part of what is supposed to be going on out here. Christ! I almost went crazy in that blasted hospital, just listening to the poor devils who realized that they were out of it. It's unbelievable. I thought everyone wanted to get hit and go home, but the minute some sawbones starts mentioning discharge papers, they grumble and growl when they learn they have to go back to civvy life and begin all over again. It's like being blackballed out of some posh club."

"'He has heard the bullets whistle,'" P-B quoted, "'and there is something charming in the sound.' I believe a man named George Washington said some such thing."

Hoyt broke in, "Well, enough of all this classic reflection. You don't have to go unless you feel ready, Mallory."

"I want to go. I've got to get a job under my belt eventually. I assure you I'm quite all right. Let's get on with it."

"Good man!"

The flight took off from a loose ground formation, and headed straight for Albert. Paterson stood out on the tarmac, huddled in a bulky British warm that had been left in his cubicle by the late Lieutenant Slyne. No one but Hoyt had questioned him about his foray over the lines, and he was left to consider the error of his ways as he watched Sergeant Opperdyke's crew dismantle his Camel and lay out the various repair operations. One wing panel had to be replaced as the main spar had been splintered by three enemy bullets. The upper covering of the fuselage would have to be replaced, the engine taken out and given a very careful overhaul, to say nothing of the damaged C.C. interrupter gear.

"I'm afraid you won't have a chance to fly again for a couple of days," the sergeant observed.

"I'm a proper chump!" Paterson confessed. "Looks like I've given everyone a lot of unnecessary work."

"That was a very good Camel, sir," the NCO chided.

"Yes, I know. You said you rigged D-6418 yourself. I remember your telling me that the day I arrived here."

Opperdyke looked puzzled. "Have you been flying D-6418 all that time? How long have you been with us, sir?"

"Oh, only five or six weeks. I came out late in January, and it's now well past the middle of February, isn't it?"

"Good heavens, sir! We've gone past the first of March. How time flies. It seems only a week or so ago when we lost Mr. Slyne and when Mr. Mallory was wounded. Now you're a very experienced pilot, and Mr. Mallory is back flying with us again. All in a few short weeks."

"Thank you, Sergeant. I don't know how experienced I am, but I certainly learned a lot this afternoon. I'm lucky to be here."

Opperdyke said quietly, "Captain Hoyt was somewhat concerned, sir."

"You're in very good form today, Sergeant," Paterson said sheepishly. "What you mean is that Captain Hoyt had to go out and rescue me. Whatever experience I have was picked up under difficulties this afternoon. I was certainly glad to see Captain Hoyt covering my tail. I thought for a few minutes that my end had come."

"The captain thinks a great deal of you, sir," Opperdyke said with some reserve, then turned and spotted the propeller of Paterson's Camel teetering precariously on two work horses. "Izzard!" he bellowed. "Get this prop into the shop where it belongs. Damn that man! Where is he?"

Paterson walked away and watched the fitters dismantling the Clerget engine, and pondered on the sergeant's appraisal of Hoyt's concern for him. Why the skipper should single him out for this personal attention was not clear; he had contributed little to the flight since his arrival, and he still found it difficult to reconcile himself to the type of work assigned to the squadron. Until this afternoon's escapade, he had proved to be a better-than-average pilot. He had damaged none of the aircraft he had flown, except for the mishap that resulted in his shooting holes in his propeller. Perhaps from now on Hoyt would worry about Mr. Yardley.

Before 'C' Flight returned from its special ground-attack mission, a bitter sheen of snow, mixed with hail, was slanting down and scraping its talons across the canvas and framework of the hangar. The wind sock was stiff with sleet, and the mechanics were slipping and sliding about the tarmac, as they awaited the return of their winged wards.

In the officers' mess Mr. Harboard was pottering about in a pair of cut-down flying boots, and peering beakishly through the window. He was anxious, disturbed, and pettish. He turned and glared at Shuffling Wally who was laying out an assortment of plates, cups, and saucers for the pilots' tea.

"Stop shuffling!" Harboard complained, and rubbed his thin hands together.

"Yes, sir," Shuffling Wally responded, and shuffled off through the door to the kitchen. No sooner had that portal crashed and closed than Shuffling Joe appeared with pots of jam and plates of sliced bread.

Harboard waited until the inelegant layout had been spread on the table, and then grumbled once more, "Stop shuffling, will you please!"

"Yes, sir," Shuffling Joe agreed, and shuffled out of the room.

Harboard took out his watch and stared at it, pottering back and forth from one window to another. Portwine, rubbing his neck and chin, came into the room and took up a watchful position at a window that looked out on the tarmac. "They're late today, sir, aren't they?" The batman rubbed his hand across a small dusty pane.

"Damned late! They were out two hours and twenty minutes this morning on a regular. Then they did two hours at noon on a special, and something like two hours on this trench-strafe this afternoon . . ."

"No, sir," Portwine corrected gruffly. "Most of that was yesterday. This is today. They haven't been out that many times today, sir."

Harboard blinked and shook his head. "You may be right, Portwine. Too many shows. One can't keep it all straight. But look at it out there. You can't see your hand before your face."

"Ah, lucky Mr. Mallory got back from hospital, isn't it, sir? They make a tight team with Mallory back, they do."

Harboard walked slowly over to the stove, aimed his rump at the glow and linked his hands behind his back. "Spring offensive! My word, if they keep worrying about it starting early, and keep sending us up for information, they'll have us so worn out, we won't be able to lift a finger when it starts."

Portwine crept up closer, his head bowed and his hands

folded over his belt buckle. "If Mr. Trent only had some fun in him, sir. When you work hard you need fun. Like Mr. MacClintock's fun with Mr. Phelps-Barrington. This place hasn't really been right since Mr. MacClintock was killed."

"Ah, you're very right Portwine."

"Then there's Mr. Yardley. He seems to act daft at times."

"Yardley. Who's Mr. Yardley?"

"Why he's the new pilot who came in from Pool a fortnight ago. Captain Hoyt has had to give him a lot of time making up for what he wasn't taught at flying school. Mr. Yardley's been a bit of a problem, sir."

Harboard knuckled his mustache back and reflected, "Always new pilots. New faces. It was only yesterday that Hoyt came, and now he's got the Flight." He rubbed his hands together trying to bring life into his thin fingers. "Here, stir up the fire, Portwine."

"I think you could do with a hot rum, sir."

"No. Drink's no good any more either. Nothing's good any more. Too many wars, Portwine. Too many wars."

"Too may wars, sir?" the batman echoed and looked bleak.

"Too damned many wars. A man ought never to come home from his first war. You know how old I am? I'm seventy-seven years old, Portwine."

"Yes, sir. So I understand, sir."

"By the way, how's your neck?"

"It's all right, sir. Hurts a bit now and then, but it's all right."

"You really want to go back flying, don't you?" Harboard waved a dramatic hand toward the window, "Even when you can open the door and can't see two feet beyond it."

"Yes, sir. I do want to go back," Portwine said, holding

his hand against the side of an old black kettle that stood steaming on top of the stove. "I think I'll make you something warm, sir."

"As you like, but you should know that there's something about you on the medical officer's desk. I believe they're going to bring you before a board in Amiens. I would be surprised if they sent you down shortly."

Portwine began mulling some rum into a mug of hot water. "Thank you, sir. I knew they'd get around to me if I waited long enough."

"But remember, when you go up before that board you must be sure of one thing."

"What's that, sir?" the batman asked innocently as he stirred the potion with a spoon to dissolve a lump of brown sugar.

"You did not shoot that blighter down—Wilson, or whatever his name was." Harboard made the point very explicit with determined shakes of his finger. "You must be certain of that."

"Yes, sir," Portwine said and squeezed an ancient lemon into the hot mixture before handing it to old Harboard. "But . . . but you don't think I did, do you, sir?"

"Did what?"

"You don't think I shot Mr. Winslow down, do you, sir?"

Before Harboard could pull his beak out of the hot rum to reply, his narrow shoulders seemed to stiffen as the high whine of a Camel, nosing through the sleet and murk, swept across the roof of the mess. The old sweat and the young aerial gunner stood with slack knees, staring up at the ceiling as two more screeches cut through the storm overhead.

"Here they come, sir," Portwine said in his indistinct throaty voice.

"One . . . two . . . three." Harboard counted and wagged a finger with each distinct roar. The individual noises built up into mass pandemonium until prop screech was devoured by engine thunder. The high, shrill triumph of flying wires balled up with the blipping of the Clerget engines until the chorus of the storm was completely obliterated. All that was outside, but with the return of the flight a mild form of insanity was put into being inside. Portwine and Harboard began to dart about, kicking chairs into position, and clearing a path from the door. Shuffling Joe and Shuffling Wally, beaming like goblins, appeared with plates of bread and huge pots of steaming tea. Captain Frost charged in from the cubicle area and worried the phonograph into life until it began to scream *You Can't Get Many Pimples on a Pound of Pickled Pork*. And with that welcome churning out, Frost added to the uproar by screeching, "They're back! They're all back . . . in muck like this! Holy Christ, what men they are!"

"None better," Harboard agreed.

"They must be perished," Frost growled and looked at the food on the table. "I hope they won't take time out there filling in those bloody silly patrol reports. They'll wind up with frostbite before they can write their names."

"Blasted cold out there." Harboard poked his face into the hot rum. "I remember one experience we had in the Himalayas back in '93 . . . or perhaps it was '94."

"Plenty of hot tea, Portwine! Buckets of it," Frost bellowed. "Nothing like hot tea after a show like this."

"Hot tea with rum in it, sir," Portwine agreed. "There's plenty of rum, sir."

"Is that the issue—SRD—or bar rum?" the MO asked.

"It's issue rum, sir. We still have half a jug of it."

"Good. I'll have one myself. Not telling what we'll be in for before tonight's over."

"But issue rum is only for the flying officers, sir," Portwine remonstrated, but thought better of it, and poured a stiff dollop into a cup and completed the potion while Frost stood with a bowl of sugar at the alert position. "This is a special occasion," he said. "Mr. Harboard has a hot rum, hasn't he?"

Before Portwine could think of a legitimate reason for this infringement of regulations, Phelps-Barrington thumped through the door from outside. He was leading Trent in with his scarf knotted as a leash, and his captive was stumbling over his immense flying boots.

"What a bloomin' show!" P-B bellowed. "Five Sopwith Camels, nose to tail in single file like the Brighton Express, tearing home in a straight line from Valenciennes. We couldn't have been one hundred fifty feet above the ground!"

Paterson held the door open for Yardley and Mallory, and slapped some of the snow from Mallory's shoulders.

"Damn good thing they didn't have the blocks set against us," Trent added to the tableau.

"What were those things going into Cambrai?" Yardley bellowed, and headed straight for the phonograph, "Camions?"

"A long, bloody line of loories," cried Mallory, "and, God, did they get ditched! Fifteen of 'em, I counted, and all of 'em went clean off the road."

"Except that one that went up the church steps," corrected Trent, "and, by God, Yardley, you crowded me so close I could see his wheel turning when he went over on his back."

"Oh, that was sport," Yardley said. "My word, you can't believe they're really men when they run. You can't believe it when they fall down and sprawl out, even when you know it's your gun that's doing it. When do we go again?"

Mallory moved over to the stove and turned his rump

toward its open door. "Probably in fifteen minutes . . .
Hello, Harboard."

Captain Frost said, stirring his rum-spiked tea, "How's
the arm, Mallory?"

Watching P-B, Trent, and Paterson snatching teacups
and wolfing great slabs of bread and jam, Mallory took a
sniff of Frost's cup. "You know damn well how the arm is.
I tell you, there's something wrong inside the bone. It's no
bloody good from the shoulder to the elbow. Am I opti-
mistic, or is that issue rum you have in that tea?"

Frost sidled away from him and joined the clamor at
the table.

"Lucky thing we spotted the Virgin at Albert," Trent
said between gulps of steaming tea. "I thought we were
going straight through to Dieppe and out to sea."

"Spotted her? She was leaning right in the cockpit beside me once," P-B announced. "A lovely virgin."

"It's a surprise to me," Mallory said through a mouthful
of bread and jam, "that they didn't take 'C' Flight for pi-
geons and start feeding us corn. I mean, the way we were
flying around that cathedral for a few minutes. I'll swear I
went through one of the third-story windows twice!"

Old Harboard finished his hot rum and said, "How
lightly you lads take virgins;" To which Mallory added
pointedly, "It never does to take a virgin seriously. Things
become frightfully involved if you do. Virgins are always
such silly blokes."

Captain Frost broke into the discussion. "We can't be
bothered with your strange little viewpoints, Mallory. The
point is, don't knock the Virgin off Albert Cathedral. She's
the ony one anywhere within four thousand miles."

"Correction." Yardley held up a jam-clotted knife.
"Three thousand. There's a rumor of one somewhere
down in Kenya."

"Unconfirmed, old chap," Phelps-Barrington protested.

Anxious to be accepted once more, Paterson recited, "Do you know where Texas is? Well, it's five thousand miles from Texas to Liverpool, and every mile is patrolled by a German submarine. The virgins that escape these submarines are placed in eighteen depots in England where they are at the mercy of any Hun who sees fit to lay an egg on 'em. If any virgins do dribble across the English Channel into France . . ."

"We pull fourteen feet of intestine out of each and every one of them, Mr. Harboard," Phelps-Barrington squeaked. "Your servant, sir."

"You're mad. Positively mad," Mr. Harboard grumbled, and stared into his empty mug.

Hoyt, cluttered with maps, helmet, and gloves, entered amid all this bantering reaction. He stood and flapped the snow off, and blinked at the group around the stove. Phelps-Barrington stopped spreading a slab of bread, and held out an introductory hand. "Stop!" he cried, and closed his eyes. "I see a man. He has polished boots . . ."

Paterson stage-whispered, "He has red tabs on his collar."

"He gazes into the future," P-B continued.

"He sees nothing."

"He sees 'C' Flight," Phelps-Barrington insisted.

"He wants information. He wants to know how many latrines have been dug at Fosse 7."

With his eyes still closed, P-B continued, "And he wants to know how many old latrines have been filled in at Fosse 7. That will tell him that the spring offensive is going to start early this year."

Paterson whispered, "He calls 'C' Flight."

"He gets the gallant captain Hoyt on the wire."

"He says, 'Hoyt, get me latrines!' "

Hoyt wagged his head in resignation and completed the

act. "I have some very sad news, gentlemen. We are washed out tomorrow."

Mallory was the first to respond. "That's bad. That means another special patrol." And Trent continued it with, "You know what they're going to do with all these specials, don't you? They're going to ruin our efficiency as a unit. We've got a damn good record, but you can't expect machines and men to carry on indefinitely without a regular schedule to work on, and you can't have a regular schedule if somebody has the gall to break in on it every time he gets an idea to do it."

"Toot! Toot!" Paterson concluded.

Harboard held out his mug to Portwine and then tossed an order to Shuffling Joe. "Tea for Captain Hoyt!"

"Thank you, sir," Hoyt said and peeled off his flying gear. He stepped out of his Sidcot, and then grinned when he saw that Yardley, having filled his puppy stomach with steaming tea, had fallen fast asleep in a wicker chair, and had begun to snore. Mallory sat splay-legged on a stiff seat, yawning and rubbing his shoulder.

"Mr. Harboard. Were you ever in a war that England *really* won?" Hoyt asked with a sigh.

"I remember some slight rumor that Mafeking was a technical victory, and then there was the expedition against Ayub Khan, but I think they knighted Ayub Khan afterward, and sent his eldest son to Cambridge," Harboard recalled, and looked at Hoyt with bleary-eyed concern. "What's the matter? Things going badly?"

"I've never seen such activity as we've got now. It's all cropped up during the last week. Jerry doesn't seem to care whether we know it or not. In fact, he waves it in our faces. GHQ just sits around and dithers. All they can say is 'Information!' and when they get it, nothing happens.

They're going to have the stiffest offensive this year, and I haven't the slightest idea what's going to stop it."

Old Harboard took on a pensive attitude. "You are quite right, Captain. I had a short talk with one of our Intelligence gentlemen a day or two ago. He told me that Gough's Fifth Army has the thankless task of holding more than forty miles of line—an area stretching between Barisis north to Gouzeaucourt—which means only one division to every 6750 yards of front. Most of these divisions are shot through with new replacements, and what is worse, British troops have been trained for *attack*, not defense. That can make a great difference, you know."

"We never should have taken over this part of the front," Hoyt said.

"No. Our forces are spread too thin. We have too many divisions in England, awaiting an invasion. Then, that fool Lloyd George has thousands of troops in Mesopotamia, and Egypt, and others doing something silly in the Suez Canal area. However, maybe the Hun will pay for his success, if he has any."

"I think it will be bloody bad," Hoyt muttered.

"Something will stop them, old boy," Harboard said. "Something always does—or else it doesn't—but it will come out all right in the books people will write afterward."

"Would I offend you, sir, if I told you you were comforting?"

"You damn well would. The sound of the word makes my joints ache."

Hoyt smiled, and went on, "You know, there's a tightness in my shoulders, and it isn't me. It's the line up there. It's pulling both ways; half the world against the other half, and it's got me in the middle. I am what they're pulling. They're pulling me apart, Harboard, and I'm too damned tired to be pulled that way. I'm damned tired."

"But that passes, Captain. Even tiredness passes. Every-thing passes, sooner or later. The only thing that goes on forever is the spirit of men. Their faces change, their uni-forms change, but the spirit is always the same. I don't know what it is. Probably in the final analysis it's two parts water, one of rum, and a dash of brown sugar."

Hoyt considered that and gulped at his tea. "What in heaven's name are you doing out here in France, any-way?"

"I haven't the slightest idea, old chap. It just seems the place to be, that's all."

"So you dyed your hair, and lied thirty years off your age, and came into the transport end."

"I suppose there are worse crimes."

"Much worse. I'll commit one myself—I'll shave. Thanks, Colonel. I feel better already."

The mess settled down to the wants and desires of men. Mallory went off with Captain Frost who had promised to look at his stiffening arm. Yardley was still sound asleep, and Phelps-Barrington was stretched out at full length on a crude wooden bench. Paterson, still wolfing bread and jam, was reading a letter that had been handed to him by one of the mess orderlies. "Good heavens!" he ejaculated. "Have I been out here in France nearly two months?"

"I don't know, old chap," P-B responded. "Where's France?"

"I must have been. Mother says so," Paterson insisted to Hoyt who was heading through the door to the cubicles. Paterson continued reading his letter until the clatter of a motorcycle roared up and coughed to a halt outside, fol-lowed by a sharp rapping on the door.

"Come in!" Phelps-Barrington yelled.

The door opened and a military dispatch rider, dusted over with light snow, stepped inside and shoved his helmet to the back of his head. "Is this 'C' Flight, Number 44 Squadron, R.F.C., sir?" he inquired.

Mr. Harboard spun slowly, and said, "Yes. What have you got?"

"It's a note for Leftenant Phelps-Barrington, sir."

"Oh, good. Right here." P-B sat up. "Hand it over, will you?"

The dispatch rider was staring at his boots, but finally walked over, stood to attention and handed the missive to Phelps-Barrington who ran a finger under the flap. He glanced up at the man's shoulder straps, and said, "You're in the Tins, aren't you?"

"Yes, sir."

"Where are they?"

"This side of Bapaume, sir."

"Who's in command now?" Harboard broke in.

"Major Farquharson is in acting command. They say he'll be confirmed. We've lost a lot of officers lately, sir."

Harboard wagged his head. "There's always a Farquharson in command, sooner or later."

"We had five in the regiment when I joined, sir," the dispatch rider explained proudly.

"That sounds like the Tins," agreed Harboard.

Phelps-Barrington skimmed over the note, and explained, "Old member-mug may be late for dinner tonight. He's been sent up on a forward observation-post job."

"You mean Johnny Farquharson?" Paterson broke in. "Is he going to be able to get here at all?"

"According to this, he thought he'd leave a loophole in case he can't."

"That's damned decent of him," agreed Trent.

"Thanks, driver," said P-B. "Tell Mr. Farquharson that we'll hold dinner until eight for him."

"Mr. Farquharson? You mean the major, sir?"

"No. I mean Lieutenant Farquharson."

"But I can't do that, sir. Is *that* message from him?"

"Of course it's from him . . . and why can't you? Do you want me to write it out?"

The dispatch rider turned to Harboard with a helpless look of resignation. "But that's the major's brother!"

"So . . . what about it?"

"He was killed on forward O-Pip this afternoon. About three P.M., sir."

8

Two days later 'C' Flight was ordered to stand by for a new type of patrol, one that aroused varied opinions and predictions.

"There must be a Jonah in this mob," Phelps-Barrington observed as he rubbed gently at the patches of frostbite on his cheekbones. "I thought Bristol-Fighter blokes were so offensive they could do any job on the front with one arm tied behind their backs. To hear them tell it . . ."

"Actually it's just another low-level bomber show," Trent pointed out, "except that it's a bit farther over. It could be interesting. I'd rather muck up aerodrome hangars than railroad yards, any day."

Hoyt took over with, "This particular place is supposed to accommodate a couple of squadrons of the Von Richthofen Circus crowd. The idea is to blast them out en masse before they can get into the air. It may prove to be a good idea."

"This smells like something General 'Boom' Trenchard has been advocating," Mallory added to the conversation. "He's been arguing that shooting down enemy aircraft in penny packets, as he puts it, is only a waste of time, and that they ought to be bashed up before they even get up to the front. But we haven't any bombers of such range, so he's been ragging the staff to concentrate on planes still in the hangars."

" 'Boom' got himself fired for that bright idea," P-B said, "which in itself may be enough to recommend it. Just what are we expected to do, Skipper?"

"Knock hell out of everything. We carry full belts of ammunition and racks of Coopers. The Brisfits will go for the shops, petrol dumps, stores, and personnel accommodations with 50-pounders. We, with the lighter bombs, will concentrate on the hangars, hoping to set large fires rather than any great explosive damage."

"Presuming, of course, that all the Jerry buses are tucked away in the hangars," Trent added with some reserve. "How is that to be arranged, or is this to be another of those comic arrangements that always go blotto when we try to pull them off?"

"Billy Bishop got away with one a few months ago," Mallory said.

"And got a Victoria Cross for his trouble," P-B related. "Now there's the part I don't like. What the hell can a man do with that bit of red ribbon on his chest? He'd spend the rest of his life explaining it."

"You don't really have to wear the V.C. ribbon, do you?" inquired Mallory. "I mean to say . . ."

"You could get six months in the Glass House at Aldershot for being improperly dressed. Just because you don't like to wear your Military Cross doesn't mean you'd refuse to put up the V.C. if you were saddled with one. Even poor old Portwine has to wear his Military Medal ribbon. They'd tie him up to an artillery wheel if they caught him without it," Phelps-Barrington declaimed. "If blokes up at Headquarters say you're a brave man, you damned well can't deny it. They'd never get anyone to do a bayonet charge again if that sort of disrespect were allowed to spread."

"And who would they get to throw themselves on 'live' bombs at the instruction centers, if war heroes refused to go up to Buckingham Palace for the investitures?" Trent continued.

"Oh, shut up!" Hoyt barked, interrupting the tirade. "We're picking up twelve Bristols over Arras, and the Jerry field is about six miles this side of Douai. We're to go down to about five hundred feet once we clear the balloon area, and approach on a curving diversionary course until we are about four miles from the field. Then we roar in at hedge-hopping height—from the rear, so to speak, and let the Bristols go in first. If the machines are in the hangars, all well and good, but if not they'll probably be out on the line because we hope to catch them between patrols. I don't know how that is to be arranged, but that's the way HQ sees it."

Phelps-Barrington flopped into a big chair and moaned, "Call me early, Mother dear, for I'm to be Queen of the May."

"I don't know," Trent said. "It may work out. What Bristol squadron are we escorting?"

" 'A' and 'B' Flights of Number 20. They're a damned hot lot," Hoyt explained.

"Why wasn't Number 22 selected? They're real fighters. They were read out in orders last week."

"That's why." The skipper grinned. "They're too bloody good to be wasted down low. They're real upper-level fighters. Number 20 has a damned good record, though, and they have been especially selected for this tactical program—and we're to work with them. If this job comes off, we may work along these lines for some time. That is unless the spring offensive upsets the applecart."

"Bombing hangars and sheds from about fifty feet?" Paterson inquired. "That ought to be fun."

"It may be if we catch Jerry at lunch," Mallory agreed

as he lit a cigarette. "But if we arrive just as they are taking off—well, it could be a rough holiday."

"Bishop raised hell with Jerry planes that were taxiing out to take off," Trent added to the discussion. "The poor buggers were caught with their trousers down. What can you do until you have a few feet of altitude? You can't fight; you can't go back and land; you have to face the prospect of zooming into a pack of scouts that are bashing about like hell. I'd rather be on the attacking side in a case like that."

"Well, we'll have to hope we get them just sitting down to lunch. The Brisfits will take care of the big sheds and shelters. We'll have to decide whether to bomb hangars or rows of planes out on the cab rank. We'll stay in action there as long as it is profitable. We'll try to distribute our bombs as evenly as possible on the hangars if there are no machines to be seen on the line. If it is obvious that the Albatri, or whatever they are flying, are lined up outside, we'll do our best, first with the bombs, and then come back in-line and pour it on with our guns. It's something we'll have to decide on when we get there and see what the situation is."

"Is there likely to be any antiaircraft fire, Skipper?" inquired P-B.

"From photos of the place they seem to have two, and perhaps three, gun emplacements—the usual thing; machine guns mounted on wagon wheels, set up to traverse fast. I wish you'd take those over, P-B. You're damned good on ground targets. Once you get rid of your Coopers, concentrate on those ack-ack guns."

"What's the signal for re-forming, Skipper?" asked Paterson, who by now was doubly conscious of the value of tight formations.

"We're in the hands of the Brisfits. They will stay in the area as long as it pays off. Their gunners will pick off all the small targets, if any show up, and their pilots will take care of any Huns that attempt to take off during the attack. We contribute what we can individually, but we stay there until the Bristol leader gives a green . . . get that now, a green Very signal. Once he fires that, we re-form as quickly as possible and head for our line. Don't worry about the Bristols. They can take care of themselves once they have gotten rid of their bombs. In fact, if you are in trouble on the way back, nose into the two-seater formation and the gunners will take care of you. They're damned good, those kids."

"This might be fun," P-B finally agreed, after inhaling on a Gold Flake. "It just might be if we could stage it just as dawn is breaking. Then we'd be sure the Jerries were in their beds and the machines in the sheds. Why can't it be an early morning show, Skipper?"

"It's been tried too many times. So far, no one has had the nerve to go in in broad daylight, and who knows, maybe we can pull it off this once. At this time of day the whole area is up and about, which should give us more individual targets to pick on. At least that is how the Top Knobs figure it."

Trent had another idea. "Why couldn't we strike just at dusk after all patrols were over?" He began bouncing a Ping-Pong ball on the rim of the table. "All the Hun pilots would be getting sozzled at the bar, the mechanics would be scoffing their coffee and sausages, and all the aircraft would be in the hangars. We could be in and away before the Jerries could put on their pork-pie hats."

"But we'd still have to get back, and by that time we'd have to face making landings in the darkness. It all depends on how much experience any of us have had landing with ground flares. Personally, I don't relish the idea with so many aircraft. One or two may get down safely under those conditions, but we don't know if the Bristol crews have had any experience. Besides, the whole patrol has been planned—and who are we to question the brains at Hesdin?"

As the Camel pilots pondered on that last bit, the telephone jangled and Paterson took down the instrument. He listened and glanced at Hoyt.

"It's for you, Skipper," he said solemnly.

"Here we go." P-B groaned and cranked to a sitting position. "You know, last time I was on leave I read a story about some flying bloke who, after shooting down whole flocks of Huns, had his tail shot off. Only on the printed page can this happen, but, as you see, he got himself into serious trouble. You know what *could* happen in a case like that, but this josser put the bus into a flat spin somehow, held it there, and touched down neatly, only bursting one tire. What would you do, Mallory, if you had your tail shot off? I mean to say, just what do you do in a case like that?"

"I'm not quite sure. I'd try to keep my head, fumble about for the instruction book and select the proper page to find out. What did old Santos-Dumond do? He didn't even bother to put a tail on his box-kite biplane."

"It's something we ought to think about," P-B mused, watching Hoyt hang up the telephone.

"That's it, chaps. We take off in fifteen minutes," the skipper said.

"I take it," P-B muttered, "someone has flown over, given the layout a good look-over, and has returned to say that everything is in readiness for our reception."

"I wouldn't know," Hoyt said, his mind on other matters.

In response to Headquarters' call, the Bristol Fighters and 'C' Flight's Camels waddled out to take up their positions on their respective fields that were about twelve miles apart. The Brisfits, those most efficient, two-seater fighters that were assuming command of the British front, moved out with businesslike precision, for they also were taking off in formation. This was a majestic sight. The slate-nosed biplanes stood throbbing wingtip to wingtip, their idling propellers glistening in the sunshine. Every man's head was up, all eyes on the leader's cockpit. They saw Captain Launchford's hand go up to the "Alert" and the other pilots began to palm their throttles up gradually. The leader's hand clenched and snapped forward, and the machines seemed to stiffen and crouch like greyhounds at the leash. The engines opened up full, the rudders waggled, and their bold colors flashed. The observers in their brown leather cocoons snuggled down inside their Scarff gun mountings and flicked impudent salutes to each other.

With these friendly preliminaries, the aircraft tore away, leaving a great swirl of dust, and from the hangar apron only the trailing edges of their wings showed. Suddenly all twelve machines zoomed together, and the earth-bound mortals caught the broad surfaces of the upper wings flaunting their jaunty cocardes and identification letters. For an instant they presented the shimmering impression of two solid triangles composed of mottled greens and browns.

They climbed away, then turned carefully and crossed over their field for their last glimpse of the hangars and for any final orders or instructions. Launchford's gunner saw a strip letter-signal laid out—the letter L—which advised the leader that no last-minute decision had been made to cancel the patrol.

The two formations met as arranged over Arras at 4000 feet, and by that time everyone had settled down to business. Guns were warmed, hydraulic pressures of the interrupter gears checked, and human rumps fitted into the undulations of the seat cushions. Below, the area changed from the flame-scarred, shell-pocked lunar layout to a pattern more defined and detailed. There were green fields, neatly drawn roads, and here and there, toylike houses, farmsteads, agricultural sheds and buildings. Small villages clustered at crossroads. Churches raised sharp spires or castellated towers. New colors, reds and yellows, flashed off tile roofs, and strings of fluttering laundry waved and flicked in the sharp breezes. Only intermittent belches of black smoke and the thump of high explosive reminded the airmen that a global war was taking place somewhere below. There was little indication of military operations this far back. There were a few practice trenches and preliminary earthworks that might be used for training programs or to provide newcomers with some idea of what they would encounter in the battle zone, but the greater spread of picture was more civilian than military. Only the businesslike blocks of temporary hospital shelters with their gleaming red crosses painted on the roofs gave an indication that death and destruction were part of the program.

Young Paterson was entranced with this new battleground. He had never been so far back in Jerry's rear, and much of it reminded him of the rural sectors of Connecticut, particularly the definition provided by the hedges and pasture walls and fences. It was still early spring and few of the vernal tints were visible, but the spread of the countryside intrigued him nevertheless. Small rivers and wriggling brooks flashed their movements; transport on the roads was chiefly civilian, and there were many individuals who did not stride in cadence or wear military gray. All this flashed through his mind as the three flights raced for their objective.

"I hope I can stick this out," the American mused. "I'd like to see this country when it is all over. It looks worth visiting on a bicycle or on foot. Golly, that would be fun."

The Bristols began to open wider, and the curving course was leading them around the back of Cambrai. They also were losing altitude fast, and details of the ground below became more distinct and defined. More opposition guns barked and tracer bullets flicked through the wide landscape breaking up the pattern into shapeless segments. One belligerent young Bristol gunner warmed his weapon against a small convoy of horse-drawn vehicles until his pilot checked him and pointed out that ammunition would be more valuable over the Jerry aerodrome.

The German aviation field lay in the fork of two lead-colored roads. A sentinel line of poplars bordered one side, and a slab-sided windmill stood in one corner, its great slatted vanes semaphoring some mysterious signal. The hangars were regulation, great shelters built of wood, in the rear of which were service sheds, stores, living quarters, and the varied hutments that made up such a complex. A short distance away was another grouping that Captain Hoyt decided housed the officers' mess and the conveniences of the commissioned ranks. There was some evidence of lawns, pathways, and flower beds. Several tall poles, painted in black and white, obviously carried telegraph or telephone wires from area to area, and the skipper was determined to give these buildings some of his attention. But before that, he found time to check on the details of the flying field. There were at least eight hangars and a broad swatch of macadam working area. There was one short line of Albatros fighters out on the rank, but most flights seemed either to be in their sheds or possibly still out on flying operations. It was difficult to know until the pilots were in a position to see into the open ends of the hangars.

The first flight of Bristols was going down as true as wide-fletched darts. They headed dead into the center of the whole layout without bothering about details. The gunners were pouring long bursts into the sheds and at small groups of men scattering from shelter to shelter. The second Bristol flight swept along over the row of hangars, and Hoyt could see the two-seaters bounce and lurch with the release of their bombs that arched in a flat trajectory for the sheds. The Bristols seemed to be flying in groups of twos, and their bombs either hit at the doorway end or the back of the hangars. Gouts of flame shot up followed by shapeless slabs of walls or roof sections, dragging lengths of twisting plank. While this took place, the gunners stood firing down, practically over open sights, at the rows of Albatros planes set out parallel to the line of the hangars. One by one they burst into flames. A Bristol Fighter roaring in low for accuracy smacked into a great slab of debris that gushed up from one of the middle hangars. The machine seemed to halt with the impact of a truck crashing into a stone wall. It lost both banks of wings, and then disappeared in the pattern of wreckage.

From the cockpits of the Camel fighters the pilots could see the Bristols skimming back and forth, systematically dropping their explosives while the single-seaters stayed a few dozen feet above them to head off any opposition from above. Paterson saw one Brisfit go kiting up, struggle to get its nose down and then completely disappear into the wide maw of an open hangar. The shed burst into flames a little later, and he realized that two Britishers had "bought it for keeps."

Despite these losses the Bristol Fighters charged about like enraged hawks, their pilots attacking profitably with their fixed guns while most of the gunners huddled behind their Lewises, cringing as wingtips and wheels passed with but inches to spare.

Phelps-Barrington spotted an antiaircraft gun mounted, just as Hoyt had explained, on a wagon wheel that spun on an axle set in a block of concrete. The Camel pilot cut out of formation, nosed under a charging Bristol and went hell-for-leather into the group that crouched around the crude mounting. He pressed his gun triggers and both Vickers spat a series of short telling bursts and the Jerry gun crew was flung in all directions.

"That ought to keep you lads quiet," he snarled, and circled the field searching for another. He found a target near the corner of a wagon shed; a gun mounted on an upright timber was directing short jets of fire at the two-seaters that were mopping up the petrol dump and stores were spare engines and other extras were kept. P-B locked his jaw, made the most of his Aldis sight, and fired one long burst that left the enemy gun unmanned. The gun crew seemed to be snatched away from the timbered base like toy dolls tied to some invisible cord. He went all the way in, zoomed hard above his target, and with grim satisfaction saw a job well done.

Paterson spent the first few seconds staring wildly at the extravanganza being played out below. He was incapable of taking an active part, being entranced with the amazing spectacle. Bombs were blowing great sheds to tangled wreckage, flames were consuming the piled up debris, and the young Bristol gunners were picking off grounded aircraft with all the aplomb of seasoned veterans. It was not until he saw Hoyt nosing down at the establishment set apart from the hangars and sheds that Paterson remembered that he was part of the attack.

"This is where I came in." He grinned and guided his Camel through two towering columns of flame and smoke, and went down fast for the officers' mess. He felt serene and calm as he pulled his bomb toggles in perfect sequence with the idea of taking the shelters one by one. He got rid of his bombs on one wing panel, and turned back for a second run, but as he made the tight turn, he felt the Camel start a dreadful sideslip. He quickly realized that she was not too stable, carrying three bombs on one side, so he rammed the throttle up the quadrant, nosed down for more speed, finally getting her reasonably level in time to get rid of the rest. He passed Hoyt with only inches to spare, and saw the skipper grinning, showing his white even teeth. As the last three bombs left the rack, the Camel became more docile and behaved beautifully despite the uneven turbulence caused by the heat and concussion.

Paterson zoomed and went into a circuit of the field looking for new targets. He saw one green-and-white Albatros crawling away from the cab rank, evidently trying to get clear for a take-off. Paterson went into a tight wing-over and nosed down like a high-velocity shell. The Albatros pilot was just trying to get his nose around into the wind when Paterson pressed the triggers. Two streams of Vickers lead converged just above the German plane's tail, and continued on until they found the padded seat and the pilot. Under that wicked flailing the Albatros went into a sharp ground loop, dipped a wing into the turf and gave a great belch of resignation. A blossom of black smoke came out from the engine cowling, and the propeller flickered to a halt.

"It's a hell of a way to get a Hun," Paterson reflected, "but it's the best I can do on this show."

Hoyt was in his element. He realized that this was one job 'C' Flight was doing remarkably well. It probably was the first time that his pilots as a group were working together as a completely trained force. Even Yardley, in his gawky, rustic enthusiasm, was responding beautifully. He could see him tailing Mallory, playing his proper role, as Mallory picked off target after target with all the skill and timing of a fencing master. Whenever anything of value appeared before Yardley's guns, he gave generously with some blundering skill, more than paying for his day's rations. Hoyt was well pleased with the manner in which his men were behaving on this most difficult and daring task.

"I'll probably never see them perform like this again. We may never get another chance to work together like this," he muttered to himself as he banked and circled, keeping an eye on his Camels and watching Captain Launchford who by now was rallying his force. Hoyt saw a group of men hurry to a lone Albatros, intent on getting the machine away to break up this devastating intrusion. He circled a great column of smoke, and then turned and went down, his blunt nose dead on the doughty enemy group. To them he seemed to come out of nowhere, and before the mechanics could get the propeller swinging, Hoyt's guns bowled them over and strewed them in shapeless heaps before the airplane. He curled away, reached for his hydraulic gear handle, yanked it up all the way and sought out another. The machines that had been ranked outside were no longer in a defined line; three were blackened skeletons, two had been pulled clear of the burning aircraft and were left standing alone well out on the field. A touring-type motorcar was maneuvering in and out trying to pull others out of the line and disperse them. Hoyt resented this and nosed down at the automobile and fired a series of short bursts. The car was hit hard and the driver lost control; the machine charged about wildly, finally ending up entangled in the wingtips of two Albatros fighters. Hoyt zoomed over the carnage and saw a green light arch up from a Bristol Fighter that carried two streamers.

"That's it!" he yelled and circled the field once more rallying his own machines and watching the Bristols roar away at hedge-hopping height, and re-form as they raced along over the curves and straight stretches of the Scarpe River that would take them back to the Arras area. The Camel leader went back as far as the Jerry officers' quarters to search for his men and was delighted to see that young Paterson by some magic means had collected the rest. They were forming up on his tail and allowing him to guide them out of the smoke and fluttering debris until they could pick up Hoyt.

"Good boy!" The skipper beamed. "It's beginning to show, just as I thought it would. Go ahead, kid. Take us home," and with that Hoyt moved in, waved to Paterson, gave him the sharp edge of his palm-signal to take command, and eased back to take over the outer corner. He waved to P-B who held down the other corner, and in that manner permitted young Paterson to lead them home from the most satisfactory show 'C' Flight had put on in months.

"Oh, we're making something of 'C' Flight," Hoyt mused to himself with deep sincerity. "How old Mac-Farlane would have reveled in this. He would have given his right arm to have done this show. This is worth all the heartaches and effort. We're a real team again."

BOOK THREE

REVELATION

March 1918

☐ Mr. Harboard's intelligence had been correct. General Gough's Fifth Army, which was composed of but fourteen divisions of infantry and three of cavalry, had been given an impossible task. His front, about forty-two miles wide, included ten miles of what was hoped would be water-soaked marsh, but the weather proved to be "attacking weather." That spring was the driest in French history. The enemy was able to wade through this space between Amigny Rouy and Alaincourt, an area that had been held more lightly than the remainder of the front. North of Gouzeaucourt to Gavrelle, a distance of twenty-seven miles, the British Third Army, under General the Hon. Sir Julian H. G. Byng, was not much better off, as they hoped to hold a front where each available division was stretched over 4700 yards.

In comparison, General Erich F. W. Ludendorff opened his "Michael" attack in the Somme area with sixty-three divisions of the German Seventeenth, Second, and Eighteenth Armies. Although his thrust had been expected, he struck before winter had actually fled, and in a district where it was thought he would be least likely to attack, as the Germans themselves had reduced the Somme area to complete ruin during their Hindenburg retreat in 1916.

The "Michael" force first pierced the Saint-Quentin–La Fère sector, but its main force was to go through north of the Somme, and after the initial penetration, the Seventeenth and Second Armies were to wheel northwest and drive the main British Army back to the coast, trusting that the Somme and the Eighteenth Army would guard their flank.

The area to be defended by the British Fifth Army had been only lightly fortified, for previous to this attack the Allies had been on the offensive, and General Gough's engineers barely had time to reconstruct the forward system before the first blow fell, and there never was sufficient manpower to fulfill that task since what manpower was available to Britain was occupied in maintaining the Navy, the merchant fleet, and the necessary industries.

General Ludendorff's assault was launched on March 21, and the surprise was intensified by an early morning mist. The enemy broke through completely south of the Somme where the defense was weakest, but he was checked temporarily near Arras; a delay that affected the whole attack north of the river.

That morning, 'C' Flight of Number 44 Squadron was trustfully abed, having been promised at least part of the day off after a week of intensive operations. But war is a tyrant, and its word can be trusted by no man. Another early morning awakening was staged in the cubicle corridor with Portwine and Shuffling Wally officiating with the call board.

"Call Captain Hoyt first," Portwine husked.

In unison they knocked on Hoyt's cubicle door. "Captain Hoyt. Captain Hoyt, sir!"

There was no answer. Portwine rammed his elbow into Shuffling Wally's ribs. "Call again. He's well away this morning."

"Captain Hoyt, sir!"

"What is it?" Hoyt finally responded.

"Special call for all flights, sir," Portwine managed.

"Oh no! Now damn it! I won't have this. I won't have my flight knocked about this way. We were washed out."

"But the major's in the mess room, sir. His orders, sir."

"Let him stay there!"

"Orders are to call all pilots of 'C' Flight, sir," Portwine insisted.

"Blast orders! Haven't they got anyone else to fight this war for them?"

"I . . . I don't know, sir."

Hoyt came to the door in his pajamas, holding a disheveled blanket around him. His insides were dull and slack, his mouth parched and encrusted with the mucus of disturbed sleep. It was difficult to straighten his knees and his feet felt as flat as those of a Billingsgate fishwife. He finally identified the two callers. "This is a blasted imposition," he mumbled, and then he raised his voice a pitch or two. "What do you mean the major's in the mess room?"

"He came over from Squadron, sir. It seems to be very important," Portwine explained.

"At this time of the morning?" Hoyt tried winding the blanket about him, but gave up and reached out for his trench coat. "I suppose I'd better go and find out what it's all about."

"An' what about the call, sir?"

Hoyt endeavored to visualize what was happening at the front, but the past few days had distorted every rational picture. There was nothing to put a finger on, so he said, "You'd better keep on with it . . . and then get someone to fetch me some hot water, will you, Portwine?"

"Yes, sir. In just a minute, sir."

While Hoyt steadied himself at his clothes rack, the two callers went to the next door. "Mr. Trent . . . Mr. Mallory, sirs!"

"Louder," husked Portwine.

"Mr. Trent and Mr. Mallory, sirs!" Shuffling Wally repeated.

There was no response, so Portwine shoved the door open and crept in. He called, "Mr. Trent, sir," and reached out to a huddled figure in one of the beds.

"Never mind! Never mind! I'm getting right up," Trent said in a perfectly normal tone of voice, and sat erect, forking his fingers through his hair. "I'll be right with you."

"And Mr. Mallory, sir?"

"Mr. Mallory will be right with us," Trent promised.

The two callers backed out into the corridor and saw Captain Hoyt entering the cubicle used by Yardley. The flight commander, belting his trench coat, went straight to the cot and shook the sleeper's shoulder. "Come on, Yardley, boy. To horse. We've got seventeen brewery breasts to groom. Bags of feather! Snap into it. Get up!"

"You be sure he wakes up, sir," Portwine pleaded. "He does act up at times."

"I know. Come on, Yardley!"

And with that, the youth bounced up like a healthy young colt, sprang out of bed still sound asleep, and thrashed the air with his long arms, talking a steady streak. It was eerie and mythic in the vague half-light of the early morning.

"Steady now!" Hoyt bellowed.

"Where, where, where?" Yardley yapped. "Remind me to tell you of a Swedish doctor I once knew."

Hoyt snatched at his pajama tail and Shuffling Wally grabbed an arm, but Yardley shook them off as a big tabby shakes off a brood of kittens. "Square feet! Square feet . . . and watch that kicking strap," he went on in a mechanical tone.

Hoyt tried a half nelson, and yelled, "Come on, Yardley! Come on, wake up!"

" 'E's fair daft this mornin' sir," Shuffling Wally observed.

Young Yardley stared at nothing and went into a gunnery sequence. "The tumbler rotates and the firing pin is withdrawn . . . weak lock spring! Need a bloody hammer!" and with that wild cry he squatted on the floor, dragging the others down with him. Aiming an imaginary pistol at something in the corner, he cried, "Mice!"

"Are there any more at home like you?" Hoyt growled, and cuffed the big youth about the ears. "Come on, Yardley, wake up!"

Yardley stood erect, rubbed his eyes with the heels of his palms, and greeted all present with a polite, "Good morning!"

Captain Hoyt emitted a deep sigh, and muttered, "Good morning."

"What is it?"

"A special. We're down for another special."

"Oh, top hole!" Yardley began thrashing around his cubicle, throwing flying gear in all directions. "Am I to go, too?"

"I think 'e's awake now," Shuffling Wally observed.

"I hope so. Take care of the others. I'm going to the mess room," Hoyt said and clenched Portwine's shoulder affectionately.

There was much the same procedure with Phelps-Barrington. He was hard to arouse, but he finally sat erect, shoved his feet out of his loose cocoon of bedclothes, looking like an enraged Roman senator.

"What's up now?" he demanded.

"A special, sir."

"Not another! Good God! We were washed out!"

"Now we're washed in," said Portwine. "All three flights."

"But we were washed out," P-B persisted.

"Yes. We were, sir, but the major's here, and Captain Hoyt's in talking to him," the aerial gunner explained.

"But damn it, they can't jump us with any more specials. We've been doing three patrols a day for ten straight days."

"It's straight, sir. Captain Hoyt's with the major now."

While Phelps-Barrington stood up, trying to make sense of the early morning call, Yardley went bouncing along the corridor loaded down with flying gear, maps, scarves, and enthusiasm.

"Halt!" Phelps-Barrington cried. "No need to hurry. There'll be another tram along in twenty minutes."

"I say!" the huge youth bellowed. "This is much better than pecking at Ovid and Pindar, what!"

"We'll have none of your bad language here, young man," P-B remonstrated. "You'll have to see Dr. Kinsolving in his study after the fourth form."

"I say. How'd you know our headmaster's name was Kinsolving?"

"All headmasters are named Kinsolving."

Paterson wandered out into the corridor in bare feet, a flying helmet on his head and a crew sweater knotted about his waist by the sleeves. He yawned, swallowed hard, and asked, "Does anyone remember exactly what this war was about?"

"Mr. Trent, Mr. Mallory, sirs," Shuffling Wally yelled again.

2

After a languorous breakfast, Hoyt ordered his 'C' Flight pilots out to the hangar, and then went to his flight office to check on some telephone messages. There was some torpid, slow-motion activity on the tarmac where a few fuzzy-faced mechanics, draped with belts of machine-gun ammunition, yellow Cooper bombs cradled in their arms, or red petrol cans dangling from greasy fingers, walked through the early morning ritual. Toolboxes were dragged across the gritty surface, and heavy tools clashed, adding a Wagnerian background to the turgid scene.

Phelps-Barrington, Trent, Mallory, and Yardley sat in a mourners' group on a long, oil-soaked bench that was propped against an inside wall. Above them a NO SMOKING notice hung at an acute angle. This Camel quartet drew on their morning gaspers, complaining of their lot. Yardley was asleep with a twisted Gold Flake between his lips, and had to catch himself every thirty seconds to keep from pitching forward on to the packed cinder floor.

"This sort of thing ought to be done right," Phelps-Barrington was arguing. "He shouldn't just barge in on us this way. He should drop cards on us first, and then wait until we return them. After all, that's tradition."

"Where's Paterson?" Trent inquired looking around.

"He's over putting Opperdyke in his place. He's becoming as sharp as Hoyt when it comes to getting repairs done. That kid learns very fast."

"It's a good thing someone keeps after those bloody mechanics," Mallory said and looked out toward the cab rank.

"She was a lovely girl, but faithless as sin," broke in Phelps-Barrington. "I shouldn't have minded, if she hadn't been so blatant about it, but she loved scenes. She simply packed her bag, ordered the motorcar around, and went back to her husband."

Paterson came over from the Camel rank and sat next to Mallory. The voice of Sergeant Opperdyke broke through the early morning air. "Come on, you lads. Put your 'earts into it. Step orf . . . Step orf."

A Douglas motorcycle pop-pop-popped up the roadway, went into a chain-and-sprocket chatter, lost some of its breath, and pulled up behind the hangar. A wide-awake voice inquired, "Is this 'C' Flight, Number 44 Squadron?"

"You turn right at the Donkey and Buskins," mumbled Yardley, still sound asleep, "and after a quarter of a mile . . ."

"I don't believe there's a pub with that name," P-B reflected. "I've heard of the Donkey and Garter but never a Donkey and Buskins."

"Whose beer do they serve?" asked Mallory.

Hoyt's voice was heard saying, "If you'll come through with me, sir. My pilots are on the bench."

"Sorry to keep you waiting, but what with the weather, we almost missed you entirely."

"No such luck," Mallory muttered.

Captain Hoyt appeared, leading a red-tabbed staff officer through the maze of the hangar floor to where the pilots were lined up. The newcomer was fairly neat and clean, but his uniform was threadbare. He had three gilt wound stripes on his left sleeve, and wore his clothes as if he was used to them. His eyes were tired, but he waved a kindly hand when the pilots stood to attention.

"Good morning, gentlemen," the staff bloke began. "Please don't get up. I'm Major McBain. Please be comfortable. I want you to take everything I say as personally to heart as you can. Sometime after midnight the general situation changed radically. We've made shoulder-strap raids all through the sector, and, frankly, I want to tell you that there's an excellent chance of having the Channel right between our shoulder blades before the week is out. What started to be minor troop concentrations in H, I, and J sectors are now mass movements. We're no longer interested in the details of them. What we want you to do is to get after them in every possible way that you can. We want them bombed and shot up. We're putting every available squadron on this ground strafe. Have you any questions?"

Yardley emitted a most eloquent snore.

The staff officer bowed: a most understanding gentleman.

Hoyt stepped forward, consulting a paper in his hand. "We're to operate on Douai. It's to be low-level work in teams of two. We're to smash hell out of anything we see. Don't bring any bombs back. When you get something particularly juicy, give it what-for, full out, and come back for another load of Coopers and new belts. This show goes on until the wash-out comes through."

"Don't let me down, gentlemen," the staff johnnie pleaded. "I walked through Douai once with no soles on my boots. This is my war just as much as it's yours, and, quite frankly, for the present we seem to be losing it."

Mallory stood up and rubbed his arm, "And it's a pretty fair war, in spots," he agreed. "Come on!"

They all rose to their feet except Yardley, so Phelps-Barrington leaned over and shook him gently. "Come on, Sleeping Beauty. Trench strafe."

Yardley sprang to his feet, trying to awaken once more, and for a few seconds gave a minor edition of his earlier antics. P-B evaded the wild, swinging arms, and cried, "No you don't. Come on, wake up. You know, bup . . . bup . . ." He pulled imaginary triggers with his fingers. "You know . . . twiddly . . . twiddly . . . plop! plop!"

The Camel pilots shuffled off to the cab rank and climbed into their planes.

In less than ninety minutes the flight was back, their mounts lined up for immediate maintenance. The mechanics swarmed all over the oil-streaked Camels replenishing the ammunition boxes, the bomb racks, and fuel tanks.

One or two machines were getting temporary patch jobs where machine-gun slugs had ripped fringed gashes through the doped fabric. Phelps-Barrington's bus required a new tire, and Opperdyke was fingering a hole in a wing strut that had been hacked by a small chunk of shrapnel. Paterson and P-B huddled before a coke brazier, drinking fawn-colored tea from bent cigarette tins.

"I was down to less than two hundred feet," Paterson said. "The ground was dotted with shell bursts that looked like balls of gray wool, and my God, the antiaircraft over Longueval was awful."

"It's quite a war," agreed P-B.

"And there were swarms of Jerries everywhere. Some were huddling in shell holes, some were marching along the roads. I suppose it was a mass attack. I fired everything I had into the biggest groups, and then tried my bombs, but I must say they didn't seem to do much damage. How do you think we're making out?"

"I don't know why, Paterson," P-B answered him, "but apparently it's some inexorable cosmic rule that there has to be one woman in every man's life who spoils all the rest of them for him."

"Shall we have 'Hearts and Flowers' with this, or do we weep silently?" Paterson inquired and warmed his hands over the brazier.

"Now remember, she doesn't have to be your first one. That's nonsense. She can be a lady or a barmaid—or a whore."

"Dear, dear, what a dreadful upbringing you must have had."

"Right. The third son of an Anglican bishop. I'm typical of the breed," P-B explained, "but this woman has to be lovely. She has to be lovely inside. There has to be a spiritual fineness in your mind for her. That is what the poets mean when they use the word 'love.' "

"And then what happens?"

"Then you get an exquisite pair of gold cuff links, sent round from Mangin's in Bond Street, with no card—with nothing—not even a breath of perfume—not even your initials—just a date. A date engraved across the face of them, and no man can go through life with only cuff links to sustain him."

Sergeant Opperdyke's voice roared above the clatter of the refueling activity. "Your 6418 is fueled and loaded, Mr. Paterson!"

Paterson took a few steps toward the flight sergeant. "Just what time was it when Mr. Mallory and Mr. Trent took off last?"

"About 7:05, sir."

Phelps-Barrington said, "Then that was Trent and Mallory we saw."

Izzard continued the program with, "Here's D-2420 fueled and loaded, Sergeant."

P-B bowed to Paterson and said, "The carriage awaits without."

By 8:10 Yardley and Hoyt were back and sitting on the long bench just inside the hangar. They were weary, sooty-eyed, slack-jawed. The youngster was wolfing a great sandwich and quarts of milky tea from a large white bowl. Hoyt sat wide-legged, examining a shapeless, unappetizing sandwich. "Damned decent of them to slice the hoofs off this beast before they lugged this sandwich over. Look at this offal!" He held up a great slab of meat that had been packed between two thick slices of bread.

"My old man loves grub like that," Yardley said, and managed a laugh.

"Tell me about him. It might take the taste of this out of my gullet."

"The old man? He's a farmer . . . and a damn good one. We have a place outside Rugby, and he raises shire horses . . . mostly for show. Dad loves 'em big, deep chested, and . . ."

"With bags of feather," Hoyt concluded for him.

"Right. Bags of feather. You should see him preparing a horse for the London show. For two days before the exhibit he bandages all that hair around their hocks upward so that it sticks out three times as much as it would if he hadn't. Oh, he's proud when his shires first trot into the ring. 'Bags of feather,' he says and rubs his hands together. 'Bags of feather.' "

"Who drives these horses?"

Yardley looked amazed. "I do, sir. Every time. I've driven in seven London shows, driving eight shires at a time. You ought to see it, sir. It's a magnificent sight."

"You, or the horses?"

"Dad wouldn't let anyone else but me handle 'em."

"There can't be anyone else in England big and strong enough," Hoyt said with sincere admiration.

"I suppose you do have to be born to it," Yardley agreed. "There's nothing like it, though. Taking them eight big dapple-grays through the gate, and into the arena with everybody standing up cheering, and some screaming their heads off. It's better than the Lord Mayor's show, or a Coronation procession."

"Bags of feather," Hoyt echoed.

"Bags of feather," Yardley agreed, and then dropped his hands into his lap. He stared out to where the Camels were being refueled and prepared for another intrusion patrol. "By George, I never knew front-line flying was like this." He gulped more tea. "I thought you sat up there at eighteen thousand feet, frozen stiff in tight formation with a lot of red johnnies around you—and all of them a Von Richthofen. Is he really any good, Skipper? All this bloody Baron, red air-fighter stuff."

"I suppose he has his place in the scheme of things, but I can't say that I've ever seen him."

"How about Captain Ball . . . and how about McCudden and Major Bishop?"

"They're all different. Ball had a little garden when he was with Number 56 Squadron. He grew flowers and kept a hutch of rabbits."

"Amazing! He had forty-three Huns and the Victoria Cross, and he wasn't yet twenty-one years of age when he was shot down."

Hoyt stared off into space. "I don't remember how many Huns he had. It's not particularly important now, is it?"

"Oh, but it's really sport, this front-line flying, isn't it, Skipper?"

A Clerget engine was heard coming in, *blip-blip-blip,* as the pilot maneuvered for a landing.

Hoyt shot to his feet. "Who's that?" he yelled.

"That's Mr. Mallory, sir!" Featherstone cried.

"Alone?"

"I don't see anybody else, sir. He's sideslippin' in over the east side of the 'drome, sir."

By 9:45 Phelps-Barrington and Paterson were back again and had joined Mallory who was hunched on the hangar bench while the refueling activity continued outside. P-B was kneading Mallory's upper arm.

"I burned the outer skin off with liniment, but it's inside, I tell you. It's something in the bone. The arm works all right from the elbow down, but it hurts like hell inside."

"You shouldn't have come back," Paterson said with compassion.

"Where the hell else was there to go?"

"You wouldn't have come back if I had been in charge here," the young American said with fervor.

"It's too bloody bad you're not in charge," snarled Mallory lighting a cigarette. "Perhaps you could have cleaned this mess up."

"No man who isn't fully fit belongs out here, especially under conditions like this," Paterson snapped and stood his ground.

"We'll work it out," P-B said and continued the massage. "Sometimes when you get yourself chewed up like this, nerve ends are cut, and you get a pain where there really isn't any pain . . . There, how does that feel? I knew a chap at home whose feet used to feel cold every time the weather turned bad, and he hadn't any feet since the Whitsun of 1904 when he got drunk and fell asleep on a railway line."

Paterson managed a half grin. "Wait until Trent sees what a mess they've made of the yards at Douai. I think the Hun must have done some of it himself. What do you suppose he's doing? Pulling out of Douai entirely?"

"What a joke that would be," P-B observed. "Maybe we're winning the war, and staff thinks we're losing it."

"We were flying just under the clouds," Paterson prattled on. "There was a strong west wind driving a great wad of low mist. I figure the swines are advancing at about a mile an hour. It was bumpy as hell but you couldn't get anywhere near a thousand feet. I tried to get rid of my bombs on some trenches. I saw one go but my bus still felt heavy, and I wasn't sure so I went down and gunsprayed a group hiding in a barnyard. When I nosed down, and started to pull out of my dive, I must have jerked the remaining bombs off for there was a hell of a blast that blew a large barn to bits."

"That's how it goes, sometimes," Mallory said, wincing.

"All right, P-B. That'll be enough, thanks. It doesn't do much good. It's inside, I tell you. Inside the bone."

At that moment two Clerget engines were heard approaching and Phelps-Barrington went out toward the tarmac. "Who is it?" he yelled.

Sergeant Opperdyke answered. "It's Captain Hoyt . . . and Mr. Trent, sir."

"Where's Yardley?" Paterson asked. "Let's see now, who did he go out with?"

"He was working with the skipper," Mallory answered, but Sergeant Opperdyke had a correction. "No sir, it's not Mr. Trent, it's Mr. Yardley."

Mallory grumbled, "It feels like it's going to snow like hell in half an hour."

"No!" snapped Paterson. "It's warming up too fast."

Opperdyke shouted again from the cab rank. "It's not Mr. Yardley either, sir. It's one of the 'B' Flight machines."

"For Christ's sake let's get organized," snapped Paterson. "Make up your mind, Sergeant."

"You two decided which one is going with me?" Mallory asked and stood up.

P-B said, "You'd better hang on here, Paterson. You're doing a better job with Opperdyke than any of us could."

"Right! I'll go with the skipper when he gets fueled."

"Well, come on then," Mallory said and crossed the tarmac still rubbing his arm.

3

Shortly before five o'clock in the morning of March 21, an enemy bombardment that included gas, smoke, and high-explosive shells from all calibers of artillery opened up against the fronts of the British Fifth and Third Armies ranging from the Oise to the Scarpe rivers, while road centers and railroads as far back as Saint-Pol were hammered by high-velocity ammunition. Diversionary bombardments were turned on along the French front over wide sectors east and northeast of Reims, and on portions of the British front between the Scarpe and Lens. Other British positions from south of La Bassée Canal to the River Lys were shelled heavily with poison gas, and battery areas between Messines and the Ypres-Comines Canal were actively engaged. At the same time Dunkirk was bombarded from the air.

All these initial assaults began at different times, but the general attack jumped off about 9:45 on a battle front of fifty-four miles—between the Oise and Sensee rivers. As visibility improved later in the day, large numbers of low-flying aircraft attacked British ground troops and artillery batteries.

The early ground attack was favored by a thick white fog that hampered British efforts, for the spotters in advanced posts could not see the SOS signals sent up from the outpost line, and German infantry had little trouble forcing its way into the foremost defensive zones. Until about one o'clock in the afternoon, fog in the advanced British area made it impossible to see more than fifty yards in any direction, and the machine guns and forward field artillery that had been disposed to cover this zone with their fire were deprived of the opportunity to lend support. Detachments holding the outpost positions were consequently overwhelmed or surrounded; in many cases before they could pass back information concerning the enemy's attack.

During the morning some reports were received indicating that the enemy had penetrated the British front line opposite La Fère, and that he had also broken into the forward positions north of the Bapaume–Cambrai road, and opposite Lagnicourt and the infamous Bullecourt. By noon it was reported that German troops were entering Ronnsoy which meant that in this sector they had penetrated well into the second defensive belt. This success continued, and Templeux-le-Guerard was taken shortly afterward, while the villages of Hargicourt and Villeret were quickly surrounded and entered about midday.

During all this, aircraft of the Royal Flying Corps were putting on a gallant show in the enemy's rear areas, beating up the roads that supplied the advance, bombing transport, harassing the movement of troops, and doing their best to hinder every element of the attack. Bad weather made their operations difficult, but under the moral lashings of threatened defeat, the pilots, observers, and air gunners added to the majestic tradition.

By 1:30 P.M. Hoyt, Paterson, and Phelps-Barrington were back together and gathered in Hoyt's hangar office.

"Well, if that was Trent who had the forced landing over Saint-Pol he must have come back on his gravity tank. If it isn't Trent at Saint-Pol, it must be that Trent is down on that railroad bridge at Lieven. I'll bet he's roaring mad; blocking the line and writing off his prop and undercarriage at the same time," Phelps-Barrington concluded.

"Whoever it was on the bridge, do you think he could have walked out?" Hoyt asked.

"Oh, absolutely. It wasn't a bad crash."

After Paterson had studied some rough figures, he said, "A forced landing at Saint-Pol was in Trent's time bracket . . . that is if they got the time right over the telephone at this end . . . but I don't see how he'd get in there without picking up some landmark that would have brought him back here."

"That's good reasoning," the skipper said admiringly.

"Well, there's no use worrying," P-B argued.

Paterson continued, "Did you talk to that damned fool Yardley, Skipper? He was flying between the brewery stacks at Vitry on that eleven o'clock show. He screwed off from me completely. Couldn't we give him a football to dribble along with one foot when he goes on a ground strafe?"

"We might try that," Hoyt said with a faint smile.

Phelps-Barrington shook his head. "He isn't in yet. He actually likes it. He's a petrol-burner. Remind me to hit him with something lusty. He's too damned healthy."

The telephone bell rang and the clerk bobbed up from just outside the door, snatched at the instrument and said, "'C' Flight office, Number 44 Squadron, R.F.C. . . . Where do you say? . . . Behind Bapaume? Yes. That's right. What are the numbers on the rudder? . . . Oh, you haven't got that, either . . . I can't hear you. Well, have you got any identifying marks at all? Oh . . . well wait till it cools off and give me the numbers on that. Yes . . . Right!" He hung up.

Hoyt ranted, "Why'd they call here?"

"Nearest aerodrome, I suppose, sir."

"Well, they haven't any right to call here unless it's one of our planes. Did they think it was?"

"No, sir. They didn't say. Just said it was a Camel."

"Well, they haven't any right to call here. I won't have it."

Phelps-Barrington and Paterson exchanged knowing glances, and gave Hoyt a compassionate look. Paterson then sighed, slapped both knees and stood up. Aping P-B he chanted, "Two by two the animals came . . . and a little child shall lead them. How do we pair up this time?"

Time: 3:30 P.M. Hoyt was alone in his littered office. Outside the activity had lessened considerably as there were only two Camels left to service. The telephone rang again, and Hoyt snatched savagely at the instrument. "Hoyt, here. Yes, sir. I'm aware of the situation, but I've got four machines down somewhere. My effective strength is just Mr. Paterson and myself . . . No, sir. I haven't got any confirmations on any of them, but I know how much petrol each one has left . . . No, sir, I'm not insinuating anything of the kind. It's all very well for you to come along at half-past five in the morning and tell us to keep up a show until we're washed out, but . . . I *know* I'm tired, sir. That hasn't anything to do with it. I want to know where my pilots are, and I can't find out keeping up this silly show at the same time. I've blown a hole in every square inch of mud from Armentières to Vitry since six o'clock this morning, sir . . . Very good, sir. That's all there is to it then, and while I'm gone, I'll have a pair of wings put on my bed so I can keep it up all night!" and with that Hoyt hung up, went to the door and bellowed, "Sergeant Opperdyke. Am I fueled?"

"All set, sir!"

"Good. And start Mr. Paterson's engine." He turned, wiped his hand across his mouth, looked the office over, picked up all the engine logs, maps, patrol reports, and hurled them at the opposite wall.

At five-thirty in the afternoon Mr. Harboard, muffled up in an old greatcoat and cut-down flying boots over which he somehow had drawn a pair of muddy galoshes, appeared in the hangar, and pottered about for several minutes. Finally, he sat down on the wall bench and stared out the door. He huddled against the cold with corpse-blue hands, as a chill wind knifed across the field and blustered about the cold canvas shed. Not one Camel was to be seen anywhere, and the old man tried to invoke some order out of the leaden scene. Silent, and morose, he watched Izzard and Bream preparing primitive landing flares that were to be set out ready for lighting should any pilot manage to struggle back in the approaching darkness.

Izzard was saying, " 'Ow about taking some of that old packing in that box over there in the corner? That ought to smudge. It's dry enough."

"Smudge ain't right," argued Featherstone. "It's got to light up properly. To do that you 'ave to sort of give it a bit of a lift so there's a draft underneath. I've made these things 'undreds of times."

Bream handed over something indistinct to Izzard. " 'Ere, 'ow about this?"

"That looks all right. Let's 'ave the petrol."

Featherstone warned. "Not too bloody much petrol, now. Remember 'ow far Texas is from 'ere, Izzard. Besides, it's engine oil that burns longest."

"Right you are . . . There's one. Come on now, let's get on wiv it."

" 'Ow many did the sergeant want?"

"Three, to make an 'L'."

Izzard mooned, "But suppose no one comes back. Gor! What a lonesome place."

"Stow that," Featherstone spat. "Somebody allus comes back. What are you trying to make of 'C' Flight? A washout?"

Bream stuck to the task. " 'Ow about wrapping this around a chunk of wood and making a draft underneath? You can nail it through both sides of the can. Or, if you knock a bomb box to bits, the pieces just fit. 'Ow's that for an idea?"

"Not too bad. You knock it to bits an' I'll nail it up."

Featherstone remarked, "They say there isn't any doubt about Mr. Trent being confirmed on this side of the line," to which Bream added, "That plane ain't even washed out!"

"That's the pity of it. Anybody else could 'ave walked

away from it, except a 'C' Flight pilot on a day like this. They say 'e 'it the compass, but 'ardly broke 'is nose."

" 'E's a bloody fine pilot, Mr. Trent. 'E used to think about flying more than the lot of 'em. What I mean," Bream explained, "is that 'e used to think about every detail of it."

"I 'ear they thought very well of 'im on the London Southwestern," Izzard commented.

"Bloody like 'im. Following a railroad 'ome, and then 'itting the bridge."

"Now you listen to me," Bream interposed. "Sergeant says 'e don't want no talk about any of this until it's confirmed. Sergeant says Captain Hoyt is sort of revving up about it. I 'eard 'im blow up on the telephone, not two 'ours ago, and I don't blame 'im, I don't. After all, they're 'is pilots, and 'e trained them."

Izzard nodded his head. "An' I'd 'ate to be senior officer in one of these ruddy mobs. I couldn't sleep, I couldn't, if I lost a pilot. Two streamers on me tail, an' all that. That's a big, bloody responsibility, that is."

" 'Old orf," Featherstone said, looking across at Harboard, "the old 'un is listening."

As the dissertation died down, the telephone in Hoyt's office began to ring, and the old man cranked his bulk to his feet. "I'll take it," he muttered, and shuffled through the door. The flare-makers listened as the old soldier answered.

"Well, what have you got?" they heard Harboard croak. "Louder, man, I can't hear you."

Sergeant Opperdyke hurried across the tarmac and into the room. "Can I be of any help, sir?"

"Of course. They seem to be calling here and want to talk to someone in command. I don't suppose I'll do."

Opperdyke took the instrument, listened for a minute or so, and then responded to Harboard's appeal. "It seems to be the same party back of Bapaume, sir. They called us two hours or so ago. They seem to have a number from a burned engine, now." He turned back to the telephone. "What is the number? It must be cool enough by now. You'll find it on the rear casing plate. Well, it couldn't have been very hot if it was that far in the ground . . . Well, all right, let's have it. Six . . . four . . . nine . . . four. Let's repeat that, eh? Right. Thank you, Sappers," Opperdyke closed disconsolately, and hung up.

"Who is it, Sergeant?" Harboard cried.

Opperdyke started to pick up the debris Hoyt had tossed around.

"I said, who is it, Sergeant?"

Before Opperdyke could answer Portwine hurried through the office doorway with a raincoat over his arm. He went straight to Harboard. "I say, sir, you have given me a start. I've been looking all over for you. I think you'd better wear your trench coat too, sir. It's getting very damp out here."

Harboard sighed and draped the coat over his shoulders. "Do you know what a terrible thing the fifth verse of the ninth chapter of the Koran says?"

"No, sir. I don't believe I do, sir."

"Well, the fifth verse of the ninth chapter of the Koran ought to be issued to every British soldier along with his razor, his rifle, and his boots."

"I agree with you, sir," Portwine replied, chiefly for something to say.

But Harboard turned to Opperdyke and asked, "What did you get on the telephone?"

"It's Mr. Yardley, sir."

"He's been killed, hasn't he?"

"Yes, sir. Just this side of Bapaume."

Befuddled and indignant, Harboard said, "It doesn't matter where, Sergeant. He's been killed."

"Yes, sir. He's been killed."

"That's all, Sergeant." Harboard then turned to Portwine and continued where he had left off, "And when the sacred months are passed, kill those who join other gods with God wherever ye shall find them; and seize and slay them and lay in wait for them with every kind of ambush."

"I beg your pardon, sir."

"Fifth verse, ninth chapter of the Koran."

"You spent a long time in India, didn't you, sir?" Portwine took hold of Harboard's elbow, and together they walked outside to the edge of the tarmac where they could see the glare from the three flares the mechanics had set out along the turfed strip.

"I've never come back," old Harboard said and blinked at the smoky glare.

"Oh yes you have, sir," Portwine insisted. "This is France, sir, and it's winter time, sir. Here, let me buckle you up tighter."

"So it is, France."

"Please wrap up a bit, sir."

"You are very kind, Portwine. You may button me up as you will. You know, for a minute or two I wondered who you were."

"Yes, sir. I understand. I followed you out of the mess, across to the farm, and all the way back here again; you do get about, you know."

"Well, don't forget. You didn't shoot Mr. Winslow down."

"Oh, thank you, sir."

4

From where they stood just outside the flight office door, they could hear the telephone tinkling again. Harboard peered over his peaked nose at Portwine, and the aerial gunner turned his head to listen as the clerk rushed in from the hangar side to answer it. " 'C' Flight, Number 44 Squadron, R.F.C.," he began.

Sergeant Opperdyke hurried over from where he had been staring out at the landing-flare operations. "Who is it, Plaisted?" he yelled.

The clerk shoved his head outside the doorway and cried, "I can't make out, Sergeant."

"Who is it?" Harboard demanded and began to move back to the doorway.

"Just a moment, sir."

"See who it is, Sergeant. Take it yourself," Harboard whined.

"I will, sir."

The clerk appeared again and explained, "Somebody's got a Lieutenant Mallard. I can't quite make out what they are saying."

Portwine husked, "Strike me pink! That's three!"

"Quite," Harboard agreed.

"But there isn't any Mallard in this flight," parried Opperdyke.

"You hope there isn't," Portwine said under his breath. "It's Mr. Mallory."

Harboard leaned over him and croaked, "What the hell did you say?"

"I said it's Mr. Mallory, sir."

"Well now, did you *have* to say it?"

"Yes sir. I know it is."

"You don't know anything of the kind, do you?" Harboard protested.

"Yes I do, sir. It's Mr. Mallory."

"How do you know that?"

"I don't know, sir."

"I'll tell you how you do. You feel it inside you. You

know just as well as when you are off your horse, feeling alone and groping about with your bare hands in the darkness, and you come up with what is supposed to be a trail, and then Sniders begin spanging over your head. That's how you know."

"That's India again, sir," Portwine reminded the old man.

Harboard stiffened with dignity. "It's not India at all. It's Afghanistan."

Sergeant Opperdyke was saying, "Well, can they spell it?"

"They're trying to, Sergeant," the harassed clerk said.

Harboard turned on Opperdyke, "Well, *can* you take it, Sergeant, or can't you?"

"Yes, sir. I can, sir."

"Well, take it then. Who the hell is it?"

Portwine pawed at Harboard's sleeve. "Look here, sir, will you please come back to the mess?"

"I damn well will not. I'm going to stay until one of those Sniders get me."

"That may be a very long time, sir."

Harboard wagged his ancient head. "I *know* it. Do you know how many years I've been waiting for some ghazi to shoot me through the kidneys?"

"No, sir. I don't, sir, but I do wish you'd come in out of the cold."

"Well, I won't." Harboard turned to the flight office door. "Have you got that name yet, Sergeant?"

"Not yet, sir."

"Well, get it."

"Hello! Hello!" Portwine cried. "Here's something. I can hear a Camel engine blipping out there."

"Is it one of ours?" Harboard whimpered.

"I can't tell, sir. It seems to be heading for our flares . . . I feel sure it's one of ours."

Opperdyke came to the doorway again and bellowed, "Everyone out on that plane, now. Smartly! Everyone now. A man for each wingtip. Let's have it." He turned back to the clerk at the telephone. "Ask them to look through the officer's pockets. His name must be on something. What about his identification disc? I'm sure Mr. Mallory had a new silver one. Tell them not to telephone unless they have something important . . . Now it's G. H. Mallory . . . He's sure? . . . Right you are. Hang up."

The clerk hung up and said mournfully, "It *is* Mr. Mallory, Sergeant."

"God's truth!" Opperdyke snarled. "Wait until the old 'un hears that." He went outside again where Harboard trapped him.

"Who is it, Sergeant?"

Opperdyke stared out to where a lone Camel was blipping in for its landing. "It's Mr. Paterson . . . out on the aerodrome, sir, and it's Mr. Mallory . . . on the telephone."

"What do you mean on the telephone?"

"Mr. Mallory crashed at Roisel."

"Badly?"

"Yes, sir, badly."

"Well, how badly?"

"They say the engine came back on his lap, sir."

"They say that, do they?"

"That's about all they did say, sir."

"Do they know how far we are from the engine in a Camel?"

Before Opperdyke could continue the pointless harangue Paterson's plane rumbled up and came to a halt with its nose well up on the tarmac and near the hangar doorway. The pilot leaned out of his cockpit and called to Izzard and Bream who had helped guide him off the runway. "I want you to make those flares blaze higher, and keep them high until the skipper gets in. I think he's all right himself, but he's coming in very slowly and I don't think he has very much left to bring in."

Harboard recognized leadership and he stood admiring the manner in which young Paterson was taking over. He respected a man who could take responsibility, but he had to ask, "What the hell do you mean, Mr. Paterson?"

Paterson unbuckled his helmet, loosened his scarf and cranked himself up so that he was sitting on the hump of the fuselage. "Your servant, Colonel. He ran into an ambush fifteen miles south of the Khyber Pass and had his velocipede shot from beneath him."

"So?"

The youthful pilot climbed down wearily and stared at the small group near the flight office door. "All right, who's confirmed missing?" he demanded, but Harboard interrupted: "In the East Suffolks, when we were in India, if we received good or bad news, we always celebrated it by drinking six double brandies—neat. Will you drink six double brandies, neat, with me now, Mr. Paterson?"

Paterson's eyes flashed. "Who are they, Colonel?"

"Trent, definitely confirmed . . . and Yardley's a certainty. Mallory? You'll have to talk to the sergeant about Mallory because he just took it on the telephone . . . but . . ."

Portwine broke in, "It's Mr. Mallory too, sir."

Paterson gave Portwine a calm look of understanding, and then asked, "Where's Phelps-Barrington? He's *got* to come back!"

Sergeant Opperdyke backed out of the dismal semicircle and began bellowing again. "I want more light from those flares. Open them up. Get more oil . . . petrol . . . anything. Never mind instructions. I've got to get my pilots in, I have."

Paterson took over again. "Don't make them too bright.

The wind's right into them, and when you hear him blip his engine, stand between the flares and the plane so that they give enough ground light but don't blind him."

"Very good, sir. Here comes another one."

Portwine edged over to Paterson and his hoarse voice appealed, "Mr. Phelps-Barrington will come back, won't he, sir?"

"He'd better," Paterson growled and turned to watch the three glare patches put up by the flares. Harboard moved to his side and Portwine took the old man's arm and together they stood listening to the rage of a badly timed engine, the screech of flying wires and the whip of a whirling prop. "We'll take it easy, if it's Hoyt," the young pilot ordered. "Don't tell him too much for the first minute or so . . . or until the first six double brandies, in fact."

The Camel suddenly appeared, dabbed down heavily near a flare and turned to churn up to the hangar until it was taxied to stand wingtip to wingtip with Paterson's. Hoyt climbed down without a word, turned and peered about, stared into the hangar and drew a crooked finger across a bloody gash that ran along his right cheek. He looked out toward the cab rank and then walked slowly to the waiting group.

"All right, Paterson, you must have something definite. What is it?" he demanded in uneven tones.

"You're very tired, sir."

"I know I'm tired, but I want a report. You've been taking charge all day. You must have something."

"I don't know whether I can tell you or not, sir. I don't know whether I can stand hearing myself say it."

"What about Trent?"

"It was Trent on that bridge."

"Well, let's have it. Where is he now?"

"He's still there."

"But that hardly broke the prop!"

"That's the way it looked, sir."

"Now don't stand there and try to tell me that that crash killed Trent."

"It killed him."

Hoyt took a sideways glance at Paterson. "Don't you address me as 'sir' any more, Paterson?"

"I beg your pardon, sir."

"I'm sorry. I didn't mean it that way. You've done a splendid job, all day. But anyone could have flown that bus out the way it is. What about Yardley and Mallory? Has anything come through on them?"

Paterson nodded solemnly.

"Let's have it!" Hoyt cried in a wild rage. "What happened? Give it to me straight. I trained these men—you didn't—and I damn well want to know what happened to them. Where are they?"

Paterson drew himself to attention and Hoyt strode over and stood eye to eye. "Don't lie to me, Paterson. I won't have it. Where's Yardley? You tell me, do you hear?"

"He's down at Bapaume," Paterson's voice quivered. "He's . . . he's burned, Skipper."

"Oh no! No! No! Please, Paterson, don't do this to me."

"I'm telling you the truth, sir."

Hoyt continued to stare. "Yes, I believe you, now. But what about Mallory?"

"He's down at Roisel. That's all we know, sir."

Hoyt bowed his head and walked away. Izzard and Bream, having extinguished the ground flares, came out of the mist and looking askance passed the flight commander. Hoyt nodded to them and said, "Thank you, Bream . . . Izzard. It was good of you to help me in. Thanks."

"It was nothing, sir," Bream said, and both men hurried into the hangar.

The group of men at the mouth of the hangar was held in thrall: old Harboard had squatted down on the greasy bench with Portwine standing nearby. Paterson sat at the far end unbuttoning the chest flap of his Sidcot, and stuffing his gloves into his thigh pockets. Hoyt came back and watched the mechanics trundle the two Camels under cover, then sat down and passed his hand across his face in a gesture of absolute exhaustion. He discovered the blood on his fingers, flicked it off, and mumbled to himself. "I don't know why I was picked for this party. I never shirked. I always did my work. They never had to check on any of us. There's never been a dud in 'C' Flight since I've been here. We've carried on just the way old MacFarlane taught us, and now look what they've done to us." His voice rose slightly, but it was still heavy with hopelessness. "They don't kill us off at our own game; they turn us into glorified infantry and chase us around all day at one hundred and fifty feet and get us all swatted down like flies."

Paterson was sobbing audibly.

Hoyt glared at him and snarled, "You'll have to stop that."

"I can't stop it."

"You'll have to stop it! You hear what I'm telling you?"

Paterson straightened up and yelled, "I can't stop it."

"All right. Where's Phelps-Barrington? Get him and we'll go over to the mess and have a drink."

"God Almighty! I can't get him. He's not back, either. How can I get any of them?" Paterson appealed.

Hoyt sat stupefied. "But nothing ever happens to Phelps-Barrington!" He stared around the thinning group. "Here, steady on that. Hold it. What's his fuel time?"

"He could still be in the air, but he isn't," Paterson moaned. "They did us all in when they denied us our teamwork. You can't have teamwork doing what we have been doing today."

"Stop it! I won't have it," Hoyt yelled again.

"I can't stand this. This has done something to me inside." Paterson stood up. "This isn't flying. This is murder. Do you know what those fellows meant to me? They meant more to me than they ever could mean to you, Hoyt. Trent, Mallory, and Phelps-Barrington were a framework, a symbol that held me together. Now they're gone, Hoyt, and I'm alone . . . and that's usually the end."

"You're alone? How are you alone? You'll never know what it is to be alone until you're dragging five men after you. I've been alone ever since I've been up front with two streamers on my tail. The men who were out here when I joined 'C' Flight are all gone."

"I think I understand your position, sir, but that's the burden of leadership. The only thing that is real to me was knowing Trent, Phelps-Barrington, and Mallory. You're not real, Skipper. You've always been something apart. Then, there's a different kind of steel in you. There's something in you that'll never be in me."

Hoyt shook his head. "You're wrong there, Paterson."

"I'd do anything in the world if you told me to. I'd go to hell behind you, but I don't think I could ever take your place. I can't even see myself carrying *one* streamer—although I have been given that honor at times."

"You're a good man, Paterson."

"I'm telling you things you ought to know," Paterson continued. "Phelps-Barrington, Mallory, and Trent . . . sensing them around me, getting drunk with them, seeing them next to me in the air, hearing them snore in the next cubicle at night. That's all there ever was to me, Skipper, and now that they're gone, I'm done too." He turned his back on Hoyt, stared out through the open hangar door and blew his nose to choke his sobbing.

Hoyt lay back with both arms along the rail of the crude bench, staring up into the darkness of the hangar roof. "Do you really know what leadership is, Paterson? It's the memory of dead friends in your heart. It's your pals working through you to help newcomers. You have Trent, P-B, and Mallory behind you." He suddenly sat up, lunged forward and buried his face in his cupped hands. "Oh God! Where are they? Tracy, MacFarlane, Sutton, Wragg, and Tommy Weatherall?"

Harboard suddenly roused, and apparently realized that he was still part of the company. Portwine leaned toward him apprehensively. "Dick Culbert's been dead forty years and Molyneux died in Malta in Eighty-four," the old man said as the aerial gunner tucked the trench coat about his thin shoulders.

The telephone rang once more, and they could hear the voice of Sergeant Opperdyke. " 'C' Flight, Number 44 Squadron, R.F.C. . . . Yes, sir. Very good, sir."

"What is it, Sergeant?" Hoyt asked dismally.

"It was Squadron Office, sir, relaying the wash-out through Wing. We're to discontinue ground-strafing operations as of seventeen o'clock, sir."

Paterson listened, and gave one wild shriek of laughter, choked it off, hurled his helmet and goggles to the hangar floor, and strode blindly away.

Harboard touched Captain Hoyt on the sleeve, and with a kindly smile on his face, said, "I've been waiting for you, sir. Shall we go now?"

"Where?"

"A fire . . . a drink . . . a comfortable chair. That's all there ever is, you know. Absolutely all."

"Thank you, Colonel."

5

The most important thrust made by General Ludendorff during the first day of the attack, was felt on the right, south of Saint-Quentin. From Fragnier, which was reached by four o'clock in the afternoon, enemy troops fought their way on to the Crozat Canal, and then took Quessy. North of this point the British 18th Division, reinforced by troops of the 2nd Cavalry Division, hung on and held their battle positions intact—although they were threatened on both flanks by the enemy's progress at Quessy and Benay—and successfully restored the situation in the neighborhood of Ly-Fontaine by a stirring counterattack. Many of the strong points in the forward zone on this division's front were also holding out, although surrounded; in fact wireless messages from these gallant defenders were received as late as eight-thirty in the evening, and rifle fire was heard in their vicinity until midnight.

Thus, thanks to the continued air operations and the determination of all British infantry—although he had made considerable progress—the enemy was still being held firmly in the battle zone in which it had been anticipated the major struggle would take place. Nowhere had he effected that immediate breakthrough for which his troops had been trained for so many weeks, and such advance as he had made had been bought at a cost that already had greatly reduced his chances of carrying out his ultimate purpose.

In view of the progress made by the Ludendorff forces south of Saint-Quentin, the lack of strength in the British line on that front and the lack of reserves with which to reinforce the situation, General Gough decided on the evening of March 21, after consultation with the GOC III

Corps, to withdraw the divisions of that corps behind the Crozat Canal. This movement involved the withdrawal of the 36th Division on the right of the XVIII Corps, to the line of the Somme Canal.

The enemy's advance north and south of the Flesquières salient made necessary a withdrawal also of the V Corps and the 9th Division, and orders were accordingly issued to the divisions concerned for a line to be taken up, as a first stage, along the high ground known as Highland Ridge, and from there westward along the Hindenburg line to Havrincourt and Hermies.

Shortly after six-thirty, 'C' Flight's mess had taken on the warmth of a happier day. The fire from the stove tossed flickering lights on the bawdy friezes, and seemed to make the characters move under some mysterious impulse. The phonograph was churning out the mellow tunes of *Lilac Domino* in a low key, and Portwine who had assumed the duties of mess orderly, feeling that any appearance by either Shuffling Joe or Shuffling Wally would be *de trop*, was moving about to the one-step tunes, and arranging the table for four.

Harboard, washed and brushed, was wearing a G.S. tunic and four rows of campaign ribbons. Paterson, who had shaved and carefully brushed his hair, wore a clean G.S. tunic and a neatly folded scarf in lieu of a collar and tie. Captain Hoyt had decided on a simple tunic, a clean shirt, and neatly pressed slacks.

"Someone's knocking on the door, Portwine," Hoyt said. "Do you mind?"

The aerial gunner hurried to the door, yanked it open and saw Sergeant Opperdyke standing outside. The NCO took off his cap, stepped inside, and said, "It'll soon be a quarter to seven, sir. Do you still want the men standing by the flares for Mr. Phelps-Barrington?"

"I want them standing by until I wash them out," Hoyt said sharply.

Paterson said, "But he's been gone five hours and fifty-five minutes, sir."

Hoyt turned and looked at Paterson, paused as a flicker of understanding passed between them, then nodded to Opperdyke. "Wash the men out, Sergeant."

As the door closed again, the mess telephone jangled and Portwine hurried to answer it. "Officers' Mess, 'C' Flight, Number 44 Squadron, R.F.C. . . . Yes . . . Yes, he's here, sir . . . Who? Half a minute, sir." He cupped the instrument and turned to Captain Hoyt. "It's the hospital at Ligny, sir."

"I'll take it," Hoyt said and held the instrument gingerly. "Yes . . . Yes . . Oh, yes, I was talking to you. about twenty minutes ago. Have you located him? Oh, he was? You're quite sure of that? Well, our medical officer has gone down . . . Oh, I see. Thank you . . . Not at all. Thanks, very much." Hoyt hung up, and straightened his tie.

"They haven't got Mallory there?" Paterson said.

"Not now."

"What do you mean? They did have him. Have they already shunted him on?"

"No. They didn't have to shunt him on. It was both his legs. He died about eight minutes after he was taken there. Steward, take Mr. Harboard's order, and Mr. Paterson's . . . and bring me a whisky and soda."

"Yes, sir," Portwine responded.

"If you want to, Paterson, you can get off right after dinner and go down by tender."

"You mean I should go down to the Pool by tender?"

"That's right. If you go down by tender you can bring back the replacements yourself. If you fly down and send them up by tender, we may never see them. One or two always come through all right, but four of them together stand an awfully good chance of being hung up for days."

"What about new planes?"

"I just had Marquise on the telephone and they can't give us four new Camels."

Portwine handed Hoyt his drink.

"How many can they give us?"

"We can get two by Thursday, and two more by the end of next week," Hoyt said, looking gloomy. "There is some talk of switching us to S.E.5s."

Paterson punched a fist into a palm. "There's always talk of switching to S.E.5s, but it never happens."

Beaming at Paterson, Harboard said, "If you go down by tender, I'll go with you. We're out of Gorgonzola cheese and we have no more Madeira in the bin, and Wingate tells me that the P.M.C. at Saint-Pol has four large tins of Huntley and Palmer biscuits he'll sell. They're the large tins," he explained, holding one hand high above the other.

Paterson said, "Why don't we all go down?"

Portwine broke that up by holding a tray of drinks between Harboard and Paterson, and then said over his shoulder to Hoyt, "Dinner's served, sir."

"Right! Shut that damned phonograph off!" Hoyt took a deep swig of his whisky and soda and bowed toward the table. The three officers turned, and then seemed to pause, as they stood looking at the table's unfamiliar emptiness. Mr. Harboard gulped his drink, put the glass on the table and picked up his plate of soup and a spoon. He walked over to the stove, stood with his legs well apart, smiled, and said, "Let's make it a hunt breakfast."

Hoyt and Paterson followed suit, and all three men stood there with their backs to the glow and began their soup course.

"Look here," Paterson spoke again with new spirit.

"We'll go right through to Saint-Omer and spend the night there. Then we'll look the Pool over and pick our meat and go on to Dunkirk and have a hell of a binge with Number 217 Squadron. I've got three old pals in 217. Chaps I knew at Toronto."

"What about Number 4 Naval? Are they still there?" Hoyt inquired. "I knew McClatchie and Charlie North."

"What is this?" Harboard broke in. "A busman's holiday? I say we go to Saint-Pol tonight. I hear the 'Dumbells Concert Party' will be there, and they have a lad who sings *Jones of the Lancers*. What's his name? . . . you know." He beat time with his spoon against the soup plate.

> *"I'm Jones of the Lancers, well rather.*
> *They say I'm the pick of the lot.*
> *Now the Guards and such fellers*
> *Use feet for propellers,*
> *But a Lancer—what, what, what,—what, what!"*

Paterson began beating time too, and closed with:

> *"Now the gunners and sappers,*
> *Are all right for flappers,*
> *But for a woman—a Lancer, what, what!"*

"Bloody good!" Hoyt beamed, and rushed his plate back to the table. "There's an American bar at Saint-Pol and Marguerite sings there. The last time I was up there, I got a bath in the hotel with hot water coming right out of the tap. I stayed in so long I got waterlogged."

"By George!" Paterson said. "I love to swim. Fresh water, you know. Lake water with a sandy bottom, the kind of water you can see right down into as far as it goes. Clean water. I like to dive into it and go all the way down and prowl along the bottom with my nose about four inches off the sand. We have a summer cottage on a lake in New Hampshire . . ."

Hoyt cringed. "I can't stand fresh water. I like the ocean. Did you ever swim in Villefranche Bay?"

"I've never been down in that part of the country."

"Cap Ferrat," Harboard said, and handed his plate to Portwine.

"That's the place!" Hoyt cried. "That's salt water, but it's as clear as any lake water you ever saw, and at night there's a phosphorescent glow to it that lights you up like Gaby Deslys."

"Lovely Gaby," whispered Harboard.

"Here! You leave Gaby to us. You take Lily Langtry," Hoyt protested.

"Out of deference to Edward, rest his soul, I *won't* take Lily Langtry."

Paterson put on an expression of mild shock. "Is this sex rearing its ugly head, or is this bathing?"

"Oh, let's have a little sex with it. Sex never hurts anything, and a great many times it has been known to do some good."

"I was in love once," Harboard said, staring up at the ceiling. "Yes, I'm quite positive that I was in love. She . . . wore a white dress that . . . swept the grass . . . and a sash of lavender silk . . . and she had very light hair with one damp ringlet . . . that curled at her temple." He hesitated and bit a knuckle. "Or was that Mrs. Gaston at Delhi? . . . Um . . . light hair? That must have been Mrs. Gaston. Kitty's hair was dark, and Kitty never wore lavender . . . Yes, that must have been Mrs. Gaston . . . Funny, I should think of her . . . or, no, that ringlet could have been Alicia Carstairs . . . Yes, I'm quite sure that was Alicia Carstairs . . . Oh, well."

Hoyt took his glass back to the table, and almost by instinct went to a window to peer out. He snapped the curtain over and came back to the stove. "Is it hell to grow old, Colonel?"

"Bless you, no. It's the only decent thing in life that ever happens to you."

"Why?"

"Because it makes you honest in your mind."

"No it doesn't. It just dulls your mind so that nothing matters to you any more. It doesn't matter to you, Harboard, that you can't remember what her name was."

"That was stupid of me."

"Not stupid at all. You can't help not remembering. That's what growing old does to you. It makes all the bright colors and all the fine music and all the laughter in life run together and become a gray stain behind you."

"It was stupid of me," Harboard insisted.

"Not at all. I can't even remember the spring of 1914. I was young in 1914, and I used to go boating with a girl who wore white dresses and had large silken bows on her shoes, but she might as well be your Mrs. Gaston in Delhi, as far as I am concerned tonight. She's so far from this place that I might just as well be seventy-seven years old myself."

Paterson finished his drink, and asked, "You don't mean to say you can't remember her name?"

"Of course I can. That isn't the point. The point is that it doesn't make any difference. It's all something else now. It never really happened."

"Did you love her?"

Hoyt exploded. "How the hell do I know? Where have I had any chance to find out what love means? I've been out here since January of 1915, and the only time I've seen a clean woman was when I went back to England to go through as a pilot . . . and what the hell do *you* know about love? You're not twenty yet!"

"Good lord! I'd hate to miss finding out." Paterson stood teetering on the balls of his feet. "I've been away from home a long while . . . considering. There was a lot of wasted time in Canada. Then, when I finally reached England I had to go through all that silly business again. Those damned Curtiss Jennys were a real waste of time. I've been away from the association of girls for months."

"It can steal your youth," Hoyt reflected.

"Back home, our house was always full of girls. Mother enticed 'em in by dozens, but they all were big wenches who played field hockey and tennis at Wellesley . . . like Amazons . . . good sports, but none of them mattered a damn."

"What about the girl in your cubicle?"

"Oh, that's Daisy. She's just a big healthy devil who makes a good pal. Talks a blue streak. I don't know whether I love her, or whether it's just some animal attraction. She does everything so damn well."

"You see, you don't recognize love when you bash into it."

"Daisy's a swell guy," Paterson admitted, "but right now I don't think I could go back to all those girls. They're all so damned young. Even the older ones. I mean the ones who are older than I am."

"You see!" cried Hoyt. "The war's stealing your youth."

"You don't understand," pleaded Paterson. "I suppose one of the cows in that crowd would have been the girl I would have married. I don't know which one, but one of them would have had her number on me, I suppose. Now, I'll never know which one."

"I shouldn't worry about it," Hoyt said pleasantly.

Portwine entered with a bottle wrapped in a napkin. Harboard bounced forward and cried, "It's the last of the Burgundy—my Burgundy. Let's hope it will take the taste of the can off the stew." He handed out three stemmed wineglasses. Portwine filled them, and stood back respectfully.

Hoyt lifted his glass to Harboard and said, "To Mrs.

Gaston at Delhi." He drank the wine down and snapped the stem of the glass.

"Here! Here!" Paterson cried. "None of that. There won't be a glass left in the mess. There were only six decent wineglasses when I counted them yesterday."

Harboard sipped, and bowed. "Thanks, Hoyt. You have a happy faculty of making me feel young." He sipped again. "I can hear the creak of the punkah rope and the tinkle of ice in tall glasses, and I can hear them coming up the steps of the veranda."

"Is this Delhi or somewhere in Burma?"

"I can see Dick Culbert and Tony Molyneux," Harboard droned on. "Tony Molyneux with his pillbox cocked over one ear and his dress spurs tinkling. Dick standing in the lighted doorway that cuts the crawling darkness like the flash of a heated sabre, and the stars up above dripping in the silken fronds of the trees like long tears. Gad, we had a mess at Benares!"

Hoyt wagged his head. "I make you young, sir, and you make me old. Let's cast an average and settle for about fifty years apiece, shall we?"

Harboard smiled. "Twenty-three and seventy-seven— that gives us exactly fifty years apiece, doesn't it, Hoyt?"

"Exactly, and I can feel every one of them tonight."

Paterson twirled his glass between his fingers. "Could we possibly lift this conversation to a more cheerful vein? Suppose we get back to that bath at Saint-Pol with the hot water that runs out of the tap. How long is that bathtub, Skipper? Can you lie full length in it, or do you have to hunch up?"

"Oh, you can lie full length. I think it was a horse trough before it was a bathtub, and there's a faint smell of the stable about it still."

"I never mind when the water's warm," said Harboard. "It brings them out, mind you, more than cold water does, but somehow or other warm water has a soporific effect and you don't seem to mind them as much."

"Then, of course," Hoyt explained, "if you let yourself get high enough, it neutralizes the other odors."

Paterson agreed. "Yes, that's true, but after you get yourself clean, the full force of the other smells hits you like a punch in the nose."

"You're too damned fastidious."

Harboard broke in with, "Oh I say, don't let fastidiousness go by the board. After all, the British Empire is founded on warm baths and stiff shirts."

There was no logical answer for that and they stood eating the mushy dessert and finishing the wine. Harboard went to a cupboard, peered about, and came back with a bottle of Drambuie. The three men lounged around the fire in three old chairs as Harboard poured the liqueur with an unsteady hand, and chanted, "Drambuie, God bless it! Prince Charlie's Nectar!"

They sat quietly, their feet to the fire, sipping the warm liqueur, sorting out their thoughts until a clatter echoing along the passage to the cubicles aroused them. Hoyt shot to his feet and turned toward the doorway leading to the passage. "Portwine! Will you, for God's sake, stop that? I say, will you stop that clatter, Portwine?"

The aerial gunner appeared in the doorway rubbing the back of his hand against his nostrils. "Sir?"

"I say, will you please have the decency to stop packing those kit bags until after we leave for Saint-Omer?"

Paterson put out his hand. "Steady, Skipper. He means well."

Portwine explained. "It's just Mr. Mallory's and Mr. Trent's, sir."

"I know damned well whose they are; and it's Yardley's

and it'll be Phelps-Barrington's next, and then it'll be . . ."

Paterson stood up and blocked off Hoyt's view of the doorway. "You'll have to calm down, you know, Skipper."

Hoyt rubbed his hand across his eyes. "Sorry. Sorry, Paterson. You're quite right, of course."

Harboard gave Paterson a look of admiration. The old man knew that at that minute the laurel of command had changed hands. He had seen this transition a hundred times before.

"I'm sorry too, sir," Portwine wailed from the doorway.

Hoyt waved a hand in dismissal. "All right, Portwine. Please carry on."

Harboard tried to relieve the tension by getting to his feet and saying, "I shall call for the tender to come around, eh?" He went to the telephone and twirled the handle three times and waited. "Hello. Motor Transport? This is 'C' Flight . . . Harboard. I want the Crossley for Saint-Omer in twenty minutes. Mark it out until noon tomorrow. Credit the petrol log for 'transportation for replacement pilots, Number 44 Squadron.' Let me have Magthorpe to drive."

"Are you sure Magthorpe hasn't piled up somewhere?" Hoyt grumbled in a low mood.

"Look here, sir," Paterson said. "You'll not do a damn bit of good by blowing up. You don't have to, you know. You're not a kid breaking up his toys, any more."

"I know. I know. I just wish I didn't have to."

"I know you're tired. Really exhausted. It's quite understandable."

"It's good of you to say so," Hoyt muttered and then took on a new attitude. "Death's a whore, but there isn't much you can do about it out here, and this little part of France is the only part of the world that exists for you and me. Everything beyond is simply a gay yarn that Marco Polo brought back."

"The war's too damned big to live up to," Paterson said. "I don't suppose there is one man in the world who can live up to it."

"You'll learn eventually. It's something that takes you and pulls you in and out of life. It's like religion; only a few people can be saints, but a million people can fall on their knees and pray. That's all we can do, Paterson. You can't get away from it. Nothing ever existed before you came here, and nothing will ever be real after you leave."

"Funny. I've lost all thought of ever leaving."

"Just like Mallory said: Where is there to go? There's nothing in the world to go back to. Suppose you live fifteen or twenty years more. Your hair will be thin, your belly will be slack and there'll always be an emptiness in your eyes because there won't be a ruddy soul in the world anywhere whom you can talk to again—except the men who have been out here with you."

"And from the looks of things most of them will be dead."

Hoyt nodded. "Yes. It's quite possibly true, but I don't think it matters so terribly much. Death was always a blank wall to me until I came out here. Now it's a sort of a doorway."

Paterson sat down and said, "Now there's a nice thought."

"He's right, you know," Harboard added, rubbing his chin. "It's a doorway to a pub; a nice warm pub with good beer and a blazing fire and a low ceiling and a smell of polished oak and of wine in old tuns and of clean sawdust. And every fine fellow you ever knew is in there waiting to buy you a drink. And let me add: mine host is a jolly fat fellow in a clean linen apron named 'God.' "

Paterson smiled and concluded. "That sounds desperately close to something."

Harboard nodded sheepishly. "Yes. I probably read it somewhere, but I can't remember where. That tender ought to be here in five or six minutes. If you chaps have anything to do, let's do it, and get off."

"That's the ticket," Hoyt agreed. "Ho . . . Portwine!"

The aerial gunner appeared and said, "Sir?"

"Pack up shaving kits and clean shirts and underwear for Mr. Harboard, Mr. Paterson, and myself. We're going to Saint-Pol for tonight, and we're going through in the morning to Pilots' Pool to bring in the replacement pilots."

"Yes, sir."

"And Portwine," Paterson said, "button that fleece lining into my trench coat, will you please?"

"Yes, sir."

"I'm damned if I'm going to put on breeches and boots," Hoyt swore.

"I can't, mine are being half-soled." Harboard grinned. "Oh, well, after all, this is the Flying Corps. What was it George Robey said in that London show? Let's see now. 'She's a very nice girl. She doesn't smoke cigarettes, or wear silk stockings, and she *positively* does not have any friends in the R.F.C.' "

"Wonderful!" cried Hoyt.

"I hope to God they never make a peacetime unit out of us. It'll spoil the R.F.C. properly. Boots and heel-clicking, and being properly dressed . . . ugh!"

"And don't for heaven's sake forget swords," Hoyt added, as he buckled on his Sam Browne belt.

Paterson went to the door leading to the kitchen, and called, "Oh, Joe! Three whiskies and sodas. Make it lively."

"Oh, no," Harboard said. "Whisky's a stevedore's drink after dinner. Make mine a brandy."

"I'd hate to be a stevedore," said Hoyt. "Make mine a brandy, too."

Paterson laughed, and yelled, "Three brandies and soda."

"That's better."

Harboard said, "Make mine a double brandy."

"That's better still," Hoyt agreed. "Make *mine* a double brandy."

Paterson shrugged his shoulders. "Well, it saves two chits, anyway. Three double brandies, Joe. Hold it! While I can still write my name, we'll take the bottle."

Shuffling Joe appeared with a bottle. " 'Ere you are, sir. Otard, sir. It's the last one."

"My word, this mess needs replenishing," Harboard complained.

Hoyt said, "Don't forget, we can polish off everything we've got left tonight, and prorate it among the new men tomorrow. After all, they're going to owe us something for the fine associations they'll have here at Number 44 Squadron."

Paterson turned to the mess orderly. "Look, Joe, pour three double brandies and soda and put what's left of those baby 'pollies of soda in a basket and let's have them on the seat of the tender when it comes around."

"Yes, sir."

Portwine came back into the mess draped with three haversacks, two walking sticks, one G.S. cap, and a Glengarry. He had Hoyt's British warm with its three pips on the shoulder straps and a pair of fur gloves. While the three officers stood nuzzling their drinks, he sorted out the gear, and then held the British warm for Hoyt to put on. When he had one arm in a sleeve Hoyt said, "I want you to stand by the telephone all night, Portwine. We shan't be back. Bring a cot in and sleep under the thing. Mr.

Phelps-Barrington is down somewhere, but we haven't gotten any word about it yet."

"Yes, sir. And Mr. Mallory, sir?"

"He died in the hospital at Ligny this afternoon."

"Yes, sir. I was afraid of that, sir."

Harboard missed this; he was busy buttoning his coat, pulling on his gloves, and prancing about with his stick over one shoulder. He broke into a new song:

> *"By Jove, you should see me on duty,*
> *All trousered, and booted, and spurred.*
> *By Gad! I'm a one-er, a ripper, a stunner,*
> *A bow-wow, a wow-wow——my word!"*

Paterson was explaining, "It's eight miles into Albert, and it's twenty miles on to Doullens by the road they're using now, and it's another twenty miles into Saint-Pol. Shall we take what's left of the whisky, too?"

Harboard chimed in, "After I've drunk half a bottle of brandy, I don't care whether I'm a stevedore or not."

"It's damned cold." Hoyt smirked. "And we shouldn't take any chances on pneumonia."

"And what about roping ourselves together? We don't want to fall into a crevasse," warned Paterson.

Harboard tried to yodel, and then added, "No. I should damn well say not."

There was a rumble outside and a voice pealed. "Hi! Where are you goin' wiv that blinkin' tender? That ain't the road, that's the garden," to which Magthorpe's voice responded, "It's all one piece to me, mate. This 'ere tender 'as been ordered by Mr. 'Arboard, 'imself——to go to Pilots' Pool for replacements."

"Well, keep orf Cookie's bit of garden!"

Portwine, still in pathetic attendance on Hoyt, kept repeating, "Have a good time, sir. It'll do you a world of good."

Hoyt stared into the aerial gunner's eyes. "Thanks, Portwine. I know you'll take care of things here." He turned back to Harboard. "Are we ready, gentlemen?"

"Just a moment!" Paterson cried, gulping the last of his brandy and stuffing bottles and small packages into his haversack. Then he linked arms with Harboard, tucked his stick under his arm and started to circle the table. The three officers had just reached the door when it opened suddenly and the squadron commander, Major Tremaine, stood stiff and officious, blocking the exit.

"Major!"

Tremaine held his gaze and steadied himself. There was a slackness about his uniform, necktie, and the corners of his mouth. It was evident that he, too, had had a few— enough to raddle his cheeks and nose, but it was also obvious that something had spoiled his evening and that he was sobering rapidly.

"Oh, it's you, sir," Hoyt snapped against the relaxation of the previous few moments.

"May I come in, Hoyt?"

"Of course, sir. Absolutely," Hoyt responded and stepped aside.

Major Tremaine moved into the light from a hanging bulb, and said, "Good evening, Paterson. Good evening, Colonel." He removed his cap and walked over to the stove. "I should have come over to you chaps earlier, but after our last patrol this afternoon, I had to go down to Wing—at Albert—and I've just gotten back. There isn't any need of my saying anything to you, Hoyt, about this afternoon. It's too Christly to talk about."

"I don't suppose they have anything at Wing about Phelps-Barrington, sir?"

"If they had, they would have called you here."

"Of course. Naturally."

"Frankly," the major admitted, "I didn't ask. I have my own troubles. Have you a spot of anything?"

Paterson took over. "Not much, sir. Just some brandy and whisky. Which will it be?"

"Make it whisky?"

Paterson dug into his haversack, pulled out two bottles, and shoved them toward Shuffling Wally who stood at the pantry. "With soda, sir?"

Tremaine nodded wearily. "Please." He addressed Hoyt again, and continued, "As a matter of fact, trouble is the only thing that GHQ is quite sure of at the moment."

"Anything in particular, sir?"

The major looked about for a chair. "What I mean, and what they mean are two separate things. Roughly, what we have been doing for the past three weeks is scurrying around like chickens with their heads off, trying to get information on the Hun push. GHQ has finally gotten it. As you know, the Germans have pretty well broken through."

Paterson came back with the whisky and handed it to Tremaine. He lifted the glass gratefully to his lips, and said, "Gentlemen."

"I suppose you have some definite instructions?" Hoyt queried.

"As definite as anyone can give in an indefinite situation of this kind. Frankly, the Hun is putting on the strongest push he has ever made, and he's expected to come right through here—and keep on going!"

Paterson said, "Keep on going where, sir?"

"Nobody has any idea."

"Do you mean to say that we're evacuating this area?" old Harboard said, fondling his blue hands.

"I wish I could tell you how *far* back, but I don't know. I do know, however, that we expect to lose Amiens."

Harboard gasped. "Good Lord!"

Major Tremaine finished his whisky, and added, "It's a wedge, with Hazebrouck or Saint-Omer for one fulcrum, and Saint-Quentin, perhaps, for the other."

"But what do you mean by evacuation?" Hoyt demanded.

"Simply that. There isn't a chance of stopping the push. The only thing we can do is to give way before it, draw the advance in, and hope to high hell that the Hun comes in too far and too fast to assure any permanency. In other words—to be brutal about it—at this stage of the game we're damn well getting bloody well licked!"

Paterson was the first to reply. "But that simply can't happen."

"Of course it can happen," Harboard insisted.

"But there must be something that can be done about it," argued Paterson. "We're not just backing out without a fight, are we?"

"You've done all the fighting over the past few weeks," Harboard said.

"You're right, Colonel. The immediate situation however also concerns us," Tremaine broke in. "It's expected that the Hun will make a desperate attempt at air dominance, beginning at dawn tomorrow. It's expected that he'll put every ruddy pilot in the air; anyone who knows a stick from a rudder bar."

Hoyt said, "Go on, sir."

"Our orders are to break it up."

"We actually get to mix with them?" Paterson pealed.

"We are expected to break it up," Hoyt said hollowly.

"We just go out and shoot every damn one down, eh?" Paterson went on. "Is that all, sir?"

"Well, no. Not quite. We are evacuating this aerodrome."

"For Christ sake!" Paterson snarled. "What goes on?"

Major Tremaine turned to Harboard. "That'll be your

job, Colonel. We're to pack officers' and men's personal luggage and kit, and get it off by"—he flipped his sleeve to look at his wrist watch—"by nine o'clock. I mean tonight. That gives you just an hour and fifteen minutes."

"And where is it to go?"

"I'm sending around the new location to you. It's almost twenty-five miles back. Chamberlain is having it pinpointed on maps for each pilot."

Hoyt slipped out of his haversack strap. "You mean we're to get all the mechanical sections and supplies out of here tonight, too?"

"Absolutely everything. All Besseneau hangars are to come down and be sent on. Anything that has to stay for lack of transport—anything that could be of any possible use to the Hun, is to be destroyed. Every pilot is to remain on the aerodrome tonight—and to remain sober. Have I been quite clear?"

"I think you have, sir," agreed Hoyt.

Tremaine stood up and held out his hand. "I'm damned sorry for this afternoon, Hoyt."

"It can't be helped—but thank you, sir."

The major turned to Paterson, "And you, Mr. Paterson, I want you to get what pilots are left with 'B' Flight, bring them over here. There's Cummings, Gracie, and Parkinson. They'll be flying under you and Hoyt." He put on his cap and tugged the peak down low. "Keep someone on watch here for anything further that might come in. I shall be at my office the rest of the night, if you want me. Thank you, gentlemen." He bowed slightly and strode uncertainly for the door. The three 'C' Flight officers watched him fade through the exit. Paterson was the first to comment. "The new aerodrome must be well on the other side of Amiens."

Hoyt shucked out of his jacket. "Wherever it is doesn't matter much, and it doesn't lighten the work we've got to do. Get me Sergeant Opperdyke . . . and get me Fairbrother, too."

Harboard cried, "Please don't tie up the telephone for a moment. I'll want to use that. Do you mind chasing on foot after your 'B' Flight pilots, Paterson?"

"Not at all. I'm on my way," the young American yelled and headed for the door.

Old Harboard went to the telephone, twirled the handle three times, and then began to speak, "Hello! Motor Transport, Number 44? Harboard speaking. Who is this? . . . Right, Sergeant. I want those two other Crossleys fueled at once. Both of them are to go down to the Squadron mess and stand by for instructions, and I want you to fuel up all the lorries and have two of them sent at once to 'C' Flight's hangar; the other four will go down to the old barn. Send a motorcycle and sidecar to our mess. Drive that yourself, Sergeant, and start the men packing up all tools and spare parts at once."

Hoyt was talking quietly to Portwine. "Never mind any more of that luggage. You get after the mess crockery, and all the cooking utensils. You might leave out just enough for hot tea in the morning. I want the mess packed up inside half an hour. Never mind any of the furniture."

"Yes, sir," Portwine answered, and hurried toward the pantry.

BOOK FOUR

CONCLUSION

March 22, 1918

It was 3 A.M. before most of the evacuation procedure had been carried out and the bulk of the squadron transport sent on its way to the new aerodrome. The Sop Camels assigned to Hoyt and Paterson, as well as the three that had been taxied over from 'B' Flight, were pegged down on the greasy hardpan where the Besseneau hangar had stood the day before. Only a skeleton force was still alert to service the war birds, as most of the noncommissioned personnel were bunked in what had previously been the officers' cubicles. There was a sullen air of uncertainty about everything. The Crossley tender that had been ordered for the proposed trip to Saint-Omer was still parked near the officers' mess, and Magthorpe, the driver, was inside sitting in a basket chair that faced the stove, keeping the fire going with short lengths of broken-up furniture. Light was furnished by three gasoline lanterns.

Portwine, wrapped in a blanket and smoking a cigarette, was huddled on his cot that had been set up under the telephone. Hoyt, and Paterson, with their outer clothing piled beside them, were dead asleep on their cots that had been brought in from the cubicles.

A few miles to the east, along the breadth of ground taken the day before by General Fritz von Below's Storm Troopers, small parties of Tommies, under cover of the ghostly night, crept out of shell holes, dugouts, and sections of battered trenches to filter back toward their previous line. Companies, or what was left of them, cut-up platoons, and even individual men, moved like wraiths across the cratered areas, their ears alert for the sound of guttural voices. The rasp of a rifle bolt, the harsh scrape of a Lee-Enfield across a parapet, or the telltale click of a cocking handle was enough to drain every ounce of movement or initiative, and there were times when they were caught and drenched by whipsaw bursts of Spandau fire. A few were able to use the bayonet effectively, but they generally avoided contact whenever possible. Many survived this hellish gamut only to be cut down by their own compatriots who were holding their sectors; anxious, determined men, unbalanced by the threat of a new attack.

Up near Vélu, a few British artillerymen had the courage to return to the guns they had abandoned during the day, by muffling the shoes of their horses with pads of sacking and dragging their weapons out far enough to use them again. This astounding exploit was carried out during the night which was wrapped in a silence made more intense by the deadening effect of the heavy mist. There was no gunfire, no rifle fire; all was as peaceful as a practice session on Salisbury Plain. It needed only the Druidic piles and monoliths to backstage the fantastic extravaganza.

"Spring's going to be early this year," Magthorpe said as he sucked on an old clay pipe. The general upheaval at the squadron had made little impression on this son of the soil. He had not had time to determine in which direction the fortunes of war were shifting. "It's in the air. They be plowing yesterday, the other side of Amiens. Of course, mind you, they always plow a mite earlier in France than they do in Kent, but them as lives on the land they plows, they knows best when to plow."

"I don't think I'd like to be a farmer," Portwine observed.

"It ain't for every man. Most men ain't up to it," Magthorpe explained. "You think you've seen some sights in this war, but 'ave you ever seen a Somerset plowing contest? Now, my lad, there's a sight you should never miss. There's nothing like a man plowing a furrow . . . as straight as an arrow across a ten-acre field. You should see them 'orses put their chests into it, knowing what it can mean. Of course, it takes a lot of beer to run a plowing contest. But what a spectacle!"

"Not so loud, now," Portwine whispered. "Our two pilots are sleeping."

Magthorpe removed his pipe in respect, and peered over his shoulder. "Ah, roight! That's the young 'un, this side, eh? The young American I brought up in January. A likely young gentleman, considering where he came from. A very interesting chap, and he knows a powerful lot about 'istory. A treat to talk to, 'e was. Jolly glad 'e didn't cop it yesterday."

"You're to stow that talk," Portwine remonstrated. "Yesterday was yesterday, and today is today."

"Yes, I know. Same as farmin'. Each day's enough for the work it brings, and if you do it properly, that's all there is to it, an' termorrer takes care of itself."

Portwine rested his head in his cupped hands. "It wouldn't be too bad if we only knew about Mr. Phelps-Barrington. There isn't any word of him at all. The other three we know about, but Mr. Phelps-Barrington just flew out of here, and that's all there is to it."

"Now, let's see. 'E was the comic one, wasn't 'e?"

"He was a proper pilot."

"Always 'ad 'is boots properly polished."

"Always had everything polished. He was a gentleman, he was. A drink, and a laugh, and a two-hour patrol with half of his bus shot away—and Amiens that night for a good time. That was Mr. Phelps-Barrington. They don't make them like him very often."

Magthorpe rubbed his grizzly chin. "And 'ow 'e could sing! Not exactly in tune, mind you, but loud and strong like 'e enjoyed 'earing the sound of 'is own voice. I used to bring 'im back nights when 'e was blotto, but, mind you, even when 'e was blotto, 'e was always polite to everyone —even to me. 'E was proper gentry, 'e was."

"It's hell the way things happen. One day everything's bright and gay and everybody's happy, and the next day you're packing kit bags and sending them over to the adjutant's office to be sent home."

"Ah, but you can still 'ear the laughter," chided Magthorpe.

Portwine almost jerked his head off its supports. "What? What's that you say?"

"You can always 'ear the laughter."

"You're balmy. How can you hear laughter?"

"Oh, it's there. In the air behind them."

"What are you talking about, Magthorpe?"

"Laughter. Young men's laughter. It don't go away with them. It 'angs back 'ere, like an echo."

"Are you going daft?"

"Not me."

"Then how can you hear dead men's laughter?"

Magthorpe looked at Portwine with a kindly eye. "Maybe *you* can't, but I can. You must remember, young feller, I brought them all up. Every larst one. I brought Mr. Hoyt up, and I brought Mr. MacFarlane who was flight commander before 'im."

"What has that got to do with it?"

"They all come up quiet, wondering what it is all about, and lookin' up into the air and 'opin' inside their 'earts that they'll be good soldiers, and then for a few weeks I takes 'em back and forth at night for a bit of binge in Amiens. And they laughs and yells and sings . . . and then after a while I takes their kit bags back." He turned around again, sucked on his pipe and stared into the fire. "But mind what I tell you; even after the kit bags go down, the laughter is there for weeks. I can still 'ear it ringing along both sides of the road, and I can 'ear it very plain when the sun goes down."

Portwine combed his fingers through his hair, and croaked, "S'truth! You'll have me that way in a minute. It's past three o'clock." He glanced up at the window at the foot of his cot. "And there's a wet fog still. You'd better poke up that fire, and we'll think up something cheerful."

Magthorpe cranked to his feet, and the wicker chair creaked and complained with the effort. "I suppose I'd better be lookin' for the old 'un. 'E's properly sozzled, and 'as been since 'e got them larst lorries off for Albert. Laugh! The old devil, 'e sent the larst motorbike off with its bathtub full of wine from the squadron mess, an' 'e says 'e won't go down 'imself until the larst tender's left with the final bit of salvage on it. Bloody old, but bloody sharp, the old 'un."

Portwine looked concerned. "You go out there and bring him back. He'll need to be warmed up."

"I'll try, but there's few, besides yourself, who can do anything with 'im when 'e's 'ad a few."

"Well, I can't leave the telephone. You tell him Portwine's got some hot rum for him."

Magthorpe grinned, pocketed his pipe, said, "Now, that's an idea!" and waddled toward the door.

As soon as Magthorpe left, Portwine made a stealthy dart toward his kit pile and carefully pulled out a bottle of rum which he held up to the light, scanning the content level. "I shall have to dollop this out carefully," he muttered, and peered into a saucepan of water that was steaming on top of the stove. He produced a small bag of sugar, a parched quarter of a lemon, and mixed his brew as he sent intermittent glances toward the door. He then set the steaming glass on the metal rack that circled the stove and continued stirring until the telephone jangled.

"Hello . . . Yes . . . Yes . . . No, this isn't the blinking artillery brigade, and I don't know where they are," he answered in his cracked voice. "I'm talking as best I can . . . What have you chaps done to the telephone system, anyhow? I think you have buggered it up completely. In fact, the whole bloody war has been out of order for about six hours . . . Never mind what I'm doing for my cold, don't you ring us up again unless you have something for Number 44 Squadron!" and with that rejoinder, Portwine hung up, picked up a butt from under his cot, lit it, and wrapped the blanket around his shoulders again.

Sergeant Opperdyke shoved his head into the doorway. "I heard it ring. Do you need any help, like me talking for you?"

"No. I can manage. Somebody's trying to get the heavies again," the aerial gunner grumbled. "Nobody's knowing who they want, or who they've had, all night long on that blinkin' telephone."

"Why don't you write a narsty letter to the company?"

Portwine ignored that. "How is it outside?"

"You can't see your hand before your face, it's that thick. I used to think the fog in London was thick, but these here French fogs are thicker than anything London has."

"But it is warming up?"

"Not much. It's bloody nippy out there."

"Medical Officer back yet?"

"Ain't seen him. He's probably ruddy drunk with his pals over at Ligny. I never hold much store by medical officers. After all, they're just doctors, and you know what doctors is," Opperdyke propounded, and then looked back over his shoulder. "Sh-h-h! Here comes Magthorpe and the old man. I'll hop it and clear out of his way."

Opperdyke held the door for Mr. Harboard who bowed and then grabbed for support at the door frame. He was very drunk, but silent and high on his dignity. Magthorpe took his arm and steered him toward the chair near the stove. "There you are, sir," he said cheerfully. "You sit there and get yourself warm. Come on, let's 'ave your cap and trench coat, eh? We'll have you snug and comfortable in a minute."

"Warm? Who said it's cold. It's so hot outside you can fry eggs," Harboard protested. "What about the punkah, boy?"

"Punkah, of course, sir," responded Magthorpe who knew how to play up to Harboard's many moods. He reached up into the semidarkness for some imaginary contrivance and began to pull rhythmically in the manner of an Indian boy pulling a punkah rope.

Harboard studied his galoshes for a minute, and then snapped, "Never mind, you fool. I'm drunk! Let's see, you're the driver, Magthorpe, aren't you?"

"Yes, sir."

"That's what I thought. Now then, Magthorpe, there's one lorry left over at the barn with a three-quarter load aboard. You go down there and tell them to come up here and wait behind the mess for the toolboxes and extra kits of the ground crew. They're to be packed aboard after 'C' Flight takes off, and that lorry is to take down the 'C' Flight mechanics. And while you're over there, if that side-car comes back—the one that had the wines—it's to go to Squadron office and take all the squadron records down to be turned over to Wing in Albert."

"Yes, sir," Magthorpe replied, amazed that the old

gaffer could still issue an intelligent order. "Right away, sir."

2

Ten minutes later Harboard had jerked out of a short snooze and was stretching his feet toward the stove. He peered about vaguely and finally caught the glow of Portwine's cigarette.

"I say, Portwine, is that you?"

"Yes, sir."

"What have you got to drink?"

"Hot rum—and, sir."

"Ah, good man. *Good* man."

Portwine shuffled over to the stove and took the warm grog from the metal shelf and handed it to the old man. "Here you are, sir. I've had it brewing for you. We've still got a bit of brown sugar."

"Good man," Harboard repeated, and sniffed at the enticing mixture. "It's not such a bad war when all men fill their proper roles, eh, Portwine?"

"That's right, sir. And there isn't much doubt what war it is tonight, is there, sir?"

Harboard lowered the glass and frowned. "What makes you say that?"

"Well, perhaps I shouldn't have, sir."

"You've been listening to what those young fools say about me, haven't you?"

"No, sir. People say too many things about me, for me to listen to what they say about anyone else."

"By George! You were to be boarded in Amiens for that wound of yours," Harboard cried.

"Yes, sir. I know I was, sir, but I've given up all thought of that. There's been so much else going on."

"Ah, yes. The Empire's having a nasty time and the

Board's probably in Paris by now from the way they've been stripping down the back areas since midnight."

"Is it that bad, sir?"

"Bad! Do you know, Portwine, that up in the Flesquières salient, somewhere near the juncture of the Fifth and Third Armies, Jerry penetrated well into our Battle Zone. The fog lay in heavy pockets all through the Omignon Valley, and about two miles north of there some survivors of the 3rd Rifle Brigade and the 8th Queens were holding on to a village named Le Verguier against a terrific bombardment. Somehow, they had gathered a number of Lewis guns, and along about ten-thirty yesterday morning, when the fog finally began to lift, they found German troops swarming before them like disturbed ants. Need I say, they were mown down by the hundreds?"

"And what happened to the Rifle Brigade blokes and the 8th Queens, sir?"

"I don't know. I got the story from a young corporal who may have been the last to come out. I suppose it all depended on whether they had enough ammunition for all those Lewis guns."

"Yes, of course, sir."

"It's all a matter of being prepared. Now I hope you were ready for that Board, eh, Portwine?"

"Oh yes, sir. I was quite ready for it."

"You're sure now?"

"Yes, sir."

"You knew what you were going to say?"

"Just what you told me, sir."

"Oh . . . What did I tell you?"

"You said I was to tell them that I didn't shoot Mr. Winslow down."

"Ah, that's right. So you remember, do you?"

"Yes, sir," Portwine said, and then paused. "You don't think I did, do you, sir?"

"Who's Mr. Winslow?" Harboard muttered. He finished his rum and shoved himself to his feet. "I can't waste time around here. I've got to get back and make sure those men are getting all the squadron files out properly. We've got to preserve the history of Number 44, you know, Portwine. Many a regiment has forfeited its chance for glory by losing its records in battle."

"Yes, sir, but you wrap up properly. It's dreadful cold out there."

After Harboard had tottered out, Portwine checked his watch and then was startled by the roar of a Camel engine being started and warmed up for about half a minute. He listened as the Clerget raged its power, stuttered, and conked out. The noise aroused Captain Hoyt who sat erect on his cot, stared about the room and instinctively reached for his flying boots.

"It's nothing, sir," Portwine assured him, "but I suppose you'd better be getting up."

"Of course. See if you can arouse Mr. Paterson."

The aerial gunner shook the high shoulder of the American lightly. "All right, sir. Come on, Mr. Paterson. Wake up . . . it's time to get up."

Hoyt got to his knees and glanced, glassy-eyed, around the room. "How bad is the fog, Portwine?" he asked as he scratched the back of his head.

"It's right down to the ground, sir, and you can't see from here to where the hangar used to be, but major's orders are for everybody to stand by, sir."

Hoyt tried to put it all together by assembling segments of his memory and fitting them into some familiar pattern. The roar of the Camel engine had shaken him out of a heavy sleep, and he was having difficulty figuring why he was sleeping in the officers' mess, and what connection Portwine had with his being there. Gradually, pieces of the previous day's events fell into place, and he rubbed the heels of his hands into his eye sockets trying to force the tragedy from his mind.

"Where is Mr. Harboard?"

"Well, he was here for a bit, but he had to go over and arrange for the squadron files to be sent down to Wing in Albert."

"I see. Has he gone down with them?"

"I don't know. I've never left the telephone, sir. In fact I haven't been out of this room."

Hoyt nodded dumbly and then asked, "How drunk was he?"

"Well, he wasn't what you might call sober, but he certainly can still give orders. I think Magthorpe's standing by him."

"Magthorpe? By the way, who is this Magthorpe?"

"One of the drivers, sir. He's the one who hears armor clanking along the road when he drives his blinkin' Crossley. He's been hearing laughter tonight, sir."

"Funny. I've never run into that one."

"He's quite a card."

"What a pair! You go out and find Mr. Harboard, yourself, and be quick about it. I don't want him wandering about in this early morning air."

"All right, sir. Right away."

As Portwine folded his blankets and prepared to go out to look for Harboard, the telephone bell rang on a muffled beat. Hoyt climbed off his cot and hurried to take it.

"No. This is 'C' Flight, 44 Squadron, R.F.C. What aerodrome do you want? . . . We haven't taken off yet . . . Well, who the hell are you, anyway? . . . We've got nothing to do with that. If you want to find out things of that sort, why don't you call up somebody who knows? . . . Oh, it's fine here. The birds are singing in the trees, the flowers are all in bloom, and the sun shines overhead while all the little children dance around the Maypole." Hoyt slammed the receiver and went back to where Paterson still huddled under his blankets. He reached for an uncovered foot and barked, "Come on, Paterson. Rise and shine. Wakey . . . wakey!"

"Lay off, Mallory. I'll get up. You don't have to twist my foot that way," the young pilot snuffled.

"It's Hoyt. Climb out of it. Up an' at 'em."

"Oh, all right. It's you, Skipper." Paterson sat up and cupped his chin in his hands. "Good morning, sir. How's the weather?"

"You can stumble over it. It's right on the ground. We're drying out a pailful for drinking water."

Paterson stared at his watch. "It's five o'clock?"

"About that."

"What are we hanging around here for?"

"Where can we go in this muck? We've got a definite stand-by."

Paterson rubbed the back of his head to arouse some degree of consciousness. "Oh, I remember. We moved the men into our cubicles, didn't we?"

"What part of the cubicles we didn't burn in the stove."

"It did turn cold, didn't it?"

"First it was cold, and then for some reason it got suddenly warm. That's what brought the fog in."

"I wonder if there's a cigarette left about somewhere," Paterson mumbled. "No chance of sending a tender . . ."

Hoyt snapped his case open under the young man's nose.

"Thanks, Skipper. Is that boiling water on the stove?"

"Practically. We'll have some tea presently, if we can find some tea."

There was a dull rumbling roar off to the east as a heavy barrage opened up. It was an emphatic salvo that had the sound of authority, a challenge that had little regard for the rest of the world.

"Here we go," Paterson said. "It's starting again."

"The bastards!" snarled Hoyt. "But high explosive is better than the mustard gas they've been firing up around Flesquières. I talked to a Royal Naval Division chap just before we bunged in, and he said they were doing all right up in that salient until the Huns began lobbing in mustard shells. They had some serious casualties, but most of them were from mustard burns. It got them around their necks and wrists. 'Damned uncomfortable,' he said."

"What sort of people are the Huns, anyway?"

"The kind that should be wiped out. They were stopped in the Forward Zone, although most of our outposts had to be withdrawn," Hoyt explained. "It was this salient on which the whole British front to the south turned and fell back on La Fère. Those Royal Navy boys must have put on a show, they hung on until ordered to retire at midnight. Even then, they only withdrew to the Immediate Zone. Bloody good, what?"

"Bloody good," young Paterson agreed.

3

By seven-thirty, a pasty yellow light outlined the windows, providing enough illumination to show Sergeant Opperdyke and two mechanics stomping up and down near the pegged-down planes. They had unbuttoned the flaps of their Balaclava caps to keep their ears warm. A motorcycle and sidecar chattered, and pulled up somewhere outside, and Opperdyke was heard to cry, "Good morning, sir."

Old Harboard was back in his basket chair staring at the glow of the stove, still stirring a glass of hot rum. Paterson was gulping tea from a pudding bowl, and Portwine had returned to his post under the telephone. There was a strong tang of scorched varnish, burned wood, toast, and the sweat of unsanitary men about the room, as Captain Frost clumped in. He stood wide-legged in the doorway and registered his bewilderment. "Holy hell! You people still here? From what I heard I thought you would all be in Rouen by this time."

"Where have you been all night?" Hoyt demanded, pacing up and down like a caged tiger.

"Do you know what I had to go through to get back here at all?" Frost raged. "I had to go within eight miles of Neuve-Chapelle, and we came in on two bare rims to do it. Every bloody road between here and Saint-Pol is stiff with men and stuff moving out. It's the God-damnedest night I have ever put in in all my life. Where's Phelps-Barrington?"

"We don't know," Harboard said solemnly. "You hear anything?"

"Nobody knows anything. Is there anything left to drink?"

"There's some rum. Here, Portwine, make the doctor a drink."

Hoyt stopped his pacing and glared at Frost. "It was Mallory, wasn't it?"

"Yes, it was Mallory."

"Did you talk to him at all?"

"No. I didn't get there until six o'clock."

"Well, what about his effects?"

"I managed to get everything there was."

"Good! Let's have it."

The MO said quietly, "You were right, Hoyt. He *was* married."

"I knew he was married, but the thing that worried me was that nurse at the Great Ormond Street Hospital."

"Well, these are the letters," Captain Frost explained, and handed over a small package. "He carried them with him, it seems."

"Thanks. We'd better take care of them," Hoyt said, and skimmed the wad into the stove.

"Did anyone go through his kit?"

"Yes. Everything else is in the clear, and the kit's gone down."

"*Ave et vale*," Frost said.

Someone was knocking on the door, and Hoyt yelled, "Come in!"

Sergeant Opperdyke appeared. "It seems to be breaking a little bit toward the west, sir." The guns roared out another salvo, and Paterson snapped to his feet. "There they go again. I haven't heard them for the past five minutes."

"They'll be nearer when next you hear them," Harboard warned.

Hoyt said, "I'll take a look," and joined Opperdyke at the door where he stood and squinted at the unfamiliar scene. "What's that over there? Is that the roof of the barn?"

"No, sir. That's the 'B' Flight hangar they didn't have room for," Opperdyke explained. "They'll be burning that in a few minutes, sir."

"Well, don't call me again until you can see the roof of the barn."

"Yes, sir."

"And I want those engines warmed up every fifteen minutes."

"Yes, sir," and Sergeant Opperdyke went off bellowing, "Pull through Number 2433. Snap into it!"

Paterson moved in and said to Hoyt, "Have you taken a look at those 'B' Flight pilots?"

"What's the use?"

"What's the use? Do you realize, Skipper, we've got to fly with them, if we ever get off this morning."

"What'll I try next? Buckets of cold water?"

"Are they still in the tender?"

"Yes."

"Well, for heaven's sake, I'm going to root them out. We've had enough of this. They come over here and drink the last of our whisky and expect to sleep it off on our time."

Another set of big guns roared their wrath and Paterson turned to Harboard. "There they go. By golly, they're a lot nearer this time. What do you say, Colonel?"

"I say that's damn close. *Damn* close."

"Hello, there's the telephone." Paterson glanced toward Portwine as the aerial gunner took down the receiver. "No . . . No, this damn well isn't the East Suffolks. This is 'C' Flight, 44 Squadron, R.F.C."

Harboard gasped and scrambled to his feet. "What the hell do you mean, this isn't the East Suffolks? Who's on the wire?"

"Brigade, sir," Portwine explained.

"What do you mean telling them it isn't the East Suffolks?"

"Well, it isn't, sir."

Harboard sat down and shook his head. "Of course it isn't. Sorry, but that means the East Suffolks must be around here somewhere."

"Oh no it doesn't, sir," argued Portwine. "Everything's been daft on the telephone since midnight."

"Oh, I agree, but they wouldn't call for the East Suffolks if they weren't somewhere in the vicinity."

The big guns raged again and the shell explosions seemed very close for a moment; one burst less than four thousand yards east of the aerodrome and sent a black column of smoke writhing high into the mist. As the group sat and listened, Major Tremaine slipped through the door. "Is Hoyt here?" he asked.

"Here, sir."

"Oh, there you are. Good morning, gentlemen. Now look here, Hoyt, if this keeps thinning out, Courtney and I are taking off within the next quarter hour. I've got nothing more definite than I told you last night. I want you to get off the ground as soon as it's feasible, and keep in the air as long as you can. Break up anything the Hun starts. That's all I can tell you, old chap. Ride him off. Stop him. Block him out."

"But what about coming back here, sir?"

"The orders are to leave a man here with indicative flares, but I think we can disregard those, because we've got infantry in our motor park already."

"What infantry?" Harboard cried.

"I think they're the Leinsters, Colonel," said Tremaine.

"Oh." The old man was disappointed.

"So, after you take off you can disregard this aerodrome entirely. What I would do, if I were you, would be to make a short offensive patrol about as far as Cambrai, or maybe a few miles this side of Cambrai, and then come back and fly over Wing HQ at Albert. They've promised me ground strips at Wing, but for God's sake, whatever you do, don't lose any more planes," the major pleaded.

Paterson politely interrupted. "Tea's ready. Will you have some tea, sir?"

"No, thanks," Tremaine said and went to the doorway, "and the best of luck to you. I've enjoyed having you with me, and I'm sorry that this has to be such a disorganized show this morning . . . but the best of luck to you all."

"Thank you, sir," Paterson responded.

"Thank you, sir," added Hoyt.

Mr. Harboard stood up, reached for a spoon and began stirring the MO's glass of grog. He looked bewildered when Major Tremaine called, "Come on, Frost. Let's get moving. I want to talk to you," and the medical officer padded after him. Hoyt and Paterson walked to the window, and then sat down on Hoyt's cot.

"What does he mean, Skipper? We're to carry on where we left off yesterday . . . bombing and strafing?"

"You know what he means. We've got to stop this bloody push!"

"I see. Well, wherever you go, I'll follow you, sir."

"We've had enough of that poohbah. Did you go through Phelps-Barrington's stuff? It's got to go down you know, and we won't know where it goes after it leaves us. He's got a mother somewhere in Chester."

"There wasn't much, Skipper. P-B had taken most of his personal stuff with him. It's hard to believe, but he was only three months older than I am."

"That's what war does to some men."

"And he had had something pretty rotten happen to him."

"Is that so?"

"I think it was a married woman."

"Now look here. That's between Phelps-Barrington and you; not between you and me. I want you to always remember that."

"Sorry." Paterson looked somber. "Everything that's left—is between you and me, Skipper. I know now that Phelps-Barrington is gone with the rest of them."

"How do you know that?"

"Because this morning I feel better about it. I have accepted it as a fact in my mind. I don't seem to need a detailed report."

"You are growing up very fast, Paterson."

"I suppose it's about time."

"Actually, you're a very young kid, you know, but you're a very stout fellow."

"Thanks."

"No need to thank me. I have to say that."

"Why?"

"Because you're my immortality, Paterson. You're the last of the lot I made. I'm only three years older than you, but you're like a son who lived when all the rest of my sons went out."

"For Christ's sake, Skipper," Paterson appealed, "a thesis on immortality at half-past seven in the morning?"

The heavy gunfire opened again and Hoyt winced as the concussion seemed to threaten the glass in the window above the cot. "Well, here they come. I suppose we'd better get into our gear."

"Don't look so gloomy, Skipper," Paterson jollied, "I know God-damned well that we're going to have dinner together tonight, but I'd like to make one last point with you. Trent and Mallory *and* Phelps-Barrington were brothers to me, but you . . . you were damn near God!"

"Please, Paterson. Will you get it out of your head? Can't you see that the only thing that kept me going and worthy of those two streamers was the fact that you chaps were on my tail? Can't you get it through your head that in the last three weeks I've trusted you more than any of the rest? Why do you think I put you in as subleader? Why do you think I spent half the night talking with you? It's because you're a kid, Paterson, and you've got a kid's ideas, and they're clean and they're full of the old poohbah, but it's good poohbah, and that's what counts."

"I don't think you ought to say that to me, Skipper."

"Why not? Why did you join up with the British? You owed us nothing."

"Nothing, except a damn fine heritage," and Paterson smiled.

"We've spread heritage and tradition all over the world, but what did it get us?"

"It certainly has left a mark of some sort."

"What I like about you is that you didn't join up to engage in glorious cavalry charges, to hear the high cry of bugles, the clink of medals, or for the smiles of women. You've always been above all that."

"Right now, I can't think what I joined up for, but I'm damned glad I'm here."

"You joined up for the purity of idealistic endeavor—and I hope I joined up for the same reason. You thought it was right, and so did I. Well, it is right, Paterson, and these are the cleanest years you will ever live, and it doesn't make any difference what anyone says afterward. The men who live through this will know it, and the ones who die won't talk. I just hope that a handful like you will live to write what we tried to do, but I'm afraid our history will be fouled by the conscientious objectors, the pacifists, and the stay-at-home cowards who usually become the spokesmen for the dead, and who try to justify their own lack of patriotism with denunciations of the cause. It has always been this way, and we probably won't be around to defend our ideals."

"For Christ's sake, don't talk like that. Don't leave me, Skipper," Paterson breathed, and reached for Hoyt's arm.

Hoyt palmed his hand away, and continued, "You are to follow me as long as you can see me, and about eight miles this side of Douai I want you to turn back and go down to Wing and look for ground strips. If there are any out, I want you to go down, land, and make arrangements for us to get the four new pilots, who are to be sent up tonight, shipped on to the new aerodrome. What I'd really like you to do, Paterson, is to go down and get them yourself."

"What do you mean, follow you as far as I can see you?"

"We probably won't be able to see anything above five hundred feet, and I don't want my tail chewed off."

"Where are you going when I go back to Albert?"

"I'll have lots to do. I'm worried about the weather. Have you been outside since you tried to rouse those 'B' Flight pilots?"

"No."

"Well, look at it."

Paterson took a look, and slammed the door in disgust. "Well, what can we do? What happens now?"

"We're going to take off as soon as we hear the major and Courtney go."

"And what about the 'B' Flight pilots?"

"Write them a note in triplicate saying we've gone to the war."

The enemy barrage opened up again, and Hoyt and Paterson were certain that clods of earth were dropping on the mess roof, but before they could investigate Sergeant what there is of it. Hardly enough to lift the sock, but it's Opperdyke shoved the door open again and hurried in. "I can see the corner of the barn now, sir. Wind's due west, sort of quivering."

"Right you are, Sergeant, and listen carefully. As soon as we leave the ground, you become acting-commander of 'C' Flight. I want you to see that these huts are touched off and burning properly, and I want you to get everybody out of here and down to the new aerodrome—and the best of luck to you, Sergeant." Hoyt held out his hand, and Opperdyke, completely off balance in the face of the gesture, stood stock still. Finally, he grinned, wiped the palm of his hand down the front of his tunic and took Hoyt's.

"And the *best* of luck to you, sir," the sergeant said, and stiffened his jaw.

The skipper turned away and saw Captain Frost heading toward him. "I say, how many cots have we here, Hoyt?" The MO stared about the disordered room.

"What do you mean, how many cots?"

"For God's sake, there are battle police all over the place, and there's an ambulance train outside looking for a casualty clearing station. I understand it was moved back about ten o'clock last night."

Hoyt scratched the back of his head, and tried to bring some order out of the chaos. "Well, the men's cots went down last night on the first lorries. They've been sleeping on the floor."

"What about officers' cots?"

"Ther can't be more than six at best," Hoyt concluded and yelled for Opperdyke. "Sergeant! Any kits left on that last lorry?"

"I'll see, sir."

Frost growled, "Well, snap it up, will you, Sergeant?" He went back to the door leading to the cubicles, and yelled, "All right. I'll take what you have in those two ambulances that are out of petrol. You can start bringing the stretchers in through that end door. Portwine, what are you doing?"

"Nothing, sir."

"All right. Clean up that blasted table, and start boiling some more water."

Harboard tottered in, and ran his bloodshot eyes over the general upheaval. "I'm looking for my haversack." He pulled himself up sharp, and said, "Hello, is that you, Skipper?"

"Yes. How are things going, Colonel?"

"I've got those three 'B' pilots under the pump. They're coming around nicely, and your fog's lifting."

Outside, Opperdyke could be heard bellowing, "All right now. Start all engines. Captain Hoyt's first . . . Switch off . . . Petrol on . . ."

One by one, the Clergets opened up, and their initial coughs, screams, and chatter gradually folded into an even roar of sustained power. Buttoning the chest flap of his Sidcot suit Paterson strode across the room, followed by Hoyt who was wrapping a scarf around his neck. Old Harboard steadied himself at the door and watched Paterson charge into the slack group of 'B' Flight pilots who were standing limp and uncertain with their backs to the slipstreams of the whirling propellers. The whiff of Castrol, smoke, and ancient dust billowed past Harboard and swirled around the abandoned mess.

"Come on you drunken louts," Paterson screamed over the abrasive rasp of the engines. "Come on, Parkinson. Shake out of it, Gracie, for Christ's sake! What the hell do you think this is? Where's your other man? You come over here and drink our whisky, and now, by God, you're going to fly with us. Get a bloody move on. Your father a Member of Parliament, or something? Get aboard there!"

Harboard shook his head and grinned as he watched the Camel pilots climb into their cockpits. He reveled in young Paterson's words and stand, but he knuckled a tear from one side of his nose as the planes waddled away, stiffened and took off with screeches of rage and defiance. When he looked back over the mess again, Captain Frost was spreading a rubber ground sheet over the table, and unloading a bag of dingy instruments.

"I take it you are going to start work, eh?" the old soldier observed.

"Who knows? I may learn something," the MO replied and shoved his cap to the back of his head.

"Good! I'll go to work, too," and Harboard turned to peer at Sergeant Opperdyke who had clumped into the room again. "Here, Sergeant, I want you to put all tool kits aboard Number 1 lorry, and then load your men aboard."

"Yes, sir. I'm supposed to set fire to this place, but I suppose it will be needed."

"You can't burn this. Dr. Frost will be operating."

"No, sir. Shall I assign the stand-by men for the ground strips, or shall you, sir?"

"You assign them."

Portwine eased into the picture and stood at Harboard's elbow. "May I stay, sir?"

Harboard looked at the sooty-eyed aerial gunner, changed his mind, and said, "I'll assign . . . You stay here, Portwine."

"It's very kind of you, sir." Portwine cast a reverent look at Harboard.

"And you let me know when you've got everybody aboard, Sergeant. And Magthorpe . . . that is Magthorpe, eh? You can start down now. Where's that motorcycle and sidecar?"

"It hasn't come back yet," Magthorpe explained.

Whatever Harboard may have replied was blotted out by the roar of a shell that exploded just a few hundred yards beyond the aerodrome. Concussion sucked out two windows, and a door slammed with a dusty thud.

"Well, that does it. Take off, Opperdyke," Harboard chattered.

"Right you are, sir."

"And mind you don't miss that detour around Albert. It is the only road that is clear."

"I understand, sir. Best of luck to you, sir."

"Oh, and Opperdyke, if you pass my motorbike send him directly to me here. I'll wait for him."

"Yes, sir," the sergeant said, and twirled on his heel, but before leaving he turned and yelled at Portwine. "Get this now . . . two white strips, crossed by day, and a 'T' of flares if it's after dark."

"Don't you think I ought to know that?" Portwine replied with faint contempt.

"Of course you know," Harboard assured him.

There was no more time for talk or instructions. The rattle and chug of trucks and ambulances replaced the uproar of the departing Camels. Portwine went to the stove and checked the hot-water situation. Frost was knotting the tapes of his medical gown, and watching the door that led to what had been the officers' cubicles.

"Bring 'em in," he said with little enthusiasm.

Strange faces, unfamiliar uniforms, and insignia appeared as two stretchers were brought in tenderly and set down along the wall. There was a long minute of silence. Portwine was the first to move. He kneeled beside a twitching figure, flipped over a tag, squinted at the information, then looked up at Captain Frost and said, "Upper left clavicle fracture, sir."

"Let me see that other tag," the MO demanded.

"Just a minute," old Harboard said, "he's one of the East Suffolks, isn't he?"

"Christ Almighty, how do I know? They're just wounded to me. Let's get him on the table, Portwine."

"You mean to say you never look at a man's regimental badges?" Harboard gasped.

4

The five Camels had taken off into the backdrop of a nightmare. There was little or no horizon on which to take a level. The fog that had appeared to be clearing when they were on the ground, now seemed to be swept up into shapeless piles with no definite corridors through which to fly. There was no streaked glare from any sunlight, and what light there was appeared to be reflected off the pus-yellow walls of the clouds. No gunfire crashed, and there was little outside distraction. Just a breathless, aimless journey to nowhere.

Half numb with concern and physical weariness, Paterson tightened his belt and realized that he was ravenously hungry. He gulped, tongued some spittle around the roof of his mouth, and tried to keep his eyes on Hoyt's streamers. Darting from lagoon to lagoon of lambent patterns, they soon lost the 'B' Flight pilots, and Paterson wondered where they would go, or what they would do without Hoyt to guide them. He peered up at his compass now and then and attempted to keep track of their course, but it was impossible, so he made the most of the odd intervals when patches of the ground were visible, trying to pick out some recognition point. Hoyt shot up into the sooty mist, but after several minutes of hopeless groping, he gave up and went back to the level that provided brief glimpses of the ground below.

"We must be eight or nine miles from our field," Paterson concluded, "but where are we in relation to our new line? It seems fairly quiet below—what I can see of it—but you can't tell until we show ourselves long enough to offer any target."

Hoyt found a rather wide clearing and looked back at his partner and flicked a friendly salute. Paterson recognized the battered area around Flesquières, and watched Hoyt turn northeast and head for the ragged ribbon of the Bapaume–Cambrai road.

"This is more like it," breathed Paterson. "Now we know where we're working."

They flew along together like men under direct communication. The road ahead was clotted with artillery, limbers, horse-drawn and motor trucks. Columns of infantrymen in single file moved along the footpaths that bordered the road. Some gunfire greeted the two aircraft, but Hoyt ignored it and went down like an arrow. Both of his guns sparkled, and a hosing of mixed ammunition sped toward the transport below.

Paterson turned away to give himself working room, and then darted in from an angle. He used his Aldis sight to pick out a confined space where some buildings had once stood, and yanked once on his bomb toggle. The Camel rose gently as two bombs left the metal rack, and he nudged the stick forward and turned slightly to follow Hoyt's course. He triggered off two fairly long bursts and scattered two groups of men who were hauling handcarts.

He saw the nose of Hoyt's Camel come up, and he followed suit, moving in close to the leader's tail assembly. They roared on, daring the intermittent bursts of machine-gun fire that raced after them. The cloud pattern was widening, and they now could fly close and snap through tight turns together with little danger. Hoyt zigzagged back and forth when ground fire sprayed spurts of tracer just ahead of them, and in turning, a small burst flickered up through one of his wingtips.

Paterson watched the area above, although so far there had been no evidence of air activity. Hoyt nosed around toward Bapaume now, and beyond Doignies the ground activity was quite obvious. Enemy troops were deploying off the roads and heading for small copses and folds in the ground from where to stage their next advances against the British positions.

"My God!" Paterson ejaculated, "the Jerries have gone clean through Gauche Wood and the Quentin Ridge. And there doesn't seem to be much of a line ahead of Villers Guislain. What the hell has been going on in this God-damned fog?" He was hungry again and felt in his thigh pockets, looking for some forgotten chocolate or a few malted-milk biscuits. Sharp spurts of pain pierced the canals and walls of his stomach, and he wondered what a whisky and soda would taste like, then laughed at the ridiculous improbability. He changed his position in the basket seat and looked around trying to ascertain how much of the murk was smoke and how much fog. There were smoke piles and pillars everywhere. Dumps were going up, and the big guns were thumping out their contribution to the battle. Fringes of small woods blazed, adding more smoke; all of it curling upward with little wind to disturb its spiraling climb.

Seeking new targets, or new enemy movement, Hoyt turned south, keeping the gash of the Canal du Nord well in view beyond his right wingtip. The ceiling was lifting and the two airmen had no trouble keeping each other in view. As the ground mist dissipated, Paterson noticed that great masses of cloud were gathering between two and five thousand feet.

"I don't like this," he grumbled to himself. "The Huns can cluster beyond those clouds and pick us off like Ping-Pong balls in a shooting gallery."

Below, the visibility was spotty, and in trying to pierce the layers of fog and smoke, it was impossible to determine what were clusters of troops and what were new patterns of earthworks. In fact, it was difficult to pick out anything that could give reliable evidence as to where the actual lines ran.

"Trent ought to be here," Paterson concluded. "He'd sort this mess out in no time. We're going to miss old Trent."

Now Hoyt was flying a wide zigzag course, darting about like a low-flying swallow. Paterson saw him start down two or three times, but once he put his sights on something, he would pull out without shooting or releasing a bomb, apparently satisfied that he would be wasting ammunition on whatever it was he had seen.

Down low the smoke was acrid and sickening, and Paterson, who felt nauseated, wished they could go upstairs a few thousand feet to get some refreshing air in their lungs. Only at intervals did Jerry send up any antiaircraft opposition, for in this fluid area there was not time to set up ack-ack batteries, and what fire screeched out came from the mobile machine-gun teams that were dispersed to give protection to the long streams of moving troops and transport.

Suddenly Hoyt found what he wanted. He turned and looked back at Paterson, raised his right arm over the rim of his cockpit, and pointed toward the ground.

"Go ahead, Skipper," Paterson said to himself. "I don't know what you've spotted, but I'm with you."

Hoyt's Camel went into a tight turn, and he headed for a straight narrow gash that appeared to be a sunken road. Paterson had never noticed it before, but sensed that it could be a road out of Villers Guislain. By the time he had checked his C.C. interrupter-gear handle and felt for the position of his bomb toggle, he saw that Hoyt had found a long, sheltered road that was packed with enemy troops who were heading for the break in the line ahead.

"My God! This'll be murder!"

Hoyt was straightening out his Camel and nosing down for the carnage. He went dangerously low, and Paterson saw his bombs flash away and take up their trajectory toward the packed gash. He eased up slightly, and then nosed down again to pour long bursts of Vickers into the charnel channel. Small outpourings of frantic men scrambled up the angled banks, trying to find cover in lesser folds, or amid the fringy brush and sparse foliage. He continued on in an undulating course, firing bursts of .303 every time he could get his nose down.

Paterson ruddered into the same pathway and caught some of the debris from Hoyt's bombs, and almost went into an uncontrolled sideslip. He fought with aileron and rudder to get back, and then pulled his own plug. The wire of the Bowden cable was slack and he had difficulty in releasing the rest of his bombs. Eventually, he sensed that all were clear and he was gratified to hear his Coopers add to the wild tympani. He tried to look back but his Camel was bouncing off the delayed concussion from Hoyt's bombs, so he had to attend to his immediate business.

Some bold soul stood his ground, and machine-gun fire screeched over Paterson's head as he attempted to follow Hoyt's roller-coaster attack, so he had to be content with putting two long bursts into the packed lane. When he cleared and could look back, he saw that what had been a well-defined roadway was almost obliterated with smoke and the widening spread of disorganized troops clambering up the road's banks, and scattering from that ditch of death.

As soon as Paterson and Hoyt could re-form, there was some slight evidence of sun streaks to the east, and Paterson was concerned again. He wished his skipper would head into some less-cluttered territory, but, instead, Hoyt worried his way up to over two thousand feet, and circled wider and wider, seeking new prey on which to pounce. Suddenly Paterson saw a large paint-mottled two-seater plodding along below them. It was obviously a Hun because it was well-marked with straight-barred crosses, but its type and wing design were not too familiar to him.

He nosed down and flew wingtip to wingtip with Hoyt until he could make him understand that there was a Jerry aircraft just below them. Finally, Hoyt spotted the strange, short-fuselaged machine, and nodded his head with enthusiasm.

"I don't know whether he wants to take on Huns, even down here, or whether we should ignore that two-seater and concentrate on stopping the ground troops, but I think he ought to know it's down there," Paterson was arguing with himself, "but what the devil is that bus? I know I have read something about it somewhere. She's got a big Mercedes engine with that ugly horn-type exhaust, and it looks as though she carries the radiator up under the center section. I wonder if that's one of the new A.E.G. planes designed for ground-attack jobs. If I could see if she has ailerons on only the upper wingtips, I'd be certain."

Hoyt zigzagged twice to lose distance, and Paterson knew that he was preparing to go down and attack from below and behind, just as he had always insisted two-seaters should be handled. Paterson tied on to Hoyt's tail and then took a quick look as the German biplane turned to keep Hoyt where he wanted him. In making the turn, the pilot disclosed that his plane carried ailerons only on the upper wings. That, and the short fuselage convinced Paterson that it was an A.E.G.

"That's what she is, and they're probably out on a ground-strafing show. Well, Hoyt will take care of them. He won't make the mistake I did. He'll go up from behind and below, and keep that gunner completely out of the play. By the way, where the hell is that Hun gunner?"

The instant he had considered all these facts, Paterson realized that something in this simple pattern was suddenly out of kilter. The act of coming up from below and from behind seemed right, but some hidden instinct started to shake him, as a puppy shakes an old slipper. He watched dry-lipped and fascinated as Hoyt came around for his final move. Then like a flash it came to him. "No, Skipper!" Paterson screamed. "Stay away from him. It's an A.E.G., and we should take him head on, or from below his nose, if possible. Don't go near his tail! That rear gunner is murder, if he gets you below him. He's got a tail-tunnel gun!"

But Hoyt had nosed down, and was starting up for his

attack. "No, Skipper! No! . . . Stay away from him. He's down on his knees using a tunnel gun," Paterson yelled, as he helplessly watched Hoyt begin his zoom toward the Jerry two-seater.

"Why didn't I remember and go around first to take out the pilot?" Paterson wailed. "We should have tackled him —as a team." The youthful American locked his jaws as he saw a deadly stream of tracer-flecked fire spit out from below the A.E.G.'s short fuselage, catch Hoyt's Camel across the top wing, and then snap down like a whipsaw. Hoyt threw up one hand, struggled to stand erect against the restriction of his belt, and then turned and waved Paterson away.

Seething with rage and frustration, Paterson nosed down at the open rear turret and lashed the German with a spanking burst of fire that torched the fuel tank almost immediately. The ground-attack machine hoicked into a frantic, clawing zoom, fell off, rolled over, and spewed a great black blob of smoke. It twisted in agony, nosed down and threw a human figure fully twenty yards away, and began its final spin.

"You swine!" Paterson screamed as he saw that Hoyt was floundering in a hopeless flat spin. He darted toward him, scarcely daring to look, but still unable to take his eyes off the tragedy. He sat watching the drama unfold, the upper half of his body tense and constricted, his belly and legs limp and useless. He saw the hapless Camel flounder, and try to get its nose around toward the Allied lines, but whatever Hoyt had done, it was too much. The right-hand wing panels suddenly snapped up, folded over, and fluttered away. Hoyt seemed to be struggling against his seat belt, but he never looked at Paterson again. The Camel's nose went down, and she started a tight spin, a graceless twirl that soon ripped the left-hand wings away:

what was left went down like a bolt from a crossbow, and fell on the bank of the Canal du Nord.

Paterson circled aimlessly, muttering and shaking his head. He waited until he saw the explosion of mud, fire, water, and smoke, marking his skipper's end. There was no question of his finish, or what would be left. Someone would come along eventually, saw the tail section away, and fill in the hole where Hoyt's Clerget had bored out his grave. It was as clean and simple as that. A streak of sunshine lanced down, bathing Paterson's wings in a saffron warmth. "Hoyt's dead," he said quietly. "I saw him go." But he did not see the three German Albatros scouts slide down the sunbeam—all firing at him—until one had overshot and zoomed in full view.

"You swine!" Paterson snarled fingering for the triggers on his spade grip. "Hoyt's dead!" He fired a short burst, and then his guns stopped. He glanced ahead to the feed blocks and saw that he had used all his ammunition, most of it against the enemy infantrymen in the sunken road. He felt the first big burst of Spandau hit him, as the Camel staggered, but he continued to fly straight on, making no attempt to evade his attackers.

"Hoyt's dead," he said every twenty seconds.

In that manner, and by the grace of his Maker, Paterson staggered on, wallowing into a patch of smoky mist and bad visibility. He sensed that he was somewhere near Bapaume, and instinctively sought his old aerodrome. He sat relaxed in the soft cushion of shock, unable to make a decision, except to fly on until something familiar swept into view.

"Hoyt's dead," he repeated once more. "It doesn't matter now. I should have told him about that A.E.G., but I didn't think . . . Now they'll get me, and that will be the last of 'C' Flight . . . There'll be no one to pick up the new pilots, and show them how to . . . But someone has to show 'em. Someone has to pull the flight together. Someone . . ."

5

A British battery of twenty-five pounders was booming over a desolate, well-churned piece of battleground. The skeletal outline of Bapaume could be seen, indistinct and eerie, through the low clouds, wet fog, and smoke. The clang of breech blocks arguing with the intermittent chatter of Lewis gunfire related the news of the day.

A few thousand yards ahead, disaster threatened, as troops, who had fought their way back out of the shambles of the Forward Zone, had returned only to find that the defenses in the Battle Zone were nonexistent. Despite their inherent gallantry, they had had little training in the art of organized retreat—staff policy being that it was undesirable to train troops for retirement as such movements would adversely affect the aggressive spirit of the men. Thus, when enforced withdrawal began, the Tommies soon lost contact with units on either side, and became isolated with tragic consequences. They had lived and fought in a straight line for the greater part of their military experience, and these new situations were a psychological shock.

The artillery fire was aimless and wasted in the early morning mist, but the ghostly curtain permitted the enemy to mass for new battle formations, and by seven o'clock they were ready to advance and attack again. The British could hear only a pointless babble in the mist, and their own artillery fire was dropping short and breaking up their hurriedly erected defenses. Within three hours, the Germans were to penetrate their left flank with no trouble because there was no one there to challenge them. Those who stood their ground held off seven consecutive attacks until they discovered that they were being surrounded on four sides.

The artillery battery men caught the uneven hiss of an aircraft engine, and instinctively moved to the roadside funk holes.

"Theirs or ours?" someone asked.

"Whoever he is, he's a damn fool, flying in this."

"I think I saw red-white-and-blue markings."

"Christ! Don't he know we're firing from this battery?"

"He could be in trouble."

"What are we in . . . a picnic on Hampstead Heath?"

"I think it's one of ours."

"We'll find out in a minute. He's just crashed in the next field."

"Come on. It might be a bloody Jerry."

The Sopwith Camel with the letter 'R' on its fuselage was flat on its belly. Both wheels were rammed up into the fuselage, and only the center boss was left on the propeller. The two artillerymen in khaki sauntered up and saw a man's arm dangling over one side, his head drooped forward against the small Triplex windscreen.

"We've got to be careful. If it catches fire, all his bloody ammunition will go up."

"Not likely. It's one of them little ones. Scouts, they call 'em."

The two soldiers pulled their steel helmets down closer over their eyes, and approached the wreck cautiously.

"I wonder if the poor bugger's dead."

"He seems to be trying to get out. His arm's moving."

"Then he probably fainted. Let's have a look."

They walked up and stared at the pilot in the cockpit. He turned his head slowly, smiled, and whispered, "Hoyt's dead."

"Well, you're alive, anyhow. Can we 'elp you, sir?"

The young pilot shook his head.

"Look! To get him out, we've got to undo that belt business. That's what keeps him in when they loop-the-loop."

"He can't stay here. Come on, give a hand."

They hauled and tugged until Paterson could be dragged over the side of the cockpit. There was con-siderable blood over the foot of his right flying boot. They lowered him gently and sat him against the side of the fuselage.

"Are you all right, sir?"

Paterson opened his eyes, and stared about. He jerked one leg, and steadied himself by pressing his hands against the stringy turf. He looked up at his rescuers. "Paterson, G.K., Second Lieutenant. Reporting . . . reporting for duty with . . . 44 Squadron, sir," he mumbled.

"He's had a bad bashin' about."

"You will want my logbook, eh?" the pilot went on.

"I think you've hurt your leg, sir. Look at the way your foot's all twisted about. Can't you feel it?"

"Is that you, Hoyt?" Paterson said, and tried to focus on the two artillerymen. "I . . . I can't see very well."

"Perhaps we'd better get a stretcher and move you out of here."

"What's the time, sir?"

"It's about half-past eight, mate. You must have been out early."

Paterson wagged his head dolefully, and took a new brace against the side of the fuselage. "We had to go out and try to stop them. But where's Hoyt?"

"Here, you'd better try a spot of water, sir. You must feel faint." He uncorked his water bottle.

"Easy now, Charlie, he's not really out of it yet. You might choke 'im if 'e can't swallow."

Paterson allowed one of the gunners to pour a few spots of water between his lips. "I know now," he said suddenly. "Hoyt's dead!"

"Ah, well, don't you get upset, sir. We'll try to get you back somewhere where it's safe."

"Hoyt's dead, I tell you. I saw him go down."

"All right, Hoyt's dead, but don't talk so loud. There's Huns all over the place."

"Do you mind if I sit down?"

"You are sitting down, sir. Does that leg hurt?"

Between bursts of blubbering and gasps of pain, Paterson continued, "Hoyt is dead, I tell you. I saw it all happen . . . Damned Hun, firing down a tail tunnel, cut his wings off. He . . . He tried to stand up in his cockpit but the wings wouldn't stay on. You can't go at A.E.G.s like that. He went down so fast . . . He's dead."

"Look here," one of the artillerymen said, "you clamp your hand over his mouth. I'm going to cut his flying suit and get his boot off. We've got to stop that blood, somehow."

"You've both been very kind," Paterson protested, "but I'm all right. It's Hoyt . . . Hoyt's dead, I tell you."

The two gunners set to work hacking at the leg of Paterson's Sidcot suit until they could examine his injury. The leg was shattered just above the ankle. How, or when, they had no idea, and cared less. They had been through this sort of battle casualty before. Blood was blood, flesh was flesh, and bone was bone. They tore out their First Field kits from their tunic flaps and bound up the hacked flesh and splintered bone as best they knew how.

"He's lost a lot of blood, but I don't think he'll be too bad if we can get him to a C.C.S."

"Where am I?" Paterson inquired between gasps and winces.

"You're all right. You're about three and a half miles east of Bapaume—not too far from the Albert road."

"Well, I shouldn't . . . be here."

"No? Well, you're bloody lucky you got this far inside, the way the line's shifting."

"I'm supposed to be on my old aerodrome."

"Well, there's no aerodrome about 'ere, sir. Are you more comfortable now? We'll have a stretcher for you in a minute."

"It's like this. Our new aerodrome is . . . about twenty-five miles back the other side of Amiens. They've got ground strips out for us. But God dammit, Hoyt's dead. I saw him go down."

"There's no aerodrome about 'ere," the other artillery-man explained. "There might 'ave been one yesterday, but there's only artillery 'ere now, and the Hun will have 'em all cold, unless we gets 'em out of 'ere fast. I tell you, sir, everything's givin' away like rotten canvas. The whole line is ripped to shreds and nobody knows nothing."

"Easy. I think he's fainted again."

"Well, that ambulance train can't be too far away. If we could get 'im to the road, 'e'd be all right. We can't do much else 'ere."

Paterson came out of his maze and continued his babbling. "I've got to get down to the other aerodrome. I've *got* to, I tell you. I want you to call Motor Transport and get me a tender. I know I'm hurt, but I've *got* to get down to the new aerodrome . . . the one the other side of Amiens."

"Steady, mate. Steady."

"Hoyt's dead, and I've got to take over."

"All right. You've got to take over. We'll try to get you down."

"I know . . . You're just saying that because I'm hurt, but I've got to get down. Hoyt's dead, I tell you, and I've got to get down. There'll be four new pilots in from Pool by tonight, and I've got to be there when they come in."

"All right. You'll be there."

"You don't understand. I'm the only one left to take over. I've got to get down and organize those four new men, and get after Sergeant Opperdyke. You call Motor Transport right away and get me a tender."

"All right, we'll get you a tender. Just take it easy."

"God, I'm tired! What happened to my foot?"

"Ah, nothing much."

"Good. You let me know when the tender gets here."

"We'll let you know."

Paterson managed a dry cackle. "Tell 'em—it's poohbah!"

The twenty-fives began firing again, and the roar of the war increased.

"We'd better get moving, sir. They're firing over open sights now. Come on, we'll help you out as far as the road . . . and a tender will soon be along."

"Right," the other artilleryman said. "One arm over our shoulders, sir. Not too far to go. We'll make it."

Paterson groaned as they lifted him to his feet. "Tell them it's poohbah."

"All right, it's poohbah, but for God's sake, let's get on with it."

"Let's get on with it," Mr. Paterson mumbled.

LOOK FOR THIS TRADEMARK
FOR QUALITY READING

CURTIS
BOOKS

Other best-selling war book titles available